Prosecutors – LA

White Jr.'s Trial

SUMMER AUGUSTINE

PEARL ROSE
PUBLISHING

Contents

Chapter 1

Sam Chapman was one of the more experienced and talented trial lawyers serving on the District Attorney's Sexual Assaults Team. He had a bad habit of saving his charm, only for juries, and not for team members. Today was no different.

"Remind me again, why we only charged him with crimes against one victim and not both victims?" asked Sam Chapman.

"Because," said Jack Wayne, a more senior attorney who chaired the committee, "The other victim is in Europe and refuses to come back to testify."

"Who is the other victim? Another prostitute?"

"Watch your tongue! She's not a prostitute, she's a very respectable woman!"

"So, why won't this respectable woman testify?"

"Listen, it's a complicated story, and it's one you don't need to worry about right now. Only one case has been charged, and that's all you need to focus on today."

"Sure, that should be easy," Sam said, sarcastically, "All you want me to do is try a case against a good-looking, young, rich guy for raping a prostitute, even though he has always had a line of women beating down his door, hoping to be his next girlfriend. How the hell am I supposed to do that!"

"With your excellent trial skills, big shot!"

"How does a prostitute get raped?"

"Hey! Straighten out your bad attitude! Any woman, whatever her reputation, has the right to decline sex; and a man who denies her that right, will be charged with rape. Understand? Besides, the victim is not a prostitute. She is a *former* prostitute. She is reformed. And, you're going to make sure the court does not permit evidence of her prior,... uh,... 'profession,' shall we say, to be introduced into evidence."

"Well, shouldn't I know the details of the other accusation, so that I can be prepared for the defense attorneys' attack on the credibility of this case?"

Just then, Katelyn Kruz, the youngest and newest member of the Sexual Assaults Team, spoke up. She was a bright young woman with the ambition to become the revered trial lawyer that Sarah Cartwright had been, before Sarah abruptly resigned from the District Attorney's Office and seemingly disappeared without explanation. There were rumors that Sarah had become so overwhelmed with the job that she quit practicing law, altogether; and moved back to Montana to work on a farm. There were other rumors that she had flown off into the sunset with a wealthy Hollywood man who promised her wealth, luxury and world travel. The mystery of her disappearance only fed the legend of Sarah Cartwright even more. Katelyn Kruz idolized Sarah Cartwright. Katelyn was only two years out of law school, and was lucky to finally get assigned to this major crimes team, where she could develop skills handling more complex and high profile cases. This case would pave the path for Katelyn to become the respected attorney that Sarah Cartwright had been. As Sam expressed his disinterest in handling this unpopular but very high profile rape case, Katelyn seized the opportunity to come into her own. She interrupted the exchange between Sam and the chair of the Sexual Assaults Team, by simply stating:

"I'll take this case, if Sam isn't interested."

The room went silent. Sam didn't object. A case this lousy could only threaten his nearly perfect trial record.

The committee chair looked around the room. No other attorney spoke up. Ten other lawyers served on the Sexual Assaults Team. All remained silent.

Jack couldn't allow Katelyn to handle this trial on her own. She was far too inexperienced; and he didn't want to assign two prosecutors to the case, because he believed that would be a waste of resources. As the committee chair pondered his response, and uncomfortable silence filled the room, Sam capitalized on his chance to get off the case. Sam suggested, "Let her handle the arraignment, I'll coach her through the trial."

The committee chair narrowed his eyes. He didn't like what was happening in his team meeting today. It felt like a rebellion. He was head of the team and people were supposed to take instructions from him. They were not supposed to whine and complain about not wanting to handle a case, or interject themselves into a matter that was too far over their heads. But that's exactly what was happening today. Despite his annoyance, Jack decided that an arraignment was simple enough to allow the eager, young prosecutor to handle. He replied:

"Just the arraignment. Sam, you're still handling the trial. The defendant's legendary father and a whole team of excellent defense lawyers will be handling this case. Katelyn can't handle this trial on her own." He then changed the subject to the next case, in order to prevent any further discussion over who would be handling the unpopular case, involving the alleged rape of convicted prostitute, Kelly Luthan.

Chapter 2

Richard White Sr., drove home in pouring down rain – rare weather for Los Angeles, but appropriate weather to mark what a horrid day it was. He had just left the jail after visiting with his son and a team of the best defense attorneys in the country. He couldn't believe this was happening. He had been a defense lawyer for over 30 years; and he never once imagined, he might have to defend his own son from such terrible charges. For the first time in his entire career as one of the country's best defense attorneys, Richard White, Sr., was afraid.

He was afraid and confused. He was baffled at how such an event could occur. He didn't raise his children to be criminals. He taught them right from wrong. He took them to church every Sunday. White Sr., taught his children to respect others and to treat others, as they would hope to be treated themselves. He taught them to live respectable lives. He gave them everything money could buy. And that money, gave his son the ability to attract the most beautiful women in Los Angeles to become his girlfriends.

White Sr., had always taught his son to respect women; and he led by example. He treated his wife like the queen of his universe. He treated her like she walked on water. He adored her and made her every wish come true. He taught his son with more than just words. He taught him through his conduct as well, that a woman was a precious gift to be treasured, and never to be harmed or brutalized.

So, it was impossible. It was simply impossible! That his son could be accused of such a crime! *Rape. Rape? How could his son be in jail for rape?* It was unfathomable. Even worse, the prosecution had also charged attempted murder, because a knife was involved. The alleged victim claimed that he threatened to kill her. And what a victim!? A woman who had been convicted of prostitution! How could this be? White Sr., could not believe this was happening to his beloved son.

As he increased the speed of his windshield wipers to match the thundering rain, the pain in his chest began to rise again. White Sr., had been experiencing it more and more often, these days. He knew it was from the stress of this case. He also knew he couldn't tell his wife about the chest pain. It would be too much for her to bear. Their son's arrest was already too much for her to bear.

White Sr., continued his treacherous drive home, navigating the obstacle course of L.A. freeway traffic, plagued with drivers inexperienced at handling their cars in the rain. He couldn't wait to get home to his lovely wife, and find comfort in her arms; but he also dreaded the thought of seeing all the pain and worry in her face, which she now carried every single day since their son's arrest. He continued his drive with images of his son still in his mind. He could still see the desperation on his face, and hear the fear in his voice. White Jr.'s words still rang in his ears, "Help me dad. Help me. I didn't do it. I didn't do it. Please help me, dad." Over and over again, his son had said, "You're the best, dad! You're one of the best! You have to get me out of here." It broke White Sr.'s heart to see his son trapped like an animal, desperate and afraid, crying like a child for his father's help. And for the first time in his entire career, White Sr., feeling so afraid.

It was much different when the defendant was your own son. The fear that you might lose the case was debilitating. That is why he had hired a team of the best defense attorneys in the country. He would watch the case closely. He would participate in every meeting, in every strategic decision, in every analysis of every shred of evidence. But he would not speak in court. Someone else had to do that, someone who didn't have so much on the line. There is an old saying that: "an attorney who represents himself, has a fool for a client." That old saying applies equally to close family members. His own son was far too close to his heart. Representing his son would be like representing himself. It could not be done effectively.

Chapter 3

As soon as the Sexual Assaults Team meeting had adjourned, Sam walked straight to the large corner office at the end of the hall. He needed to catch the District Attorney before he left his desk. By Sam's calculation, the District Attorney would still be at his desk, engaged in his morning ritual of returning dozens of calls to important people around the city, including his constituents, the media, high ranking police officers and the mayor.

Sam did not hesitate to interrupt that morning ritual. He was far too proud of his win-loss record to allow a case like this to screw it up. He was hoping to convince the District Attorney to allow Katelyn Kruz to take over the entire case.

As Sam spoke, the District Attorney listened to him thoughtfully, without interruption. Normally, he would never consider such a ludicrous suggestion as to allow an attorney of Katelyn's experience to handle a case this complex; especially, with all the problems this case had. But this case was different. The defendant was the son of his old friend, Richard White, Sr., a prominent defense attorney whose reputation preceded him, both in the courtroom and around the city. He was a well renowned attorney, benefactor, and an all-around good guy. He was respected by all the judges in the courthouse, and loved by all who knew him. He exuded such charm, that it was hard for any of the prosecutors to hate him, like they hated so many of their adversaries in the courtroom. Instead, they loved him as a person, and respected him as an attorney.

The District Attorney knew that many of the prosecutors on his staff hoped to land a job at White Sr.'s prestigious law firm, after gaining enough trial experience in the D.A.'s Office. White Sr., was good to his staff. He paid them well and offered great perks. He regularly threw lavish parties, to which only a very select few prosecutors were invited. Sarah Cartwright, for example – an extremely talented trial lawyer who White Sr., had been recruiting to join his firm, before she suddenly resigned from the District Attorney's Office and disappeared. Also, the District Attorney himself never missed a party. He and White Sr., had been good friends since law school. The divergent paths, down which their careers had taken them after law school, never changed that fact. They kept things professional and appropriate on the job, never allowing personal friendship to compromise their professionalism; but off the job, they were still great old buddies who visited each other frequently and attended the same social events.

White Sr.'s close friends called him "Rick," and he was affectionately referred to around the courthouse, as "White Sr." They called him White Sr., because he was the first "White," in his law firm's name: "White, White & Smith."

White Sr., was the father; and White Jr., was the son. White Jr., was also the defendant in this rape case; a case, the District Attorney himself doubted. But upon the instruction of a well-respected attorney, whose integrity the District Attorney knew to be impeccable, White Jr., was arrested for raping a prostitute. He was arrested and indicted before the District Attorney had an opportunity to call his old friend and warn him. While, the D.A., could not order the dismissal of the case as a favor to his friend; he could do him the small favor of assigning an extremely inexperienced attorney to the case, and allow it to appear as if the jury let him go, not the D.A.'s Office.

He should have felt guilty for considering the possibility of intentionally handicapping the prosecution's case, but it was very difficult for the District Attorney to believe that the All-American kid he watched grow up, was guilty of this crime. The young man had everything – good looks, lots of money, his father's charm (which White Jr., only used on women, not juries). He was frequently seen with the most beautiful blondes as his girlfriends.

The only thing the boy seemed to lack was a strong work ethic. He preferred surfing, driving fast cars and partying, to working. He never worked hard enough to become the great defense lawyer that his father had become. However, his lack of motivation to work did not make him a criminal. It was just too hard to imagine that White Jr., was actually guilty of a crime such as this; but the crime had been charged, and the District Attorney saw no politically correct way to get rid of the case, other than to let the system go through its motions and see what verdict the jury returned.

So when Sam suggested that young, inexperienced, Katelyn Kruz, take over the case, the District Attorney sat quietly, feigning a facial expression designed to make Sam believe that it would be difficult to convince him.

Then, forcing the sound of reluctance and skepticism into his voice, the District Attorney finally said, "I don't know, Sam... ," knowing very well that Sam would persist.

And Sam persisted, "You know we cannot win this case. You might as well let a young Deputy D.A., sharpen her skills trying a case against the best team of defense lawyers money can buy. When else will she have an opportunity to practice her skills against such legends as these? And you don't have to worry. I'll coach her along the way. I will help her with witness preparation, trial preparation, anticipating the defense strategy, all that!" Sam continued enthusiastically.

Leaning back in his chair, with a thoughtful expression, the District Attorney allowed Sam to go on. After making Sam sweat it long enough, the District Attorney conclusively answered: "You make a good point, Sam. This is an excellent opportunity for her to sharpen her skills. There is no better way to become a good trial lawyer, than trial by fire. And since this is going to be a learning experience for her, on a case we know can't be won, let her make her own mistakes. We learn best from our losses. So don't waste too much of your time coaching. If she has a question, answer it. But don't develop the trial strategy for her. Don't prepare the witnesses for her. Do not prepare the questions to be asked of witnesses; and do not prepare the opening statement or closing arguments. Do not tell her what to do in jury selection. She needs to develop her own strategy, and learn from her own mistakes. That can only happen if she performs all those tasks herself, and watches how her decisions affect the case."

Chapter 4

White Jr., was escorted to the courtroom, shackled in chains. Due to the attempted aggravated murder charge, his wrists were handcuffed in front of him, and a long chain connected the handcuffs to ankle cuffs. He had to shuffle into the courtroom with small, half steps because of the restrictive shackles. The jailor who escorted him into the courtroom made no exceptions for someone he thought was a spoiled little scumbag, who was most likely, guilty of the crimes charged. The jailor presumed that White Jr., was guilty of all charges. He assumed that White Jr., was just another arrogant, spoiled, rich kid who believed that his money, and his father's talented defense work, gave him a free pass to do whatever he wanted in life.

On their way from the jail to the courtroom, the jailor, pretending to be clumsy, stepped on White Jr.'s foot and bumped him against the wall with a hard thud. He insincerely apologized each time, "Sorry man, I'm clumsy sometimes. But that didn't hurt too bad, did it?"

White Jr., kept his head down and mumbled, "I'm fine," as he tried to keep as much distance away from the clumsy jailor as possible. After several of these mishaps, he learned to watch the jailor's movements and tried to get out of the way before another accident inflicted more injury. His toe felt like it had been crushed, and his head felt sore from the impact it had made with the wall.

Even more painful than the clumsy jailor's accidents, was entering the courtroom, as a shackled defendant. All eyes fixated on White Jr., – some wide with shock at the sight of him so humiliated; others narrowed with suspicion and contempt; but the worst of them, twinkled. The twinkling eyes of eager journalists, salivating at White Jr.'s potential demise, were worse than the prosecuting attorney's determined face.

As soon as White Jr., reached counsel table, his team of defense lawyers encircled him; and he felt much safer. He knew his father was going to get him out of this. He knew the judge was going to set bail, which his father would immediately post, thereby releasing him from jail, pending trial.

But Katelyn Kruz had other plans for White Jr. She planned to make a name for herself convincing the judge, against all odds, and against a legendary defense team, to deny bail and order that White Jr., be held in jail, pending trial.

White Jr., watched the door that connected the courtroom to Judge Johnson's chambers. He knew Judge Johnson well —a logical, well-reasoned, fair judge, before whom White Jr., had appeared as defense counsel, on many occasions. Watching that door was like waiting for a burst of air, after being submerged in water. As soon as Judge Johnson emerged from that door, it would only be moments until White Jr., was set free on bail.

When the door finally opened, and the judge entered the courtroom, White Jr., almost vomited. *It was Judge Kline. Why was Judge Kline in Judge Johnson's courtroom?* Judge Kline was a female judge with a nasty reputation. Despite the guaranty by the U.S. Constitution that all defendants were innocent until proven guilty, Judge Kline had a reputation for treating men, facing sexual assault charges, as if they were guilty until proven innocent. It was rumored that she hated all men; and that she used her judicial power to get back at them all for the days she believed she had been mistreated, as a young female attorney. She first began practicing law during a time when very few women were lawyers. Times were much different now; but this old feminist still had a serious chip on her shoulder. She was rude to male attorneys, and she was ruthless in the way she handled sex crimes. She was known as, "the man-eater." And today, "the man-eater" would be deciding whether White Jr., would be released on bail, or held in jail pending trial.

"All rise and come to order," announced the bailiff.

"Sit down!" snapped Judge Kline, as if standing were an insult, instead of the sign of respect it was intended to be. She had the worst judicial temperament.

As White Jr., sat and his stomach turned violently, a member of the defense team put a hand on his shoulder and whispered an explanation in White Jr.'s ear: "Judge Johnson has been rushed to the hospital in a medical emergency, but he's in stable condition. We only expect Judge Kline to cover his cases temporarily. If things don't go well today, we will wait for Judge Johnson's return, then request a bail hearing. Don't worry, kid, everything's going to be all right. Your father and I won't let them hold you for long."

The explanation did not abate White Jr.'s nausea.

"How does the defendant plead!" snarled the judge, as she glared at White Jr.

"Not guilty, Your Honor," said Larry Pason, the member of the defense team with the most experience and best record defending sex crimes.

"What's the State's recommendation on bail?" quipped the judge, almost before Larry even finished his sentence.

Katelyn stood, and began her well rehearsed speech:

"Your Honor, the defendant has substantial assets, and tremendous incentive to flee the jurisdiction, pending trial. His assets are so significant, that we expect him to flee to a very comfortable and luxurious destination that does not observe extradition. It is the State's fear that the defendant will escape justice, forever. He is considered extremely dangerous, as..."

"Objection! That's preposterous, Your Honor! My client has no criminal history, whatsoever! The charges have been fabricated by a prostitute seeking to extort money from my wealthy, good-looking, well-mannered and well-respected client. I..."

"Who asked you, yet!?" barked the judge, with a snarl and an elevated voice. "It's not your turn to speak! It's the State's turn to speak now. And look at that jury box. Do you see anyone there? Do you? Of course not! Because this isn't a trial! I'm the only one here, and the code of evidence does not apply to these proceedings; so, your objection is not only overruled, it's completely inappropriate!"

Then turning to the prosecution with less venom in her tone, the judge stated, "Ms. Kruz, please continue with the State's recommendation."

Katelyn continued:

"Your Honor, as I was saying, the State considers this defendant to be particularly dangerous because he brutally raped a woman, with the use of a deadly weapon – a knife to be specific. She barely got away from him, after he threatened to kill her. Do not pay attention to his lack of a criminal history. Rape and attempted murder, alone, are serious enough charges to consider him a danger and a threat to the public. His lack of a criminal history, and his pampered lifestyle make the threat of jail even more frightening to him than it is to a hardened career criminal. No, Your Honor, his personal circumstances and history do not make him less likely to flee. They make him more likely to flee.

"Even worse yet, Your Honor, Mr. White, Jr., is a former criminal defense attorney himself; and the victim in this case, is his former client." Perfectly timed silence allowed the words to hang in the air, lingering with the sound of disgust in Katelyn's voice.

Then, raising her voice to match the zeal in her argument, Katelyn continued, "As if rape and attempted murder are not atrocious enough,..." She paused and pointed at the defendant, as she declared: "That man preyed on his own client! A woman who trusted him. A woman who was vulnerable, and who had relied on him to protect her own interests. She never would have suspected that her own lawyer would rape her and try to kill her!

"The State very strongly recommends that you hold the defendant pending trial, without bail. He is a threat to the community. He is a threat to the victim, and he must be brought to justice. Justice requires that you deny bail.

"Thank you, Your Honor."

Katelyn sat down with the rigidity of a military officer, her hands resting on counsel table, and folded conservatively in front of her. She looked straight at the judge with the steeled, expressionless resolve of a hard-core prosecutor, as the defense lawyer rose to speak.

"Your Honor, with all due respect, the prosecution has greatly exaggerated the circumstances of this case. It is my client who is the victim. Please look at my client, as he sits here, even further victimized by a criminal justice system gone awry – a criminal justice system, which has arrested the wrong person. This court need only take one look at Mr. White. You will see, there is a scar on his face. That scar was not there before the alleged victim – who is a convicted prostitute – fabricated this story. It was she, who slashed him in the face with the knife. It is she, who is the criminal. After the encounter, she drove herself, not to the police, but to the District Attorney's Office, with the knife still in her hands, immediately after the incident. There is no 911 tape of a call by a frightened woman who barely escaped a dangerous situation with her life. There are no 911 calls from neighbors or any other witnesses reporting a woman screaming help, or frantically running away. We would expect a woman whose life had just been threatened, to panic, to be frantic, to dial 911, immediately. But instead, this woman acted with cold, calm, calculated deliberation.

"Your Honor, the convicted prostitute did not go to the police. She did not behave in a manner consistent with what one would typically observe after a rape. Instead, her behavior was calculated. She went straight to the District Attorney's Office to report the alleged crime. In all my years handling sexual assault cases – and I have handled thousands – I never once observed a case, in which an alleged rape victim drives straight to the District Attorney's Office, after the alleged rape, to report the crime! And one need not even wonder why she behaved so bizarrely. The intent and the motive are clear in the action itself. That convicted prostitute, who accepts money in exchange for sexual intercourse, had a plan. It was her plan to convince a *lawyer* – and I mean *lawyer,* not *police officer* – to convince a lawyer that a rich man assaulted her. The motive? Very clear. In that prostitute's mind, she thought: 'convince the D.A.'s Office to prove him guilty, and all my lawyer has to do, is calculate the damages I will receive.' That's a case any attorney would take on a contingency! Nothing out of her pocket to sue a wealthy man on her fabricated story. The D.A.'s Office proves liability. The prostitute and her lawyer collect the check.

"In her cold, deliberate calculation, a street-wise prostitute was able to convince the District Attorney's Office to order the arrest of the victim of her own crime – my dear client who sits here, judged already before he has ever had a chance to exercise his constitutional right to trial by jury, before whom he is presumed innocent. But today, the prosecution asks you to deny him that right. They ask you to find him guilty before he is tried. They ask you to incarcerate him pre-trial for several months, as this is a serious case, which will take several months to completely investigate. Your Honor, it is this court's duty to balance out the power of the executive branch, which appears before you today, in the form of an overzealous prosecutor seeking to convict and incarcerate my client – in a case wrought with doubt – before he is even tried.

"Your Honor, there is so much doubt in this case, and a possible misuse, really, of the D.A.'s power, that this truly is a case, which would warrant release on his own recognizance, without requiring any bail. But my client wants to prove to this court that he has every intention of appearing at trial to clear himself of these preposterous charges. He has asked me to request that you set bail. He will post bail, Your Honor, in whatever amount this court deems appropriate. It is my humble recommendation, that nothing over $1 million is necessary. We ask nothing more of you today than to honor the Constitution of the United States of America. Thank you, Your Honor."

Katelyn bolted out of her seat before the defense lawyer even sat down. She was eager to rebut the defense lawyer's characterization of events, and hoped to speak before the judge made up her mind:

"Your Honor, if I may. The defense team is brilliant. They are so brilliant, they can read a woman's mind. They can think of all kinds of terrible plots on her behalf. That's fantastic defense work. But it does not change the fact that that man is dangerous," Katelyn insisted, while pointing at the Defendant.

Katelyn continued with a sarcastic tone, "And oh yes, his honorable and generous offer to post bail, which the defense claims is unnecessary, well Your Honor, that's my point. He does not care how high the bail amount is, because he can, and he will pay whatever it will cost him to buy his freedom today, so he can disappear to a tropical island, never to return and face justice..."

Judge Kline turned her attention toward the defendant, as Katelyn's rebuttal argument trailed on. She allowed Katelyn to finish her argument, though she was no longer listening. At the conclusion of Katelyn's rebuttal, Judge Kline turned to the defense attorney and asked, "Mr. Pason, is it true that the alleged victim is a former client of the defendant?"

"Well, Your Honor, I'm not in a position to..."

"Stop that, Mr. Pason. Don't play cutsie with me. If someone convicted of a crime, was represented by your client, that fact will be public record. No privilege exists to protect that fact, not on behalf of your client, and not on behalf of his client. So tell me now, is it true that the alleged victim is a former client of the defendant?"

"It would appear so, Your Honor."

"It would appear so? It would appear so?" the judge repeated with thick sarcasm in her voice. "Why does everything only 'appear so' to a defense attorney, and never 'is' so? Shall I take that as a 'yes,' Mr. Pason?"

"Yes, Your Honor."

"Mr. Pason, this is not the first time your client has told a story about being violently victimized by one of his own clients. As I understand the story that went around this courthouse not very long ago, your client asserted attorney-client privilege to hide the identity of one of his clients, who had robbed him and assaulted him so badly, that your client ended up in the hospital. Today, your client would have this court believe that he again, has been victimized by a more intelligent thief, one who slashed him in the face with a knife, for the purpose of extorting damages in a civil trial, to follow the criminal trial, she so cleverly convinced the District Attorney's Office to pursue. While I will say, there is a question here about who assaulted who, it is a question the jury must decide. And they will decide that question before your client has an opportunity to flee. Bail is denied.

"But, Your Honor! – "

"Next case."

"But, Your Honor! The Constitution of the United States! – "

"Order! Order in this Courtroom!" hollered Judge Kline, while slamming her gavel several times. "I have decided the terms of your client's custody, Mr. Pason, and I have already called the next case. Please leave counsel table and allow the next set of attorneys to take their places."

Larry Pason and every defense lawyer at his counsel table (including the defendant) knew that when Judge Kline slams her gavel, her next act is to hold someone in contempt of court. So they quietly gathered their things, and with body language slouching in defeat, they moved away from counsel table.

★ ★ ★

Katelyn walked triumphantly out of the courtroom towards the conference room, in which the Sexual Assaults Team meeting was about to begin. She was happy the team was meeting today. And what luck! It was just after her triumph in the arraignment of White Jr.

The Sexual Assaults Team was comprised of ten elite prosecutors plus one young attorney showing enough promise to be invited for a test-run on the team. It normally took years before the invitee could be assigned to handle even a pre-trial hearing. Katelyn was the first young invitee to be allowed, so early in her career, to handle an arraignment like the one she just left. It was the dumb luck of Sam Chapman's arrogance, which she had to thank for this huge step towards advancing her career. Katelyn was a bright young woman with the ambition to become the revered trial lawyer that Sarah Cartwright had been. Nobody outside Sarah's closest inner circle knew why she had so abruptly resigned and disappeared, leaving only a "Dear John" style letter on the District Attorney's chair. Her sudden departure only seemed to add even more mystique and *"ah"* to her legendary status as an amazing trial lawyer, who had accomplished so much, in just a short 6-year career.

Though she never met her, Katelyn idolized Sarah Cartwright. Katelyn was barely two years out of law school, and was lucky to finally get assigned to this major crimes team. It offered the chance to develop career-building skills that could only be acquired by handling complex and high profile cases. Getting even just the smallest responsibilities in White Jr.'s case could pave the path for Katelyn to become the respected attorney that Sarah Cartwright had been.

Katelyn turned the corner to enter a conference room down the hall from where the arraignment had just taken place. She was the first to arrive, and she took her usual seat.

As the other attorneys began to gather around the conference room table, Katelyn sat with a wide grin on her face. Jack Wayne, the Committee Chair, spoke to her first, "You look happy."

"The judge held White Jr., without bail, pending trial."

"That's great, Katelyn! Great job!" exclaimed Jack Wayne, with pride.

"Don't congratulate her too much," said Sam Chapman, as he pulled out a chair to sit down. "She got lucky. Judge Kline was covering Judge Johnson's courtroom, today."

Katelyn's smile fell from her face.

Sam continued, turning to address Katelyn, "You were overzealous, Katelyn. You sounded like a bloodthirsty prosecutor, in there. Any other judge would've felt like you were over-playing your hand. That's how you lose credibility. With the facts of this case, you should have asked for a respectable amount of bail, instead of getting all bloodthirsty, like you did in there. This is just one case. Don't lose your credibility as a prosecutor, getting too excited about one case."

Katelyn's mouth hung open as she stared at Sam, doe-eyed and speechless. She was caught off guard by this sudden blast of criticism, and too junior to know how to reply.

But Jack's voice came quickly to her defense: "This sage advice is coming from the guy who was too scared to try the case himself."

Sam shot Jack a scowling look, as Jack continued, "Congratulations Katelyn, the District Attorney has decided that you will be handling White Jr.'s trial. Sam will be your coach."

Katelyn beamed with ambition and disbelief. She sat up straighter in her chair as a wide excited grin spread across her face.

The Committee Chair looked back at Sam, "And you, better coach her *before* trial. None of this Monday-morning quarterbacking shit. Ok?"

Sam looked directly in the Committee Chair's eyes, and with a little too much calm and poise, he said, "I will coach Katelyn with as much effort as the District Attorney expects me to coach her."

It was subtle, and the words Sam used were carefully selected with enough diplomacy to fool everyone else at the table; but Jack heard the defiance in Sam's voice, and he knew the deeper meaning in it. He wasn't in that room when Sam convinced the District Attorney to allow such a young, inexperienced prosecutor to take over the case, but he knew about the history between White Sr., and the District Attorney; and Jack was smart enough to figure out that a favor was being done for the District Attorney's old friend.

Jack shook his head to clear these frustrating thoughts from his mind. His next thought was of Sarah Cartwright. He cursed her in his mind. How could she just disappear the way she did, after ordering White Jr.'s arrest, and leave such important work unfinished?

In that moment, Jack decided to call Detective Jones. If anyone could find Sarah quickly, it was Detective Jones.

Chapter 5

It was a clear dry day in Oklahoma, where Kelly Luthan now lived. Kelly had returned to Oklahoma before the arraignment. She left Los Angeles the same day she had given grand jury testimony against White Jr. After leaving the courthouse, that day, she drove straight to her studio apartment, packed everything she owned into her small, red, Toyota Corolla, and began the long drive back to her hometown. She couldn't get to Oklahoma fast enough. Her drive was long, and relentless. She only stopped when necessary, resting minimally, and only as required to keep the drive safe.

Kelly had not considered the possibility that she might be required to return to L.A., for a trial. She always assumed that a plea bargain would be reached. She knew White Jr.'s father was an amazing defense attorney who would negotiate a very lenient deal with the District Attorney's Office, resulting in White Jr.'s release from jail. She didn't want to be around when White Jr., was released. She also didn't care whether or not White Jr., would spend any real time in prison. When she first reported the alleged incident, she was not exactly motivated by a desire to bring him to justice; rather, she was mostly motivated by the desire to avoid getting arrested herself for slashing that knife across his face. The last thing she wanted was to be charged with another crime, which would tarnish her reputation even further. So far, nobody back home knew how she had supported herself during the years she had spent in L.A., hoping to become an actress. The entanglement she had with White Jr., only made it more likely that her shameful past would follow her back home. She had to do everything in her power to keep the saga of her L.A. life, back in L.A. Each day Kelly woke up in Oklahoma, she thought to herself, *so far so good.*

Life was good now. Kelly had rekindled an old flame with her high school sweetheart, Johnny Goodminn, who had never stopped loving her during all those years she'd been gone.

★ ★ ★

One week before Kelly left L.A., she called her parents to let them know, she was coming home. Word spread like wildfire throughout the small town, in which Kelly had grown up. Johnny heard the news; and he was ready for her. During that entire week, he eagerly awaited Kelly's arrival. Johnny took time off his busy schedule as a general contractor. He spent the whole week waiting at the local diner for the day she would roll into town. From his favorite booth, he could see the one and only main road in town. It was an old highway that passed right in front of the diner.

Johnny had a plan. He would park his old red pickup out front. It was the one he and Kelly had made so many memories in, back in high school. She was sure to see it on her way into town. Though Johnny had a brand new pick up now, and a nice car, he specifically chose "Old Red" to park in front of the diner. He hadn't driven that pickup in years. He was happy it was still running. All it needed was a new charged battery, and it ran like new.

Johnny was hoping the image of that old truck would draw Kelly into the diner to see him. If that didn't work, it would not deter Johnny. From his favorite booth in the diner, Johnny would be able to see Kelly drive by. And if she did, he would just hop into his pickup and follow her to her parents' house.

Each day after her parents had received the news that Kelly was coming home, Johnny arrived at the diner as soon as it opened at 6:00 a.m., and stayed until it closed at 10:00 p.m. He never ate so much in his life. He didn't want to take up a table for the whole day, without making appropriate purchases. So, he ate breakfast, lunch and dinner there. He also ordered snacks and dessert in between. He would drink coffee, too. He drank tons and tons of coffee. And he would stare at that old highway, waiting for his one true love to come home. That week, the waitress nicknamed Johnny's favorite booth, "the Command Post." Whenever she'd put an order in for the cook, she'd say: "It's for the Command Post." And the cook would know that it was Johnny's order. Johnny was a regular; so, nobody had to ask him how he liked his eggs or how well he wanted his steak cooked. The chef at the diner already knew.

On the third day that Johnny sat waiting for his one and only love to come back to him, the waitress sat down across the table from him. Johnny was not surprised. The casual atmosphere of the local café permitted this cordiality between waitress and customer. Not wanting to be rude, Johnny slowly pulled his eyes away from the window, but kept the street within his peripheral vision.

Diane smiled warmly at him, "I'll watch the command post for five minutes if you want to take a quick break, visit the little boys room, check on your employees, whatever you need to do. Don't worry. I'll stand watch and call you immediately if I see her drive by."

Johnny smiled back. "Thanks. You're the best, Diane!" But he didn't dare leave the diner. He left his command post only for a quick restroom break. And the same routine developed between them, each day after that, for the duration of Johnny's wait.

Finally, Kelly Luthan drove into town. On her way into town, she slowed down and looked around, admiring the buildings that were so familiar, letting her mind wander down memory lane. Then she saw it – that old red pickup truck. There it sat in front of the diner where she and Johnny had shared so many milkshakes. Could it be? Was that Johnny's old truck? And was he still driving that thing? Kelly slammed on her brakes and whipped her steering wheel to the right, quickly pulling into the diner before she missed its parking lot. The squeal of her tires jolted Johnny's attention up from his coffee cup and out the window. Johnny saw her and jumped to his feet. He was standing when Kelly walked in.

"Johnny! Is that you!?" Kelly squealed.

And Johnny hit his knees, "Finally! Kelly! You've finally come home to marry me!" Johnny had dropped to one knee and held out the same little diamond ring he had proposed with, after graduation. But she had turned him down then. She turned him down to chase a Hollywood dream. And Johnny swore to her that he'd keep that ring and wait for as long as it took for her to get tired of that stuff and come home.

Now, standing in the diner so many years later, Kelly stood, speechless. Tears filled her eyes, and rolled down her cheeks. He meant it! He really meant what he said, all those years ago. It was an unexpected but beautiful surprise. She had held so many regrets resulting from her choice to leave her high school sweetheart to move to L.A., seeking a career in acting. Though she found work as an actress, it was limited to small meaningless roles that weren't worth the sacrifice she had made. And to see that Johnny still loved her, after all this time, she was never going to let go of that again.

Kelly ran to Johnny, kneeling, as she approached him, practically knocking him over, as she threw her arms around him. Kissing him, she cried, "Yes! Yes!" Tears of love streamed down her face, as she continued hugging him and kissing him. Catching her breath, she looked into his face, and held it with both hands, "Yes, Johnny, I've come home to marry you," she finally said, as she stared into his eyes, with a baffled but loving smile, still wet with the tears that had rolled down her face.

Johnny held her tight and kissed her, "I can afford a much bigger ring now, but I want you to have this one, too."

"It's perfect, Johnny. It's just perfect. I don't need a bigger ring. I love this one!" Kelly exclaimed, as she laughed and cried.

Then, Melvin, the owner of the diner came out from a door that connected the diner to the tavern. "I think this calls for a toast!" he declared, as he popped open the bottle of champagne he held in his hand. Everyone in the diner celebrated with Kelly and Johnny that day; and Kelly called her parents to come join them.

★ ★ ★

But today, the subpoena Kelly had just received, threatened to ruin everything. It notified her that White Jr.'s trial would be held in a few months. Kelly knew that a trial would elicit questions about her character and her conduct, if not in the courtroom, certainly in the L.A., local media, as she had seen when White Jr., was first arrested. A trial would reveal her past. If Johnny ever found out about Kelly's past, it would utterly destroy him. It would destroy her. It would destroy their relationship.

Staring down at the subpoena in her hands, Kelly felt panic rising in her chest. She had to come up with a story for why she had to travel back to L.A., *alone*. How would she explain this to Johnny? He would never let her go by herself. When he put that ring on her finger, he swore he'd never let her out of his sight again. He swore he would never again allow the bright lights of Hollywood to steal his love away. She knew she could not make up a story about landing a role in a movie. If she said that, he would tell her to choose between him and L.A. It would be the end of them. Now that Kelly was over her silly Hollywood dreams, she loved Johnny more than anything in the world. She couldn't lose him. She regretted all that wasted time they had spent apart while she was chasing silly dreams in L.A. She regretted the filthy lifestyle, she allowed herself to deteriorate into, while trying to make ends meet in L.A. She knew that if she had just stayed home with Johnny and accepted his marriage proposal after high school, she could have had a much better life.

Kelly looked down at her ring now, as she stood surrounded by boxes filled with supplies for the new café she would be opening in a week – a dream made possible because Johnny borrowed money to help her open her own business. She looked around the empty café that would soon be open, and her eyes welled up with tears. This new life, which she believed, was the only way to escape her past in L.A., was made possible because of Johnny. All that time she spent, trying to figure out how to come back home to achieve this, she never once guessed, that all she had to do was ask dear, sweet Johnny to help. If she had known that, she never would've gotten caught up in that mess with White Jr. Now, she stared down at the subpoena in her hands, terrified. She was terrified that she might lose all this, terrified that she might lose Johnny's love, terrified that the whole town would find out, that she had once been a prostitute.

Chapter 6

Detective Jones entered the café where he was meeting Jack. He quickly located him and walked over to his table. When Detective Jones sat down, Jack didn't even say hello.

"You need to call Sarah Cartwright," Jack demanded.

"Why?"

"You need to tell her it's time to stop living happily-ever-fucking-after in the south of France. She needs to get back here and perform her duties serving justice."

"Sarah's not coming back."

"Tell her she has to."

"She's not coming back."

Jack slammed his fist on the table, raising his voice, as if yelling at Detective Jones would somehow reach Sarah, and he insisted: "She has duties here. She needs to come back!"

"Why are you so upset? What's the urgency?"

"Because," explained Jack, "Sam Chapman was supposed to handle White Jr.'s Trial. But that arrogant asshole was so worried about his precious win-loss record that he went to the D.A., and weaseled his way off the case. The District Attorney has used that as an opportunity to take care of the son of his old, law school buddy by assigning a young, inexperienced prosecutor to the case. I was doubtful enough when Sam was assigned to the case, even with his talent and trial skills. White Jr., is sure to walk away from this with Katelyn on the case. There is only one person I know who could win a case like this, and it's Sarah Cartwright."

"But she couldn't try the case anyway, she interviewed the victim with me, she'd be a potential witness," argued, Detective Jones.

"There are ways around that," explained Jack, "Besides, at the very least, she could be coaching this young Deputy D.A., on how to handle herself. She needs to be here."

"She's on her honeymoon. She's not coming back for this trial."

"Honeymoon? You mean, she married the guy?"

"Yeah."

"Sarah Cartwright married David Nolan?"

"Yeah, that's why I went to Europe. I was at their wedding."

"Now, hold on a minute, Detective. Are you saying, that after Sarah dismissed a criminal case pending against David Nolan – which, very notably, involved White Jr. – she flew to France with David Nolan, married him, and now refuses to come back?"

"Yep."

"Does that not strike you as odd?"

"Nope."

"Nope?" mocked Jack.

"Nope," repeated Detective Jones, unaffected by Jack's tone, and elaborated, "Nolan turned out to actually be the victim in that case."

"You're certain?" asked Jack.

"I'm certain," answered Detective Jones.

"So, let me get this straight," began Jack, in a voice filled with suggestion, "David Nolan was initially the suspect in a criminal investigation. During that investigation, it was revealed that White Jr., was a participant. Then, somehow, it was later decided that David Nolan was the victim, not the suspect. And, upon Sarah's instruction to police, White Jr., was sent to jail; and almost immediately afterwards, Sarah ran off to Europe and married David Nolan?"

"That's an oversimplified version of the story," argued Detective

Jones, "but yeah, that about sums it up."

Jack pressed Detective Jones further, "Did we ever establish, with certainty, that David Nolan was, in fact, a victim in that case, and not actually a co-conspirator of White Jr., in a large scale white-collar crime scheme?"

"Of course, we did," answered Detective Jones, simply.

Jack replied with a calm, defied only by his words, "That's right, all on the word of a convicted prostitute. How could I forget?"

"Hey!" objected Detective Jones, annoyance finally rising in his voice. "It was on Sarah's word, too. I didn't just take what a prostitute said, as if it were gospel. What are you suggesting? And how's that important, anyway? It's usually a criminal who witnesses another criminal's act. Don't pretend like you've never relied on one criminal to convict another."

Jack narrowed his eyes, pensively. All sarcasm and tension gone from his voice now, he replied with an honest question of his own: "How certain are you that White Jr., is guilty of the crimes he's been charged with in the Kelly Luthan case?"

"I'm absolutely sure."

"Because Sarah told you he was?"

"Yes."

"But despite all the reasons why Sarah believes he's guilty, she will not testify against him, and she will not assist the prosecution in bringing him to justice?"

"Those are the facts."

"Those are pretty shitty facts, Jones!"

"I can't change the facts. But you know Sarah as well as I do, she has good reasons for everything she has done."

Jack changed the subject, "Now, there is the matter of the potentially exculpatory evidence we have yet to disclose to the defense."

"Exculpatory evidence? You mean evidence that suggests White Jr., is innocent?"

"Yes."

"What evidence would that be?" asked Detective Jones.

"White Jr.'s involvement in the David Nolan case."

"How could that help White Jr.'s defense?"

"Well, it calls into question Sarah's motive to frame White Jr., for one thing! It sheds light on the credibility of the prosecutor who interviewed the alleged victim and ordered White Jr.'s arrest! Isn't that obvious?"

"No. I thought you were pissed off when Sarah left, because you thought if she had stayed and pursued charges against White Jr., for his involvement in the David Nolan case, it would have been easier to prove White Jr., guilty of the rape and attempted murder of Kelly Luthan."

"I did, until Sarah ran off like an escaped convict herself! And with the other person of interest in the case, no less! She needs to get back here, Jones! Get her back here before I have to disclose this evidence to the defense."

"What's to disclose? No police reports were written about White Jr.'s involvement in the David Nolan case."

"Even worse! Get her back here!"

Chapter 7

That night, Detective Jones called Sarah. It was 6:00 p.m. in L.A., and 3:00 a.m. in France. He forgot to calculate the time difference.

Sarah heard her cell phone ring, and quickly reached for it, hoping to answer before the sound woke David. She whispered, "hello," as she carefully slipped out of bed trying not to wake David. As Detective Jones announced himself, she walked towards the small ballroom of their beautiful chateau, atop the hill in Eze, France. The ballroom was far enough away from the bedroom that David would not hear her speaking on the phone. The marble floor of the ballroom was cold under her feet; so, she walked quickly passed the pillars of marble, which were beautifully decorated and accented with gold, until she reached the deep, red velvet, Victorian loveseat. This was her favorite place to sit in the ballroom. The velvet was soft against her skin and felt good when she picked her feet up off the cold, marble floor. The loveseat was situated to one side, angled perfectly to frame one of the six sets of French doors, which opened up to a grand balcony overlooking the Mediterranean Sea. On a clear night, with a full moon, she could see the water, even in the dark. Tonight, there was a full moon, and the yachts below were lit up with the occupants who were still enjoying their parties. It was an exquisitely romantic scene outside her window. She wished David were awake. But instead, this elegant scene was wasted on an ugly reminder of the dirt and grime she had left behind in Los Angeles. Detective Jones was on the phone talking to her about a criminal case.

Detective Jones filled her in on the conversation he had with Jack; and concluded, "So, you have to get back here before he discloses that evidence to the defense. It will look bad that you dismissed that other case, disappeared with the defendant, and refuse to come back to participate in any part of prosecuting White Jr., in this case."

"I disagree."

"With what?"

"The evidence is not exculpatory, it is inculpatory."

"You mean it tends to prove he is guilty of raping Kelly Luthan, it does not tend to prove he is innocent?"

"Correct."

"But Jack said that would only be true if you were here, not hiding out there, like a... um, these are his words, like an 'escaped felon.'"

Sarah laughed. "He's taking this a little personally, isn't he?"

"Actually, no, he's just upset that you're not taking it more personally."

"Please tell Jack, that my opinion of his dilemma is this. He does not need to disclose the evidence because the standard of whether or not evidence is exculpatory, is objective, not subjective. That means, you look at it from the perspective of an average defense lawyer. The question is not, whether this excellent, brilliant and legendary defense team might be able to make inculpatory evidence look exculpatory. The question is whether the evidence is in fact, objectively exculpatory. My opinion is that the evidence is not exculpatory; and therefore, the US Constitution does not require the prosecution to disclose it. Therefore, Jack can leave me alone and let me enjoy my new life in France, while he continues to slave away at the D.A.'s Office. I've paid my dues. I've served my time. It's time to pass the torch to a younger, more eager prosecutor and let her find her glory bringing this scumbag to justice."

"But she's not getting any help, Sarah."

"What do you mean?"

"White Jr.'s going to walk. Nobody in the D.A.'s Office is giving her any guidance on how to try a case this complicated. And she's never tried a rape case before, let alone a rape case involving a victim who has been convicted of prostitution."

His words struck Sarah in the gut. She felt sick to her stomach at the thought that White Jr., might escape the charges; but she was also apprehensive about traveling back to L.A. She had a more serious, personal concern to worry about now. She couldn't let that scumbag, White Jr., drag her back to L.A. – even if he was a defendant in a case the State couldn't win without Sarah. Caught between two difficult choices, she decided to end the call, "It's late here, Detective. I'll talk to you about this later."

Detective Jones heard the dial tone before he could say another word.

There were very few people who knew the history between Sarah Cartwright, White Jr., and David Nolan. That history was the reason Sarah had ordered Detective Jones to arrest White Jr., so quickly. It was immediately after the former prostitute had made her claims against him. The arrest was made without delay, and without fully investigating the statements of the alleged victim, Kelly Luthan. This created a severe handicap in the State's case. An arrest made before completing a proper investigation leaves open questions that brilliant defense lawyers can exploit, by answering them in their own way, with their great ideas. Sarah knew this was a vulnerability in the State's case; however, she could not guess what specific vulnerabilities might arise, because she did not stay in L.A., to investigate the case any further. This left Sarah with a nagging feeling of unfinished business, and a fear that White Jr., would not be convicted and incarcerated for the lengthy prison term these serious charges would require. But Sarah had a new life that she needed to protect, now. She didn't want this case to disrupt that life. She turned off her cell phone and set it down on the velvet loveseat. She then walked onto the balcony for some fresh air, hoping to shake off the stress of the detective's call.

Sarah stood on her grand balcony overlooking the Mediterranean

Sea, in the middle of the night. She walked to the railing and stared down at the water and the yachts below. The view was majestic, even at night. She put her hands on the stone railing, closed her eyes and tilted her chin up, feeling the warm sea breeze. She kept her eyes closed and took a long deep breath. She needed to feel the warmth and comfort of the south of France to clear her mind of the things she left behind in L.A. When she finally felt relaxed enough, she went back inside and walked towards the bedroom where she longed to be close to the love of her life.

When Sarah reached the bedroom, she saw that David was still sound asleep, lying on his back in the same position she had left him. Sarah loved how sweet and innocent he looked while he slept. She took off her light pink silk robe and slipped back into bed with David. They usually slept in the nude. Sarah pressed her naked body against David's nude, sleeping form and she sighed with pleasure at the feel of his skin against hers. She kissed him on the lips and he smiled. She watched his sweet face to see if she had woken him. His eyes were still shut, and the deep, steady rhythm of his breath did not change. Her kiss made him smile even in his sleep. This made Sarah smile too. She then nuzzled in next to him, wrapping one leg and one arm around him as he slept. Sarah listened to the sweet sound of David's slumber, trying to get back to sleep herself. But she was restless, and turned on. Lying next to David always turned her on. They never went to bed and fell asleep, without first, making love. Now, she was awake in the middle of the night, but he wasn't.

Sarah nuzzled in closer to David and kissed his neck. A gentle moan, as light as a sigh, escaped his lips. He always made that sound when she kissed his neck. Sarah lifted her head to look into David's face. He was still asleep. This melted her heart. *Wow, he even makes that sound in his sleep*, she thought. Sarah lied back down and nuzzled her face into the nook between David's jawbone and his collarbone. She then caressed his chest as she kissed his neck. The deep, steady rhythm of his breath still did not change. She gently traced his muscular chest, drawing her hand downward over his rock solid abdominal muscles.

Slowly, and gently, her hand continued its downward descent until she reached his groin. She gently caressed his manhood, as she began kissing his chest. She felt him grow hard under her touch, as her caress turned into a gentle massage. Feeling his desire in her hands, she slowly wrapped her hand around him and began to stroke.

As she stroked him, David's breath changed, from the steady rhythm of sleep to heavier, deeper sighs of pleasure. But his eyes remained shut. Sarah began to kiss him harder now, pressing her lips against his neck and sucking. She lifted her mouth and opened it around his jawbone. David's eyes began to open slightly, as she gently traced her teeth against his jaw line. With his hard erection still in her hands, she continued stroking him. He was not completely awake yet, but on the verge of waking up. She heard him mumble, "No, mmm, still sleep…ng." Sarah giggled. She pressed her lips against his ear as she stroked his manhood a little harder, and she whispered, "It's not a dream, my love. Wake up." David's eyes flung open. He turned his face towards her with surprise. "Sarah!"

"Mmm, hmm, Yes," she answered seductively, still firmly gripping him and stroking him.

David tilted his head back with pleasure. "Oh yes, Sarah. Yes."

Sarah pressed her soft breasts against him and David moaned, "Ah." Lying on his back, enjoying the feel of her hand, his desire grew to such heights that he had to take control.

David rolled over, pinning Sarah beneath him, as he kissed her hard on the lips, in an open mouth kiss that devoured her mouth. Pressing his mouth against hers in a deep, passionate French kiss, David wrapped his arms beneath her naked body, and pulled her against him, pressing his hard desire into her womanhood, slowly entering her. Sarah's mouth opened in ecstasy as her head tilted back. David pressed himself into her further and deeper, with a slow sensuous motion that matched the passion of his kiss. Then he began to thrust slow and deep, as he pressed his face against hers. He moaned with pleasure in her ear and the sound of her passion matched his. He thrust deeper, harder, faster, as Sarah's cries of pleasure became louder. He continued, as he whispered in her ear, "I love you, Sarah. My wife, my life, I love you." Sarah responded with a loud cry of pleasure, "Ahhhh," as she grabbed him tight with her arms and her legs, and he continued his sweet rhythm, delivering ecstasy with every thrust; and David continued to make love to Sarah deep and hard, until finally he felt the pinnacle of her pleasure, as she came all around him; and he released his own orgasm into her, trembling with pleasure until he lost all his strength and slumped down against her body, panting heavily until they fell fast asleep in each other's arms.

★ ★ ★

As the morning light beamed through the skylight of their luxurious bedroom, in their chateau atop the hill in heavenly Eze, Sarah and David began to stir in their soft feather bed. David kissed Sarah and she slowly opened her eyes. "Mmm, Good morning, love," she purred.

"Good morning," he replied, as he nuzzled her. She was lying on her back. He was on his side, with his arms and legs wrapped around her, as if she were his body pillow.

Wrapped in the luxurious comfort of her husband's arms and the silk sheets of their plush bed, Sarah murmured, "I'm not ready to get up yet,"

"Me neither," said David.

Sarah turned her head towards David, buried her face into his chest, and shut her eyes again, a content smile spreading across her face.

David looked at his wife lovingly, and with vague images of the night before teasing his mind, he sleepily asked, "Did we make love, last night?"

Sarah's smile grew wider. "Yes..."

"No, I mean after we fell asleep. In the middle of the night, did we make love, a second time?"

Sarah giggled deviously, "Yes."

David's eyes widened, as he stared at his wife, "I thought that was a dream!" he exclaimed.

Sarah burst into laughter, "I know."

As the dreamy memory became clearer in David's mind, he asked with sudden realization, "Hey! Did you wake me up with a hand job!"

Sarah laughed even louder now, "Yes! Ha, ha, ha."

"You naughty, naughty woman! You took advantage of me in the middle of the night!" David began tickling Sarah as she squirmed around squealing and giggling, mischievously. It was rare that Sarah ever initiated lovemaking; not for lack of desire, rather for lack of opportunity, as David's sex drive was so strong, she hardly had an opportunity to initiate. Sarah's out-of-character conduct from the night before surprised David, but he loved it!

David continued tickling Sarah as she squirmed around. "Explain yourself!" he demanded. "Explain how you can live with yourself, taking advantage of a man while he slept!"

Sarah shrieked and giggled and squirmed.

David continued tickling her. "I said, explain yourself! How do you disturb a man while he tries to get his sleep!"

Sarah laughed, "I was horny!"

"Horny? I'll show you horny!"

David pulled Sarah underneath him and began kissing her all over. His kisses tickled. Sarah squirmed to try to get away. "Oh no, you don't!" David wrapped his arms around her tighter, entrapping his wife in his loving embrace, as he attacked her with kisses; then the playfulness of his kiss became softer, more sensual, more passionate. Sarah gave in to his sweet, sensuous passion, as her squirming stopped, her body relaxed, and she gave her mouth and her body to his, as he took ownership of what belonged to him. And they made love again.

★ ★ ★

At the breakfast table that morning, Sarah's thoughts became occupied by the phone call she had answered the night before. She tried to push it out of her mind. She had been able to keep the dreadful thoughts at bay, during her precious moments with David last night and earlier this morning; but now, in the sober light of day, while eating breakfast, the phone call and the things the detective had said began to haunt her.

Sarah was always a firm believer in truth and justice. She executed her duties at the District Attorney's Office with as much zeal as anyone could give. She felt guilty about not being there now. She felt guilty about ignoring an entire case. But as she looked across the table at David, she knew, that her priority was to him, and only to him. He was her hero. He was the man she saved herself for. He was the man she would spend the rest of her life with, and he was the soon-to-be father of her unborn child. Sarah was pregnant. She could not jeopardize her pregnancy by enduring the stress of flying to L.A., to help perfectly capable prosecutors handle a case that would carry a long enough prison sentence to take care of White Jr., once and for all.

Thoughts of her pregnancy made Sarah look down and place her hand on her stomach. David looked across the table at her, with a look of concern, "What's wrong?" he asked. "Do you have a stomachache?"

Sarah felt a twinge of guilt. She had not yet told David about her pregnancy. She hated keeping a secret from him. She loved him so much and she wanted to share every moment with him; but this time, she wanted to make sure it was a viable pregnancy before she got his hopes up again. Last time, David and Sarah had been ecstatic when the pregnancy test turned up positive. David's eyes lit up brighter than she had ever seen before. He was the happiest man alive. He began making plans for the nursery the same day they learned of the pregnancy. But then, two days later, before they could even schedule the appointment with the doctor, Sarah began bleeding, with what appeared to be an extra heavy period; except, it was painful. She knew what must have been happening. She lost the baby almost as soon as she had found out she was pregnant. David was devastated. When she told him she thought she was having a miscarriage, the look she saw on his face revealed to her that it was a blow, which had taken all his joy and all his happiness. He remained sad for several days, thereafter.

The doctor had confirmed the miscarriage, explaining that he estimated that she had only been pregnant for five weeks, and that miscarriages frequently occur during that time period, due to the fact that the pregnancy was never viable to begin with. Nonetheless, David and Sarah had felt devastated by the feeling of loss.

So this time, she would wait before telling David. She wasn't sure how long, but she knew it was still too early now to get his hopes up.

Sarah cleared the worried look off her face, gave David a winning smile and said, "No, I'm just stuffed." She then quickly moved towards him, took his face with both hands and gave him a kiss. She could easily distract David from any thought, with just one kiss. It worked. He flashed his beautiful smile at her, and forgot all about the conversation they were having.

"Let's go down to the yacht," he said.

Sarah smiled brightly. She loved being on their yacht. What a perfect way to forget about everything. She would spend the day sunbathing and making love to her husband, on their magnificent yacht, moored in the Mediterranean Sea.

Chapter 8

In California, rape shield laws prevent defense attorneys from presenting evidence of a rape victim's sexual history, unless the defense can convince the court that special circumstances exist. White Jr.'s defense team believed, that without question, this case involved special circumstances warranting an exception to that rule. They waited until Judge Johnson was back from medical leave before they filed a motion to allow the evidence of Kelly Luthan's conviction for prostitution to be admitted at trial.

Sam had seen the motion and knew that Katelyn would need help responding to it; but the D.A., had already instructed him to not offer her any help with this case, unless she asked. The same day the motion had been filed, Sam stopped by Katelyn's office, and gave her a generic, "how do you do?" She gave a polite response, indicating that she was fine, but she did not ask for his help on the motion. So he didn't offer. He just carried on about his business.

★ ★ ★

Katelyn poured every bit of her energy into researching every case she could find interpreting California's rape shield laws. She stayed at the office until midnight, several nights in a row, preparing her written response to the motion. She had to win this hearing. If she won, it would level the playing field. It would turn this case into an ordinary rape case, instead of one that involved a prostitute as the victim, which thereby made it nearly impossible to prove, as most jurors would automatically have difficulty believing that a prostitute had been raped.

While typically, a deputy district attorney had very little time in her day available for researching case law and drafting written responses to defense motions, this case was special. Despite spending most of every business day in the courtroom handling other cases, Katelyn found time after court was adjourned each day to sit at her desk and work for hours on end, day after day, researching the law and preparing the best written brief she could file in response to the motion. After several grueling weeks of researching, writing, and practicing her oral argument, Katelyn was ready.

★ ★ ★

The hearing on the defense motion to allow the evidence began at 8:00 a.m., on a Friday morning. Larry Pason, White Sr., and five other defense attorneys were gathered at counsel table for the defendant. Katelyn Kruz was the only attorney sitting at counsel table for the State. All the cases she had researched were printed and handy, in case she needed to refer to any of them. Even though only one rule of evidence was at issue, she had the entire California Code of Evidence by her side, as a security blanket. The oral argument she had prepared for this hearing was typed and in her hands. It had been outlined and highlighted, with notes in the margins. These papers were sitting squarely in front of her. She grasped the sides of this pile of papers as she waited for the hearing to begin. Also within reach, was a copy of each legal brief, filed by the prosecution and the defense. She wanted to be as prepared as possible. Katelyn was nervous, but she was determined.

Procedure dictated that, because the motion was filed by the defense, the defense presented its oral argument first. Larry Pason began:

"Your Honor, I trust that you've read our brief thoroughly and that you have thoroughly reviewed all the cases cited therein. I will not repeat what is set forth in writing, but I will highlight a few important facts as I begin my argument.

It is very important to keep a few things in mind. First, the alleged victim has been convicted of a crime of moral turpitude – prostitution to be exact. Second, after the alleged incident, the victim had a knife in her possession. That knife was bloody. It was my client's blood on that knife, not the prostitute's. There was not a scratch on her.

Your Honor, this is no ordinary rape case. We are not seeking to discredit an ordinary woman with a sexual history that is typical of this modern era – an era, which has no room for arcane laws that punished promiscuity in women who did not remain chaste until marriage; an era that no longer allows the criminal justice system to put the victim of rape on trial for her past. We do not ask you to defy our modern era to impose old laws. We do not challenge today's laws. We do not challenge the California Supreme Court's unanimous decision upholding California's rape shield laws. We simply ask you to acknowledge the stark factual differences between that case and this one. In the case of *People v. Fontana*, the California Supreme Court did not allow evidence that a 19-year-old girl had sexual intercourse with her boyfriend the same morning that she had been attacked by a convicted rapist. That victim had merely engaged in sexual intercourse with the boy she loved, a normal thing that a modern day 19-year-old in love would do. This case is far different from that. This case involves an armed, street-wise prostitute, with a cold and deliberate plan to extort money from my client.

We ask this court to allow the defense to present evidence that the alleged victim has been convicted of prostitution. We ask the court to allow this evidence, not for the improper purpose of proving consent to sexual intercourse, not for the improper propose of proving that the prostitute acted in conformity with her prior profession on this occasion, and not for the improper purpose of proving she had a predisposition for committing acts of prostitution. We ask you to allow the evidence of the conviction for prostitution to be admissible at trial in order to prove motive, opportunity, intent, plan and knowledge – all of which are the type of facts the code of evidence allows us to prove, through the use of evidence of the alleged victim's prior sexual history.

Your Honor, the alleged victim is in fact, the perpetrator. She seduced my client for the purpose of creating evidence of a sexual exchange. Then, while my unsuspecting client believed he was engaged in a consensual transaction with a prostitute, she suddenly slashed him in the face with a knife, which she brought to his house, for the purpose of making it appear as if a struggle had ensued. Then, she drove straight to the D.A.'s Office, determined to convince them to arrest my client immediately. And she was savvy, Your Honor. She was so savvy, that she was able to convince them to order an arrest, without first completing a proper investigation.

No ordinary woman has the wherewithal to concoct and carry out a plan like that! But that is exactly what happened to my client. Only a woman with vast experience and knowledge about men and sex, only a woman who is casual and careless with her own body, selling it as if it were merchandise, would have the will, the knowledge, and the conniving nature to plan and execute such a scheme. The jury must know about her past as a prostitute! If this very important fact is excluded from evidence, my client will be denied the opportunity to present all facts necessary to confront his accuser. It would be the same as denying him a right to any trial at all. He is the defendant in a criminal case, and must be afforded the opportunity to completely present his side of the case. My client's side of the story cannot be explained without introducing evidence of Kelly Luthan's prior conviction for prostitution.

The jury needs to know that the prostitute knew how to handle herself in a situation such as this, through her prior experience, and thus, she had knowledge. The jury needs to know that the alleged victim is a convicted prostitute; who therefore, has the experience to plot and plan the extortion of money from a man, through the use of sex and seduction. The jury must be told of her practiced and professional use of her body for financial gain, because it proves she had motive to fabricate these charges, in furtherance of her plan.

The jury needs to know that a prostitute used her occupation in order to create the opportunity to execute her plan to extort a large sum of money from my client – far more money than what her occupation alone would provide.

Kelly Luthan's prior conviction for prostitution speaks to all of these facts, and to her intent to frame my client. Her conviction for prostitution is relevant to prove things the law permits us to prove with that evidence; that is, motive, opportunity, intent, knowledge and plan. Kelly Luthan's conviction for prostitution proves she had the knowledge and ability to plan this elaborate scheme. It proves she had motive to frame my client for her financial gain.

If my client is denied the ability to present this evidence to the jury, he will be denied his constitutional right to a fair trial. He will be denied his constitutional right to fully confront his accuser. The only thing separating our fine country from the tyranny and brutality of old English laws, and even current laws in other countries, are these guaranties by the United States Constitution. The absolute guaranty and right to confront one's accusers, and the absolute guaranty and right to a fair trial, are among the primary reasons our forefathers founded this great nation. To deny my client these rights, is to do injustice to our precious constitution. You may as well put that old, but sacred document into a shredder if you deny our motion, Your Honor. We implore you, with the utmost sincerity, you must grant our motion to allow evidence of the conviction of Kelly Luthan, for prostitution.

Thank you, Your Honor."

Larry Pason sat down, and Katelyn stood up. She took a deep breath to calm her nerves. The defense lawyer's oral argument was so good that he nearly convinced her he was right. She forced that thought out of her mind and remembered the argument she had prepared. She began:

"Your Honor, the defense has one purpose and one purpose only in presenting this motion. They seek to put a rape victim on trial to distract the jury from the fact that it is their own client who is on trial. I am disgusted and appalled at how many times Mr. Pason has called Ms. Luthan, 'the prostitute,' during his oral argument today. If you permit this evidence, imagine what he will do at trial. He will continuously refer to her as 'the prostitute' and the jury will forget that they are here to judge White Jr., for rape. They will become confused. They will start to believe they are here to judge Kelly Luthan for prostitution.

Your Honor, the defense seeks to put a rape victim on trial for conduct she has already answered for. She pleaded guilty to the misdemeanor crime of prostitution – the one and only crime in her criminal history. She completed her sentence, never violating her probation a single time. She never returned to the criminal justice system again, which is refreshingly unusual, really, for most people convicted of crimes. After her conviction, she gained respectable employment as a paralegal in a law firm. As far as we can tell, she never again engaged in prostitution, after that one conviction. It had been a full year between the time of her conviction, and the time that White Jr., so brutally raped her. The fact that she was able to gain possession of the weapon and escape with her life, is a fact we should celebrate. It is not a fact we should use as an excuse to violate the rules of evidence, which exist in order to prevent the great injustice of putting the victim of a brutal crime on trial, instead of the man who brutalized her.

Ms. Luthan is now living the simple life in Oklahoma, struggling to make ends meet, like all the rest of us. She is a human being. She made one mistake in her life, for which she has already paid her dues. Let's not drag her through the mud again, and violate her in this courtroom, the way White Jr., violated her that day.

The rules of evidence do not permit evidence of a woman's prior sexual conduct to be admitted in a rape case in order to prove consent. But that is exactly what the defense is trying to prove with that evidence. They seek to prove that Ms. Luthan went to the defendant's home seeking sexual intercourse. They ask you to allow evidence that she has previously been convicted of prostitution, in order to prove that she consented to sex on the day in question. That is not allowed by the rules of evidence. They can tell their story and present their theory of the case – that a wealthy man is a sitting duck for greedy women who may frame him for rape so that they may collect damages after he is convicted. They can present that theory without proving that the woman in question is supposedly an expert at sex. It is true that the code of evidence distinguishes between the purposes for which the defense seeks to introduce the evidence.

I agree that certain types of facts can be proven by showing the victim's sexual history; while other types of facts cannot be proven through that evidence. Mr. Pason has accurately distinguished between the things you can prove with evidence of prior sexual history and the things you cannot. He states that he does not attempt to use the evidence for an improper purpose. However, that statement is not correct, Your Honor.

This Court must ask itself one question: Why does the defense want to prove she is a professional at sex? Does it tend to show she had motive to frame him? Or, does it tend to show she consented to sex? The only answer the court will come up with is this, her sexual professionalism is meant to prove she consented to sex on the day in question; and to prove she had a predisposition for engaging in casual, meaningless, or financially beneficial sexual intercourse – each purpose is an improper use of the evidence. Establishing that she is a prostitute does not serve the proper purpose of proving motive. Motive can be proven by pointing to the defendant's wealth, not the victim's past.

Prior sexual history cannot be presented in order to prove consent or a predisposition to commit the act. Nevertheless, that is exactly what the defense seeks to prove with this evidence. But more so than that, Your Honor, they seek to blind the jury with one fact that the jury will never see passed. They seek to blind the jury with the fact that, once upon a time, the victim engaged in prostitution. This could make some of the jurors feel that it doesn't matter if the defendant is guilty or innocent, because the victim has already been a prostitute, so who cares if she had one more degrading sexual encounter? But that's a dangerous thing to allow juries to think. It's the type of thing that allows rapists to walk away free, only to commit another rape against another, more vulnerable, more innocent woman. The prejudicial fact of Ms. Luthan's prior conviction will completely distract the jury from the job they are meant to perform, and that is to decide what actually happened that day. This court must not allow the defense to use such prejudices to disrupt the administration of the criminal justice system. This court must honor the code of evidence, which is designed to allow court proceedings to proceed fairly.

Mr. Pason asks you to give his client a fair trial. You will. The code of evidence provides a fair trial. I ask you to follow the rules of evidence and to deny the motion, which, plain and simple, is a request for permission to violate the rules of evidence.

Thank you, Your Honor. That's all I have." Katelyn sat down and waited for Judge Johnson's response.

Judge Johnson listened carefully to both sides. He allowed the defense attorney to respond to Katelyn's argument in rebuttal; but instead of listening, he used that time to ponder his decision. This was a very close call. He had never, in all his years on the bench, had such difficulty deciding an issue. The defense had made great points in their argument, which were very convincing. But that young prosecutor brought up a very important issue. The court had to decide what the defense was truly trying to prove by presenting the evidence. Certainly, if the evidence proved both consent to sexual intercourse, and motive, it would be admissible. The mere point that the evidence speaks to both the inappropriate fact, as well as the appropriate fact, does not render the evidence inadmissible. Judge Johnson spent the time during which the defense attorney gave his rebuttal argument, to think; and he pondered the question: *Does the fact that a woman is a prostitute tend to prove she had motive to frame a man for rape so that she may collect damages from him?*

The other nagging issue on the judge's mind was one that neither attorney addressed. Judge Johnson pondered the fact that this was the second story White Jr., had told about a client victimizing him. No one will ever know the circumstances of the first incident. While one can presume that the client whose identity was never revealed was in fact the perpetrator (because they never came forward), the fact that White Jr., had had two violent entanglements with his clients, strongly suggested something was amiss. These nagging issues occupied the court's mind.

If White Jr., had deep dark secrets between himself and his criminal clients, the judge would have a hard time justifying granting him such a strong advantage at trial – an advantage, which would probably guaranty a "not guilty" verdict. Judge Johnson looked at young Katelyn Kruz sitting alone at counsel table with inquisitive, nearly vulnerable eyes, very obviously nervous about how the court would rule. Then, he looked at the team of seven outstanding defense lawyers seated at the defendant's counsel table. This fight was already unfair. It was already tilted heavily in White Jr.'s favor.

Judge Johnson was a fair judge. He wanted every trial to be conducted in such a manner that the truth would be allowed to flourish. He decided, in that moment, that that is exactly what the general rules in the code of evidence provide. They create a platform designed to bring the truth to the surface and to keep prejudices at bay. He decided he would not grant an exception to those rules today.

Judge Johnson delivered his ruling, as follows:

"Mr. Pason, lightning never strikes the same place twice."

"What do you mean, Your Honor?"

"Your client found himself in similar circumstances, with another one of his clients…"

"But, Your Honor! That's not before the Court!"

"I know it's not before the Court. That's why I'm telling you what's on my mind. I'm getting it on the record so that if I'm making a mistake here today, you can take it up with the court of appeals."

Larry Pason immediately knew what that meant. It meant the judge was ruling against him, so he tried with all his might to change the judge's mind before he uttered the one word that would destroy the defense theory of the case, the word: 'denied.' Larry Pason respectfully interrupted the judge:

"Your Honor, earlier encounters with different clients have no relevance to this motion, or to any part of this case."

"Maybe you're right."

"Your Honor, you know I'm right."

"Well now, don't get excited. I'm not basing my ruling on that fact. I just raised it so you had your evidence that the judge who heard this motion, whether relevant or not, was aware of facts involving the defendant asserting attorney-client privilege to hide the identity of a different client who violently assaulted him; and that today, the defendant's theory is that another former client of his, has violently assaulted him; but that he remains purely innocent of any wrongdoing under either of those circumstances. And that this judge believes, lightning does not strike twice. So there, you have your record, which you can take up on appeal, if it ever becomes necessary. Now for my ruling, and the reasons why:

"This Court finds that the defense seeks to present evidence of the victim's prior sexual history for the purpose of proving she consented to sexual intercourse, or for the purpose of proving that the victim had a disposition for acting consistent with the acts of a prostitute. That is not permitted by the code of evidence. Such evidence is highly prejudicial to the State's case. It's probative value, for any relevant fact at trial, is outweighed by the prejudicial effect it will have. The motion is denied."

Katelyn's face lit up. She couldn't believe it! She won the hearing! And nobody could say she just got lucky because it was Judge Kline deciding the matter. Now, she felt like she had a chance of winning the trial too! She was elated.

Larry Pason did not attempt to argue after the court stated its ruling, but he was hoping to draw some sort of victory out of today's terrible loss. "Your Honor, there is still the matter of our Motion to Reconsider Judge Kline's ruling regarding custody, I was hoping the court could set a bail hearing today."

The judge replied, "This morning, I signed an order summarily denying your request for reconsideration, Mr. Pason. I am not in the habit of overruling other judges in this courthouse. I am not the Court of Appeals."

Although, Judge Johnson had reviewed the transcript of that hearing and believed that Judge Kline was far too strenuous (as he would not have held the defendant without bail, but would have allowed him to post bail), Judge Johnson had a very strict policy against allowing defense attorneys to pit one judge against the other, using them as a mini-appellate process, in motions to reconsider or in requests for bail hearings, after such matters had already been determined at arraignment.

Larry Pason continued to plead with the court, "Your Honor, with all due respect to Judge Kline, I believe she reached an unfair decision, which is different from what you would have decided, had you been available and able to preside over your own courtroom that day. My client should not suffer such an unfortunate circumstance. The facts of this case warrant bail. Even Judge Kline stated that she believed there were serious questions as to who assaulted who in this case, but nonetheless she denied bail. This will result in my client spending several months incarcerated pending trial, which we believe will result in an acquittal. It would mean he spent all that time incarcerated for a crime he did not commit! Your Honor, you must rectify this injustice. My client must have an opportunity to post bail!" Larry zealously concluded.

The judge responded, "Other than your disagreement with Judge Kline's decision, do you have any other reason why I should set a bail hearing on this matter to reconsider the custody terms imposed by Judge Kline? Are there facts you have discovered which you were unable to present to Judge Kline? Is there a change in circumstances, which warrants a rehearing?"

"We have no new facts, Your Honor."

"Then, I will not grant a re-hearing. This court is adjourned."

As the judge tapped his gavel, White Jr., doubled over in his chair as if someone had punched him in the gut. He put his head down against counsel table and began to sob. White Sr., sat beside his son and put a hand on his shoulder. He gently patted him in comfort, though he himself felt bewildered and betrayed by a system he once respected and trusted. It took all his strength and resolve not to join his son in despair, and crumple to the floor in hopelessness. Today, the defense had received two devastating blows, one right after the other. They all had thought, for sure, Judge Johnson would release White Jr., pending trial and grant their motion to allow evidence. He was always a fair judge who was very serious about protecting a defendant's constitutional rights. Today was an anomaly. White Sr., could not believe what was happening. The pain in his chest returned, and it felt as if it were spreading to his left arm. He sat in his chair, trying to catch his breath, as his son sobbed uncontrollably next to him.

White Sr., couldn't tell anybody about the chest pain he was having. He was afraid a doctor would tell him he could no longer work on his son's case. The pain usually passed after a few moments. By now, White Sr., had developed a habit of waiting for the pain to subside.

It was such a devastating day in court that nobody thought it was strange that White Sr., remained seated at counsel table, long after the jail deputies had taken his son to the jail, and the judge left the bench, and the courtroom staff had exited the courtroom. Members of the defense team remained and waited to console White Sr. They asked if he was all right and if they could do anything for him. He waived them off and told them to go on without him. He just needed a few minutes to collect himself. They respected his wishes and each of them slowly exited the courtroom, leaving White Sr., alone.

White Sr., closed his eyes and said a little prayer, "Dear God," he began, "Please let me live long enough to clear my son of these charges."

A few minutes later, the chest pain was lifted and he was able to stand up and walk to his car. He drove home in the pouring down rain, again. *Why did it always rain so heavily on terrible days like this?* He wondered. The weather most certainly fit his mood.

When White Sr., got home, he saw his weary wife and quickly sought comfort in her arms. She wrapped her arms around him and he rested his head against her chest, as he began to weep. She understood that this meant, it had been a hard day in court. She was afraid to ask what happened. When he was ready, he spoke:

"They held our son in jail because he's too rich. They won't allow evidence of the victim's filthy past because it too strongly proves she's lying. I've never had a more terrible day in my life." The elderly lady held her husband in her arms and rocked him, hoping to comfort him. She tried not to let him hear her cry, as tears streamed down her face.

Chapter 9

Word had spread through town that Johnny and Kelly were back together again. They had been the town's golden couple back in high school. He was the captain of the football team, and she was the captain of the cheerleading squad. They had been king and queen of the homecoming dance, as well as senior prom. Johnny wasn't the only one who had been heartbroken when Kelly had turned down his engagement and left town. The whole town felt like it had lost something special. Now that the two were back together, it was a moment to celebrate. And the grand opening of Kelly's new café, aptly named "Kelly's Kafe," was the perfect event for all to come congratulate the happy couple.

The day was a huge success. Kelly was certain that every resident in town had come in that day. She made delicious mocha lattes, cappuccinos and coffee milkshakes. All their customers were ranting and raving at how they'd never tasted such great coffee drinks before. Every piece of pie for sale had sold out. Kelly's grandmother had the best pie recipes in town, and she baked the pies that were sold at the café. The pies were proudly displayed under a sign that read: "Grandma's Prize Winning Pies," and everyone knew what that referred to. Kelly's grandmother had been winning the pie contest at the 4th of July bake fair every year, for as long as Kelly could remember. And now, those pies were helping her new café become a great success. All the people closest to Kelly pitched in to help her with the grand opening. Her mother helped at the cash register. Her father ran to get more supplies when they began to run low, and Johnny took the day off so he could devote all his time to be there with Kelly, lending an extra hand with whatever was needed.

At the end of a long day, full of non-stop customers, Johnny closed the door behind the last few customers, and cheerfully bid them goodbye. It was 10:00 p.m. It had been a very busy grand opening. The helpful family members left soon after that. Johnny closed and locked the door behind them and couldn't wait to get back to the kitchen, where he could hear Kelly rummaging around, refrigerating the food from the display case and cleaning up. Johnny and Kelly were the last two people still in the café.

Johnny flipped the "open" sign in the window over to show that Kelly's Kafe was now "closed." He drew the blinds shut in each window, one at a time, growing more and more anxious to take advantage of the opportunity to be alone with Kelly. He walked back toward the kitchen to see Kelly standing on a stepladder, reaching up to grab more paper cups to re-stock the supply for the next day. Johnny stood in the doorway of the kitchen and watched her. She was still a striking beauty, even more striking actually, because now she was more womanly than he had remembered. She now carried a stronger sex appeal than the innocent girl who had left him behind. Johnny wasn't sure if that was something he liked more, or less about Kelly. He missed the sweet innocence of the girl whose virginity he took under the high school bleachers many years ago. It was the most private place two teenagers could find at the time.

Although he missed the girl she used to be, Johnny could not deny that he enjoyed the hot nights they spent together, now. He was a man, after all. Though at times, it would leave an ache in his heart. He couldn't help but wonder what had made her change. Little things in her behavior were triggering these questions in his mind, frequently. When he would begin to wonder about such things, he would force the thought out of his mind. He couldn't stand to think of what, or who, had made Kelly seem so much more experienced now.

Pushing that unnerving question out of his mind, Johnny stopped and stared at the beautiful woman he had never stopped loving, grateful that she was finally back. He watched her short skirt rise as she reached upwards for the cups. Although a gentleman would help his fiancé, Johnny didn't feel like being a gentleman tonight. He felt like enjoying the view.

Kelly wore a closely fitted, short, white skirt with a tiny, white tank top, also closely fitted. The scant clothing revealed her beautiful, tall, thin body, and long legs, which were narrow but not scrawny. Her legs were nicely defined with delicate muscle tone, but still maintained feminine sex appeal. This beautiful body had been hidden under the apron she had worn all day long. Now that the apron was finally off of his beautiful fiancé, Johnny decided he would stand there and indulge himself for a moment, instead of offering to help Kelly get the cups that were just barely out of her reach. It was more fun to watch her stretching upwards with various attempts, letting out a soft grunt of frustration each time.

After watching her several failed attempts to reach the cups, Johnny let out a masculine chuckle. Kelly whipped her head to the left at the sound of Johnny's adoring laugh. Johnny was leaning against the wall now, in a relaxed pose, his feet crossed at the ankles and his large, muscular arms crossed in front of his strong chest. He had a silly grin on his face, reflecting the perfect mix of tenderness and masculinity in a perfectly chiseled face – a face, which was blessed with the classic good looks of a strong square jaw line, and one darling dimple on his right cheek. His perfectly handsome face was framed by dirty blonde hair that was still as thick as it was back in high school.

"Well don't just stand there and laugh at me!" Kelly said playfully. "Come help me!"

"Oh, if I come over there, it won't be to help you get those cups down," Johnny said, with promise in his voice.

Kelly smiled deviously, "What will you do, if you come over here?"

"Mmm, I'm still thinking about it..."

Kelly then froze in place, her soft playfulness transforming into a vixen's seduction. She kept her right arm raised in the air, as she slowly turned her head away from Johnny, maintaining a sideways glance, leaving her eyes the last to break contact. Throwing her head backward, seductively, she looked up as she reached higher and higher, as far as she could stretch her tall thin frame. As her hand slid upward, she pressed her breasts against the hard steel frame, and slowly caressed the steel shelves. Just as she reached the point where her body could not have reached any higher, she slowly turned her face towards Johnny, pressing and sliding against the steel like a cat purring against its owner. Then, teasing him some more, she turned her face away from him, keeping her body pressed against the hard steel, caressing it with her body, in a seductive turn towards the opposite wall, facing away from him, again. She moved like a stripper making love to her dancing pole. Then, slowly wrapping her hands around the metal poles, gripping them tight, she slid her hands down the cold hard steel, as she squatted low on the top step of the ladder. The movement forced her skirt up so high it revealed her butt cheeks and the white lace G-string she wore. Pausing long enough to emphasize the view beneath her skirt, she tossed a quick glance over her shoulder at Johnny with a raised brow before slowly turning her head to face the shelves. Then, releasing her hands, she caressed the metal in an upward direction again, as she slowly stood, reaching towards the cups. As her hands neared the cups, she arched her back and pressed her breasts deeper into the shelving, "Aha," she moaned seductively, as she slowly turned her face towards Johnny, enticing him with steaming bedroom eyes. "Will you please..." she batted her eyelashes, emphasizing the word, "please," as if begging for more in the bedroom, "Please... come help me."

Johnny was not turned on. He was perplexed. Though most men would consider themselves lucky that their girlfriends could so quickly turn on the erotica, Johnny wasn't sure he liked it. It was moments like this that shocked him back into wondering, where they hell she learned how to act that way. This was not the Kelly who had driven away from him so many years ago, a bright eager young girl who'd never been with anyone but him. Kelly's sudden change, from the playful woman he loved, into a scheming seductress, made him feel like he was watching a cheesy pornographic movie, not the love of his life. Johnny loved and treasured Kelly. He wanted their lovemaking to be pure and sweet. He didn't want it to feel like a B-quality movie. However, he was careful not to say anything that might insult Kelly or discourage her from being seductive and sexy, out of fear that she would stop trying altogether. This left him unsure of how to tell her that this did not turn him on.

Kelly was biting her finger now, staring at Johnny suggestively. At that, Johnny decided to stop her silly display. He walked over to her and picked her up in his arms.

"Come on, let's go home." He pulled her skirt down so that she was decent again, and he carried her in his arms to his truck. "I want you in our bedroom, not this kitchen."

Johnny chose to react to Kelly's overly sexual, and less than attractive behavior, in the way he'd grown accustomed to reacting to it. He would simply take the lead and re-direct the course of their exchange. Johnny had strong muscular arms and a gentle, though firm mannerism, which allowed him to take control of most situations without any resistance. Instead of discussing his feelings with Kelly, he would "change the subject" so to speak, with actions instead of words.

Instead of passively watching her seduce him in low budget movie fashion, Johnny would be the man and take the lead – whether that was taking her down off that stupid ladder tonight, or, as he had done on previous nights, rolling over to get on top and moving her into a position he preferred (usually missionary), that's what he would do to "change the subject" of a physical conversation he was not fond of. Tonight was no different. He lifted Kelly off the ladder, walked her over to his pickup, and placed her in the passenger seat. This changed the mood into something he was more comfortable with. He became the man in control, and she became the precious woman he loved, again.

On the drive home, Kelly slid across the bench seat to be close to him. She seductively stroked his thigh and played with his hair. This was an intimate gesture that he enjoyed. As they drove along, Johnny turned his face to kiss Kelly, quickly, never keeping his eyes off the road for too long. The drive was short because the town was small. When they parked, Johnny picked Kelly up again and carried her to their bedroom. He kissed her passionately along the way, opening the front door blindly with one hand, as he fumbled to get the key in the lock. Kelly and Johnny kissed romantically as they entered the house. He carried her up the stairs then dropped her gently on his soft bed. He climbed on top of her, each of them still fully clothed.

Johnny put both hands on each of her outer thighs, caressing upward, raising her skirt with a gentle stroke of his hands. She held him and kissed him as he did this, while his fingers curled under the seam of her lace underwear. With Kelly lost in his kiss, Johnny pulled her underwear down slowly, caressing her long legs all the way down, until he reached her ankles, sliding the delicate lace off and tossing it to the floor. Lying on her back, she remained relaxed and waited for Johnny's next move. Johnny smiled. This is how he liked her. Patient. A little submissive. He then used his hands and his mouth to work magic that transported Kelly to a state of mindlessly ecstasy. Johnny kissed her clitoris and she sighed. He licked her and she moaned. He continued licking her as she grabbed his thick hair in her hands and sighed loudly with more pleasure. Johnny indulged in this moment. Too many times before, it had felt as if she had only been tending to his pleasure and not taking her own. Holding her down by her hips and subjecting her to his tongue, gave him the opportunity to ensure that he was the one delivering pleasure to her. He continued his relentless licking, and her eyes closed in ecstasy as she gripped his hair so tight. With his mouth digging deeper and deeper into her, he reached up with both hands to feel her breasts. He pulled the tank top down so that her breasts popped out the top. He began to fondle her bare breasts, as he continued licking her pleasure zone. The feel of his hands and his tongue, in unison, delivering pleasure to all the right places, magnified the ecstasy coursing through Kelly as her head thrashed from left to right and she lost awareness of anything other than the pleasure she felt. Johnny worked his magic hands and his skillful tongue relentlessly. Kelly's sighs of pleasure heightened into screams. Her screams of pleasure came out in short panting breaths, "Ah! Ah! Ah!" And Johnny carried on, licking, fondling, caressing. He rubbed his right thumb around her nipple in the same gesture that his tongue swirled around her clitoris. And Kelly's body began to shake. He continued delivering her pleasure until her whole body went into convulsions, her cries of pleasure getting louder and louder, until finally she sighed and her body stilled.

Finally, he brought her to the point of satisfaction, he'd been aiming for. Johnny lifted his head and moved his body, so that his face was close to hers, now. He lied down next to her and wrapped his arms around her. He sweetly kissed her lips and her cheek and her neck, as she lie panting, trying to catch her breath. He held her in his arms and pressed his face next to hers.

When she finally caught her breath, Kelly asked: "What about you?"

Johnny replied: "Tonight was for you. You worked so hard today. I don't want you to worry about me. Just sleep."

Kelly looked at him, eyes wide with surprise. And Johnny reassured her. "Sshh. Just sleep, my beautiful woman. Just relax and go to sleep."

Kelly relaxed against Johnny and closed her eyes. Johnny held her tight in his strong muscular arms, pressing her delicate body against his sturdy six-pack abs. The feel of his strength overwhelming Kelly with feelings of safety and security, she fell asleep easily that night.

Johnny held the woman he loved, in his arms, as his mind filled with thoughts that preoccupied him. He was certain this had been the first time she reached orgasm during their intimate moments, since she had been back. He wondered how he could do this again through traditional lovemaking. When they made love, it always seemed as if Kelly remained distant, never giving in completely to the pleasure of sex, but somehow keeping him at arm's length despite their physical closeness. It was almost mechanical, as if she were merely performing a job. This disturbed Johnny. Everything about their relationship was perfect, except for the sex. The disconnect in the bedroom haunted him. He wanted to feel an emotional connection with her during sex, like that amazing bond they had shared so long ago, when she had given herself to him. He knew it was silly to think that she would have been abstinent all these years. He knew he had to be reasonable and accept the fact that she'd been with other men. But he hated how much it had changed her. He was desperate to get the woman he loved back. All the way back – heart, soul, body, mind – everything. He wanted the complete Kelly back; and he was determined to figure out how to truly get her back.

Chapter 10

It was 6:00 p.m., after a long day of hearings, and Katelyn sat at her desk pondering the issue of voir dire for White Jr.'s trial. Every criminal trial starts with voir dire, a process involving the selection of 12 people from a pool of potential jurors. It is also casually referred to as, "jury selection." Katelyn knew that she had to adjust her voir dire strategy for this case. Her only question was: *How?*

During voir dire, the first 12 jurors are randomly selected from a large pool of jurors sitting in the courtroom. Selection of the first twelve, is pure luck of the draw (or the unlucky draw for those who would prefer not to serve). Those first twelve are seated in the jury box and will be the ones to serve on the jury, unless excused for cause by the court, or excluded when an attorney uses one of three preemptory strikes, which each side is allowed to use for any reason. The jurors are questioned about their biases and prejudices. Each lawyer is allowed to ask questions exploring whether or not the potential juror will be unfairly prejudiced against their side of the case.

The purpose of voir dire is to select the 12 most unbiased people to judge the facts of the case, without allowing their personal lives or predispositions to interfere with their judgment of the evidence. For example, a police officer or a prosecutor is likely too prejudiced, by the nature of their work, to serve on a jury in a criminal case.

While the legal purpose of jury selection is to end up with 12 of the least biased people to judge the case, every attorney has an alternative strategic purpose for voir dire. Each attorney formulates questions for the jury designed to do two things: (1) bring their biases to the surface, just before they judge the case; and (2) identify those jurors who are most likely to favor their side of the case.

Katelyn had never handled a sexual assault case before. Her only experience so far had been with driving while intoxicated cases and other misdemeanors. The trial of White Jr., involved subject areas, in which Katelyn had no experience, and therefore, no clue how to strategize and prepare for voir dire. She had always overheard the best trial lawyers discussing the importance of voir dire in other cases. She had heard them say that cases can be won or lost, based on mistakes lawyers make in voir dire. She was aware that common mistakes made by attorneys conducting voir dire included asking a sensitive question the wrong way, thereby causing offense to members of the jury who would hold it against the lawyer throughout the trial. And this case certainly involved sensitive issues.

Katelyn was nervous. She had no idea how to prepare for voir dire. She considered asking the reluctant, Sam Chapman if he would help, but she was certain that would be of no use. As she sat there nervously ruffling the blank page onto which, she had yet to write down a single thought, the phone rang.

"Katelyn Kruz, how can I help you?" she answered.

"Hello Katelyn, my name is Sarah Cartwright."

Katelyn gasped, *Sarah Cartwright?* She thought, *The Sarah Cartwright?*

"Um, uh, hel-- hello."

"Do you know who I am, Katelyn?"

"Yes. Of course I do!"

Sarah smiled on the other end of the line, looking out her French doors into the late evening. It was 3:00 a.m. in France.

"I heard you could use some help preparing for White Jr.'s Trial."

"Yes! Oh my God! Your timing is perfect. I can't believe it! I was just sitting here wondering how to prepare for voir dire! I've never done this before, well, I mean, I've done it before, but just not in a rape and attempted murder case," Katelyn chattered on nervously.

She couldn't believe her idol was on the phone offering to help her prepare this case.

"Ok. Rule number 1, take a deep breath, relax. Nobody can think straight when they're nervous."

Katelyn took in a deep breath and tried to relax.

"Now, let me start with a few general rules about voir dire before we go into the specific questions. First and foremost, your sole purpose in voir dire is to get the jury to like you. Make no mistake about it, this is a popularity contest. I know you've heard all that garbage about trying to identify jurors who will be biased in your favor. But that's never going to work. As soon as you identify who favors you, the defense sees who does not favor them, and they use their preemptory strike on that juror; and vice versa. So really, most cases do end up with the least biased, among those left in the room, after each attorney uses their three strikes. So don't stress out over the questions you'll ask, or the fabulous job you'll do convincing them you're on the right side of the case. Instead, gain their trust."

"Ok. How do I do that?"

"Smile. They have to like you. Many of them are nervous about being there themselves, wondering how they're going to make such a significant decision about someone else's life. So you have to give them a warm, welcoming smile to make them comfortable. Your job in voir dire is to get them to believe that if they follow your lead, they will surely make the right decision.

And Stand. Do not sit at counsel table when it is your turn to address the jury in voir dire. You have to build rapport with them. You have to create that connection, which makes them want to follow your lead. So when it's your turn to ask questions, you walk over and stand squarely in front of the jury. Do not stand behind the podium. That creates a barrier separating you. You're trying to build a bond. When you're standing squarely in front of them, smile. Wait for them to smile back before you speak. In that fraction of a second that you've paused, you've gained their attention and they're ready to listen.

When you do speak, the first thing you should do, is thank them for fulfilling their civic duties coming to court that day to serve justice. In each of your questions to the jury, when you inquire about their biases, you will ask them if it will interfere with their civic duty to apply the law and serve justice. You're repeating the same theme, over and over again in your questions – that the only thing you're asking them to do today, is the right thing, to serve justice."

Katelyn was writing frantically as Sarah spoke. She was taking down every detail of the advice she was given.

Sarah went on. "Now, let's talk about the sensitive questions you'll be asking them. I'm going to let you prepare the questions on your own, then I'll review them to help you make sure you phrase them in a way that will come off the tongue smoothly in front of the jury. You have to practice your questions, and make sure you remain poised and eloquent at all times. That's what will make them willing to follow your lead.

In this very sensitive case, you have to be the first one to raise the issue of the victim's past, and get them comfortable with the idea that even a woman with a past like that, deserves as much protection under our laws as any one of us does. Get each one of those jurors to make a commitment to you, during voir dire, that they are able to follow the law; and that they will not allow any prejudices they may have, about a woman with that type of past, to interfere with their unbiased judgment of the facts of this case. You also need to do this in order to take the wind out of the defense's sails. If the jury hears it from them first, the defense will spin that fact and exploit it in their favor."

"But I've already won a motion to exclude that evidence!" Katelyn said excitedly, hoping that would make Sarah proud of her.

"Don't rely on that ruling, Katelyn. It will be a huge mistake."

"But the judge has already ruled that the defense cannot present evidence of her prior conviction for prostitution."

"Katelyn, listen to me. You are not up against Joe Schmoe. You are up against the most brilliant defense attorneys in the country. They will not allow the judge's ruling to stop them from getting that evidence to the jury."

"But how?" Katelyn asked, bewildered.

"I can't even predict how. That's how brilliant they are. You have to be prepared for this, Katelyn. The only way to win this case is to get each of those jurors, in voir dire, to commit to judging this case on the facts, and not on the victim's past. Those who cannot make that commitment will be stricken for cause, because the judge will find them too biased to sit in judgment of the case. That will leave you with all three of your preemptory strikes to use on other jurors. It will set the stage for open mindedness. It will even the playing field for a fair trial for the prosecution."

Katelyn sat at her desk nervously listening to Sarah. She just couldn't imagine how to strike that balance. Her stomach turned with anticipation.

Sarah heard footsteps enter the ballroom. "Sarah?" she heard David ask in the dark.

"I have to go now Katelyn, you prepare those questions, as I've asked you to, and I'll call you at this same time next week. Bye."

Sarah hung up and Katelyn sat at her desk, even more nervous than she was before Sarah had called. This changed everything, her whole trial strategy, the way she would prepare the witness, everything. She had already told the victim what great news it was that the court had denied the defense motion. How would she tell her now, that she must prepare to answer questions about being a prostitute? And how was she supposed to bring that up, delicately? Katelyn didn't know what to do.

★ ★ ★

Sarah quickly erased all the recent calls on her cell phone and smiled up at David as he crossed the long hall into the ballroom. "I'm over here, darling," Sarah called out to him.

"Sarah, what are you doing up at this hour? I rolled over and you weren't in bed."

"I know sweetie. I had told my mom I would call her today at 6:00 their time. I didn't want to wake you."

"Ok." He said, as he approached the deep, red, velvet loveseat. Sarah was sprawled out onto the loveseat, her back resting against the armrest, and her bare legs extending along the soft luxurious sofa. Sarah was wearing a white silk teddy, covered by a matching white silk robe, which ended at mid-thigh. The breeze from the slightly opened French door blew open her robe. She practically glimmered in the moonlight. David loved the view. His mind was on far different things than asking why she had to pick this hour to call her mother, when France and the western United States shared other more decent hours in common.

David approached the couch and made himself comfortable on top of Sarah. "Mmmm, this is a nice spot you've chosen."

Sarah smiled and wrapped her legs around David. "It's much nicer now," she purred.

David kissed Sarah gently on the lips. Then grabbed a handful of her thick, long dark hair, to pull his wife towards him. He pressed his body against hers, as his kiss became more and more passionate. With his free hand, he touched her thigh where the silk robe ended, and slid his hand upwards, bringing the robe and the teddy with it, exposing his wife's nudeness underneath. The cool sea breeze tickled and caressed Sarah's skin, as the smoothness of the silk lingerie tantalized her body, the titillation heightening at the feel of David's touch of her skin. With his muscular body pressed against hers, Sarah didn't need any more foreplay than this, tonight.

That initial touch of her husband's hand sent electrifying pleasure rushing through her, and the thrill of anticipation aroused all of her erogenous zones. Sarah fumbled with his silk boxers, pulling them down, frantic to free the hardness beneath. His kiss was passionate, his firm grip of her hair was passionate, and his sensual caressing touch was, oh so, sweet. She needed him, and she needed him now.

David understood her desperate plea in the way she fumbled and yanked at his boxer shorts. As soon as he was freed, he thrust into her, deep and hard, as his tongue thrust further into her mouth, moving with the same force and passion of his groin. She moaned into his mouth and arched her back, pressing her soft breasts deeper against his chest. David moaned with pleasure and thrust again. His passionate kiss muffled Sarah's cries of pleasure. He kept thrusting and thrusting and thrusting. His deep kiss was strong, relentless, equal to the force of his sweet glorious erection thrusting deeper and deeper into her, as she moaned. He thrust faster and harder, and she grabbed him tighter with her arms and legs, returning his devouring kiss with the same passion. He kept thrusting harder, faster... harder and faster. "Yes, Sarah, Yes!" David grunted, breathlessly. "Ah! Yes!" He thrust harder,... faster,... harder,..."Ah!"... "Oh!"... He gave her more, until,... finally,... her head thrust backwards, as she screamed, a long cry of ecstasy... then she sighed, a sweet high-pitched moan. David continued his thrusting. He wanted to give her even more pleasure as she continued to orgasm. He loved the feel of his wife in orgasm beneath him, in his arms, all around his cock. He wallowed in the sweet sensation, as he continued thrusting and she kept moaning loudly, her head thrashing around violently, as he prolonged her orgasm. One long, jagged breath escaped her lips as her body shuddered and shook, and her arms and legs turned to putty; and David came spectacularly inside his wife, his body shaking with ecstasy as he and his wife continued coming, in unison. Finally, her body calmed and his body stilled, and they blissfully and slowly came down from their orgasms together. Panting breathlessly, they caressed and kissed and held each other, as they sank deeper into the couch an entangled web of bliss, until they fell asleep on that loveseat, the rest of the evening.

Chapter 11

Kelly's Kafe was open six days a week, from 6:00 a.m., for the early morning coffee drinkers, until 11:00 p.m., for the late night dessert eaters. Kelly was in the café today happily working as hard as ever. This was her place and she loved it. It didn't bother her that she had to work six days a week from sun up until sun down. As soon as the café was making enough money to hire employees, she would do so, and she would relax then. But for now, she was happily putting her heart and soul into making this a success.

Kelly smiled brightly when she heard the jingle of the bell dangling from the front door, as it opened.

"Hey, babe," said her favorite customer. It was Johnny.

Kelly skipped over to him and wrapped her arms around him, giving him a warm hug and kiss. "I love you."

"Love you too. And I miss my baby, you've been working so hard."

"It doesn't feel like work. I love this, Johnny. Thank you so much for helping me."

"Anytime. I want my baby to be a success. You know I would support you with anything you wanted to do, don't you?"

"Yes. I know it, now."

"Hey!" squawked an elderly woman, from her seat at the other end of the counter, "Will you two love birds give someone else some love! My coffee cup's empty!" she demanded, as she tapped her coffee mug against the counter.

Kelly hurried back to her station behind the counter and grabbed the coffee pot to fill the cup of "Old Lady Nelson," one more time. Old Lady Nelson, as the town affectionately called her, was a widow who had now developed a habit of spending hours at Kelly's Kafe so that she wouldn't get lonely at home. It was mid-day, during the slowest time of business, and Mrs. Nelson was the only customer in the café. She usually read the newspaper, and kept Kelly company, while Kelly waited for more customers to come in. Sometimes she got cranky, but Kelly loved her just the same.

"Mrs. Nelson, you really ought to try one of the fancier drinks I make here. All you ever have is this regular, old-fashioned drip coffee. Why don't you let me make you a mocha cappuccino? You would really like that!"

Mrs. Nelson waved Kelly off with her left hand, and picked up her newspaper. Kelly giggled and walked over to where Johnny had sat down at the other end of the counter.

"How can I help you, sir?"

"Gimme some of Grandma's Prize Winning Pie! Make it cherry. And a cup of coffee like Mrs. Nelson is drinking."

"What? You too? Let me make you something special."

"Nah. Just plain old black coffee with my pie. That special stuff's for all the high school kids that swarm the place when school gets out. Let them drink it."

"Yeah, I guess it is a generational thing in this town. But I promise you, once I get you hooked on this stuff, you'll never quit." Kelly batted her lashes at Johnny, with a sweet grin.

"Baby, I'm already hooked." Johnny leaned across the counter and kissed her, an innocent peck on the lips. Then he said, "Sweetheart, you know I normally like to help you on Saturdays, but we're just so busy with this project. The guys got lazy and fell a little behind when I took a week off to help you with the grand opening. Now, I have to crack the whip and make them work Saturdays to get us back on schedule to finish this job in time. The only way I can do that is if I'm there."

"Don't worry, honey. You've helped me more than enough. I can manage here myself, today."

Johnny looked at Kelly with adoring eyes. He just loved this woman so much. Her beautiful face, her unbending spirit, her gung-ho attitude. He was proud to call her his fiancé. He was also beaming with excitement about an idea that had come to him, during his drive towards the job site, that morning. He now had a plan for exactly how he was going to bring his fiancé back to him, as completely as he needed her back, emotionally and sexually.

It was not the pie and coffee that brought him to Kelly's Kafe that day, but the desire to lay the foundation for his plan, as soon as he could. As Kelly set the pie down in front of him, he put down his coffee cup and looked into her smiling face. Then, he asked her, "Darlin, tomorrow is the only day off we share together. Do you mind if I take you somewhere special instead of going to church?"

Kelly smiled. Johnny didn't realize that, never missing church on Sunday was his rule, not hers. But she teased him a little. "Well,... I don't know..."

"Come on, please," Johnny was almost begging like a little boy hoping to convince his mother to take him to Disney Land. He looked so sweet. Kelly couldn't toy with him any longer.

"Ok!" She grinned widely. "Where are you taking me?"

"It's a surprise. I gotta go, babe. I'll come help you lock up tonight." Johnny kissed Kelly on the lips again and he was gone.

She watched him walk out of the café. Her gaze remained on him until he was in his truck, and his truck was out of sight.

"You look like a lovesick puppy!" snapped Old Lady Nelson.

Kelly just smiled and stared dreamily down the path Johnny's truck had taken, long after it was out of sight.

★ ★ ★

The next morning, Johnny was frying eggs and Kelly was flipping pancakes, at home in Johnny's kitchen. Kelly had immediately moved into Johnny's house after his surprise marriage proposal. She hadn't even unpacked her things at her parents' house. After their celebration at the diner, Kelly drove straight to Johnny's house with him, and made that her home. It was a big, white house with four bedrooms, a well manicured lawn and a huge backyard, perfect for the kids Johnny always talked about having with Kelly. The large gourmet kitchen was perfect for cooking. When Johnny had the house built while Kelly was still living in L.A., he had told the subcontractors to make the kitchen a woman's dream. "Find me the best appliances, find me the prettiest granite, design it with all the characteristics you've heard all your wives and mothers say they've always wanted in a kitchen," Johnny had said. The three men listening to his demands had looked at him, perplexed. "But you're a bachelor!" One of them had pointed out. "Hopefully, not for much longer," Johnny replied, "she should be coming back, any day now." Then, Fred had responded by simply patting Johnny on the back with understanding. He didn't have to ask, who.

That was three years ago.

Now, finally, Johnny's dream had come true. He and Kelly were now standing in that kitchen he had made just for her, not knowing when, but knowing for certain, that she'd be back one day.

"Why do you always insist on frying the eggs?" asked Kelly.

"Because, I can make them exactly how I like them, just barely done, not sunny side up, and not quite over easy, but easier than over easy. Nobody else seems to know how to get them exactly that way."

"Ok. Master of the egg pan, please make a few for me that are cooked barely more than over easy, but not quite over medium."

They both laughed and shared a quick kiss in front of the stove, as each one tended to the pan they were cooking with.

"I can't wait to find out where you're taking me today," Kelly smiled at him.

"You're going to love it. At least, I hope you're going to love it."

"I will," Kelly reassured him.

After breakfast, Johnny and Kelly climbed into Johnny's truck and drove past the church, where the whole town was sure to be for the next few hours. Johnny drove her up the hill and around the corner to the highest hilltop in town. It was called "make-out point." Kelly laughed and laughed as she saw where Johnny was taking her. He pulled to the edge of the hilltop so they could look out his windshield at the best view you could find anywhere in town.

"I love it! You were right Johnny, I love it!"

Johnny smiled. "We're not there yet."

"What?"

Jonny unbuckled his seat belt, walked over to the passenger side and opened the door for Kelly. He held out both his hands. She leaped into his hands, as she had done so many times before, in their high school days; and he lifted her out of the truck and placed her gently on the ground.

"We can't make-out, here," Johnny said, "The Sheriff patrols this place too often."

Those words. Kelly couldn't believe it. Those were the exact words he had said to her so many years ago, on that very special night.

Johnny took Kelly by the hand and said, "Come on. Let's leave my truck here to throw them off our trail. Let's go for a walk, instead."

Again, the same words Johnny had said to her, the night they walked two miles until they found the privacy they were looking for behind the grandstand bleachers at their high school football field.

Kelly knew what was happening now. They were re-living the moment Johnny had taken her virginity. She was overwhelmed with the emotion that came flooding in. She tried not to cry. Her smile was as bright as the sun, as she blinked back tears. They hardly spoke during that same two-mile walk they had taken back then, walking hand in hand, anticipation rising.

This time, Johnny was more prepared. He had a picnic basket packed with a champagne bottle, strawberries and champagne glasses; and a soft blanket to lie underneath them so that they wouldn't get so dusty this time.

As they approached the bleachers, butterflies fluttered wildly in Kelly's stomach. It felt like the first time. She felt like a nervous schoolgirl again. Johnny led her by the hand. "Come on," he said, "Under here."

Kelly followed, her hand still in his tight grip, giving her comfort and security. She knew back then that she could trust Johnny forever. It was this safe, secure feeling that she felt now, and which she had felt then, that made her give in to him that night. Today felt the same. Kelly followed Johnny under the bleachers, and it was as if she had traveled back in time, as she passed underneath.

Johnny found the spot they had carved their names after they made love for the first time. He dusted it off with the handkerchief that was in his pocket.

"It's still there! Come look!"

Kelly walked over to where Johnny was, ducking to see what he had found. And there it was, still carved into the underside of the seat. It read: "Johnny loves Kelly, forever."

"Right here. This is exactly where we were, Kelly. I'll lay the blanket here."

Johnny laid the blanket down, and each of them laid on top of it.

"Should I open the champagne?"

Kelly giggled. "Ooh champagne. So grown up."

Johnny smiled and popped open the bottle. "Come here," he said. And Kelly scooted closer to him. He poured two glasses and handed one to Kelly. They were lying on their stomachs. Kelly was kicking her feet as she giggled and sipped champagne.

"Will you marry me, Kelly?"

"Yes."

They clicked glasses and sipped champagne.

"You won't run away, this time?"

"No, Johnny, I promise. I'll never run away again."

"I should have a tracking device installed in that ring, in case you do."

They both laughed and Johnny put down his glass and wrapped his arms around Kelly. He kissed her as she giggled.

"Are you nervous? Don't be nervous."

Kelly giggled. "I'm just a little nervous."

Johnny held her tight and kissed her neck. "Ah." Kelly whispered, closing her eyes. She was still kicking her feet with the champagne glass in her hand.

"Give me your glass," Johnny whispered.

Her eyes still closed, relishing the lingering feeling of his kiss, Kelly handed Johnny her glass.

Johnny set her glass next to his, and whispered, "roll over."

Kelly rolled over onto her back and waited. Johnny got on top of her and kissed her on the lips softly. She kissed him back. His soft kiss became a little deeper, more indulgent, softness slowly becoming possession, possession intensifying into desperation. Kelly returned the desperate passion in her kiss, reaching her hands up and running them through his hair. And finally, he felt the passion he'd been seeking from her. Johnny then slowed their kiss to the gentle softness with which it started, ending with a gentle peck before pulling away and looking deep into Kelly's eyes. He was going to take his sweet time. He wanted his Kelly back.

Johnny kissed her on the neck, and her mouth opened as she sighed with pleasure, giving her neck to him. His kiss dropped to her collarbone and became gentle as a light caress. She lied there relaxed on her back, with a smile on her face and her eyes closed in bliss.

His gentle kiss traveled downward towards the top of the low-cut sundress she wore. He trailed soft kisses along the skin of her breasts where the sundress exposed her cleavage; his gentle kisses tracing the seam of the dress from left to right, then right to left, never lifting his lips from her skin. The soft kisses felt like a sweet caress. He pressed his mouth into her cleavage, kissing her harder there. With his mouth still pressed against her skin, he softly placed his hands on the bare skin that now heaved as her breath became deeper. He spread his fingers across her breasts above the sundress, gently moving them downward and over the material until the tips of his fingers reached the seam at the top of her dress, where he let the index finger of each hand, hook underneath the thin fabric, which barely covered her nipples. He slipped each index finger beneath the material of her dress on each breast and below the bra underneath, gently pushing the fabric down and out of the way. As her breasts popped free, he grabbed one with his mouth, gently taking her in, suckling, licking, sucking, as his hands continued to move the straps of her dress and bra downward.

With his mouth, he continued fondling her breasts, from one side to the other, as his gentle hands slid the straps down her arms. His mouth never ceasing its hungry indulgence of her soft breasts, he slipped his hands down her torso until the dress and bra were dangling around her waist. Continuing his sweet suckling of her breasts, he slid his hands around her back and unsnapped the bra. He cast it aside and reached back to unzip her dress, never taking his desperate mouth off her body. As he unzipped the dress and slid it further down her body, his fingers curled into her underwear and brought them down with it. His mouth moved downward following his hands. He kissed her side. He kissed her stomach and trailed kisses across her perfectly flat abdomen. His mouth reached her hips and traveled down her legs, as he slid the dress down her legs, to her ankles, then her feet. Finally, reaching her feet, he removed her dress and underwear completely, and his hands were free to explore her body.

Johnny lifted his head to watch Kelly, as he caressed her legs with both hands, from her ankles, upward toward her knees. He wrapped his hands around her knees, caressing her softly with a circular motion, moving his hands inward, and slowly gliding them up her thighs. Kelly stared into Johnny's eyes lovingly, waiting with anticipation.

Johnny stopped at the top of Kelly's inner thighs. He looked into her eyes, and whispered, "Can I?"

Gazing up into Johnny's eyes, Kelly nodded slowly without speaking.

With one hand, Johnny first caressed the skin at the apex of Kelly's thighs. Then with his middle finger, he separated the lips, and pressed gently against her clitoris, circling it as he pressed a little harder and deeper with each movement. Kelly's eyes widened as she stared into Johnny's face. He never took his eyes off her face as he moved his middle finger, then slid it slightly downward and pressed it inside her. Her eyes got wider and her mouth opened, and he pressed deeper into her. He slowly drew his finger outward, then pressed hard inward, then outward, then inward. Her wide eyes glazed over with pleasure. He continued this motion as he watched and felt Kelly's pleasure escalate. His finger quickened its pace of the inward and outward motion, as Kelly's breathing sped up to match the pace. He added a little more strength and she cried out in pleasure. He moved his finger inside her faster, harder, faster. "Oh Johnny, yes! Yes, Johnny, yes!"

Suddenly he removed his finger, and she begged, "Please, more please." Johnny quickly removed all his clothing, then pressed his finger inside her again as she grabbed his arm, hoping to keep it in place. She didn't want him to stop yet. So he continued penetrating her with his finger. As Kelly began to reach climax, Johnny quickly removed his finger and swiftly slipped his erection deep inside her, before she noticed his finger was gone, pressing his hard cock inward and outward as fast as the rhythm with which his finger had penetrated her. Kelly grabbed onto him with both hands, wrapping her arms around his strong muscular back and shoulders, as he pressed his body against hers and wildly kissed her lips, her neck, her cheeks, he pounded into her desperately. "Oh, Oh! Johnny! Oh!" she screamed. "I can't believe it!" she panted. "I can't believe it, it feels so good!" Johnny kept penetrating Kelly. He wouldn't stop. He was not going to stop until he knew she came. He pressed his hard cock deep inside her, moving inward and outward with determination. His pace was fast, his force was hard, and she screamed louder. He pounded harder and faster, he would not relent until she came. "Oh! Johnny! Johnny!" she kept screaming. He pounded her hard and fast, intensifying the movement as each of her screams became louder. Johnny panted breathlessly into her ear, "I love you, Kelly. You're my one true love. I love you now and forever." And that's when Kelly came with the most powerful orgasm she'd ever felt in her life; the pleasure burst out of her, a warm sensation permeating her body, exploding first inside her vagina then spreading outward, coursing through her veins, filling her arms and legs and entire body with warmth and pleasure and ecstasy she'd never known before. Johnny felt her pleasure surround his manhood and he knew. He knew finally, he had the woman he loved back. Kelly's body fell limp beneath him. Her arms dropping from the tight grasp she had clung around Johnny, her eyes closing, her head tilting back, and a long sigh of ecstasy escaping her open mouth, "Aaaaaahhhh." That sound, that look of ecstasy on her face, pushed Johnny over the edge. Johnny's pleasure burst out of him, filling her with his cum. He grabbed her face with both hands and pressed his mouth hard against hers, kissing her with deep passion as he kept coming and coming. Then he fell on top of her, panting heavily, wrapping his arms around her, holding her tight, as they both lie there exhausted from the powerful orgasms they both had.

Chapter 12

After that Sunday under the bleachers, Kelly and Johnny's relationship was pure bliss. Johnny had taken Kelly across the threshold and truly brought her back home. Sex between them was now amazing – every single time. She would now allow him to lead, and would indulge in the pleasure he gave her. The barrier, which previously prevented her from creating a loving bond with him during sex, had fallen. She no longer behaved robotically, as if she were merely performing a task focused only on making him ejaculate. Now, whenever they had sex, they made love, true love. This is what Johnny had been missing. And he was so grateful that his idea worked. Taking her back to that precious moment they shared, had the effect of wiping away years of bad experiences. He had brought her back to the girl she was before she left Oklahoma. The time was finally right to start planning their wedding.

But there was a problem. Kelly had to go back to L.A., and she couldn't tell Johnny why. She wasn't even sure if she should tell him it was L.A., she was going to. What if he followed her?

Parked outside Kelly's Kafe, just before opening, Kelly took a folded piece of paper from her glove compartment. It was folded into such a small square it could almost be mistaken for lint. It was the subpoena commanding her to appear and testify at White Jr.'s trial. Although the young prosecutor had told her not to worry, her conviction for prostitution could not come out during the trial, Kelly worried. It was unfathomable for her to believe that Johnny could accompany her to L.A., and never learn about her conviction. She could never allow him to find out, she had been a prostitute. She had to come up with a story. She then looked up at her beloved café, and wondered how she was going to staff the café while she was away. What excuse could she make, that was worthy of leaving the man she loved behind, and leaving her business, for what could be up to a few weeks?

Kelly carefully placed the folded square back into her glove compartment, in the pocket of a folder where she kept her proof of insurance and registration. This was the only place she could think to hide it. She could not save the subpoena's details regarding time, place and courtroom number into the calendar on her cell phone, in case Johnny saw it there. The trial was now only weeks away, and she had to think of something.

Kelly called a friend she used to room with in L.A. It was her friend Ann, who also worked as an actress in Hollywood. Ann was good. She always landed good roles. Ann could turn on her actress abilities in a pinch, to get them out of (or into, whichever they preferred in the moment), any situation that arose.

The phone rang twice.

"Hello?"

"Ann. It's Kelly."

"Hey! How are you! Oh my God, it's so good to hear your voice!"

"Nice talking to you to. I hate to cut you off but I'm in a hurry, and I need your help."

"What is it?"

"I need you to call my house at midnight tonight."

"Why?!"

"I need you to use your acting abilities to sound frantic, desperate, and in need of urgent help, the kind I could never ignore. The kind that would make me drop everything, my business, my fiancé, my family, and rush to your side to help you through your drama."

"Like what?"

"I'm sorry, I'm in too much of a hurry to think of something now, so I need you to think of it. You'll have to write the script and perform the role. But whatever you do, don't be frantic in L.A. Be frantic in any other city. Actually, nowhere near California. Pretend to be anywhere in the United States, just not California. I need an excuse to leave my home in a hurry and be gone for two weeks."

"Kelly," Ann's voice was filled with concern, "Is everything ok?"

"Yes. I just…"

"No. I mean, is he hitting you or something?"

"No! No. That's not it at all."

"Kelly. You can tell me."

"No. I just can't let him know that I have a trip planned to L.A. That's all. I'll explain everything when I get there. I'll be there in a few weeks."

Kelly watched Old Lady Nelson pull up and park in front of Kelly's Kafe. *Damn,* Kelly thought to herself, *Just like clockwork, that old lady is always here 5 minutes before 6:00 a.m.*

"I have to go now, Ann. Please. I'm counting on you. Bye!"

Chapter 13

David and Sarah walked out of their imposing double doors and down their long, stone staircase to find their favorite driver waiting next to the town car. The steep and curvy roads that wound up to their hill, so high above the Mediterranean Sea, was not suitable for travel by limousine. Instead, they used a town car. In fact, you never saw limousines in that region; rather, the wealthy either drove their own sports cars, or were driven around in a town car.

David and Sarah each had their own sports cars, but preferred to be driven. They enjoyed holding hands and paying attention to each other, instead of being forced to pay close attention to the potentially dangerous windy roads – which is what driving themselves around in one of David's yellow Lamborghinis, would require. David hardly ever drove a Lamborghini anymore, because Sarah preferred having all of his attention while someone else drove them to their destination.

Today, as they walked towards the town car, their driver greeted David, "Sir, I have dry red wine, today; and dark chocolate. I thought you would like something different than your typical champagne and berries."

"Yes. That's perfect, Jean Claude. Thank you. So what special trip can you surprise us with today? Sarah seems to know the secret, but she won't tell me."

Sarah smiled, wryly. She did know, but it was something that would blow David's mind, so she was going to keep it a secret. She was excited to see the look on his face when he first realized what he was looking at.

"Oh, no, no, noo!" protested Jean Claude, "She does not know. This is a secret for the two of you." It would be easier to keep the secret, if he let David believe he wasn't the only one who had to wait for the surprise.

Sarah and David settled into the backseat of the town car, and David opened the bottle of wine. Sarah had to take a glass; otherwise, David would get suspicious. She stared at her glass with worry; then decided a few sips would be ok. She wouldn't finish the glass.

As the driver wound David and Sarah down the hill, they sank into the plush leather seats of the town car, Sarah's left hand in David's, and a glass of wine in her right. David made small talk with the driver, as Sarah looked out her window at the amazing scenery that the south of France offered. The natural beauty of the gorgeous cliffs rising above the Mediterranean Sea, was decorated by ancient Roman architecture, beautiful churches, adorned with real gold, castles and fortresses, which people of earlier centuries used to defend themselves atop the high hills. And of course, the water, the crystal clear blue water, so clear you could see straight down to the bottom, even from the highest cliff. It was the bluest water, Sarah had ever seen.

Sarah felt David's hand squeeze hers a little tighter, which brought her attention back to him. She pulled her eyes away from the amazing scenery and looked at David. He smiled at her with his sweet closed lip smile, and his pretty blue eyes twinkled. *As pretty as the water out there*, Sarah thought to herself. David didn't have anything to say. He just wanted to see his wife's pretty face. She smiled back at him lovingly, and the driver drove on.

As they approached a small quaint-looking house, Sarah began to feel excited. They were almost there. Their driver had arranged for them to visit a private individual who never allowed any visitors. But the driver was in such good graces with the homeowner, that the homeowner trusted him to bring over only those individuals, whom the driver would highly recommend. After all, the gentleman would get lonely without any company. This gentleman was a collector. He was a collector of very fine art. His collection began with this small structure, which he made his home, despite the fact that he was wealthy enough to live in the largest estate in the French countryside. The small structure had been a restaurant during the days of Picasso, Renoir, and Monet. When they were all starving artists, they paid for their food at that restaurant with their artwork. The original paintings, with which these renowned artists paid for their food, still hung on the walls. It was such a well kept secret that only a few people in the world knew about the place. This secret survived the Second World War, when the Germans were stealing the finest art from all over France. The old restaurant was now this eccentric art collector's home. It was not open to the public. This was an extraordinarily rare opportunity.

The homeowner answered the door, himself; and greeted Jean Claude with a handshake and a kiss on the right cheek. He shook David's hand, and kissed Sarah's, "Please, do come in."

When they walked in, they were astonished by what they saw. All around the house, every inch of wall was covered. David's mouth slowly opened in awe, and his eyes rounded with amazement as they scanned the countless paintings emanating gloriously from their frames. David loved art. He still hadn't comprehended what exactly he was looking at, because he'd never heard of these paintings or this place. He had never heard of a secret stash of unknown works by these famous artists. David automatically assumed that the man was a painter himself, so talented that he could paint to emulate these amazing artists.

Forgetting himself, David walked directly to the nearest wall lined with several magnificent paintings. "This is amazing! It's just amazing!"

David paced along the wall and inspected each of the paintings closely. "I can't believe it, you painted all these!?"

The man roared with laughter. "No, sir. No. I wish I could be so talented!"

Sarah giggled as she watched David's face light up like a child. She waited for the man to tell David what he was looking at.

"Well, where did you find them?" asked David.

"Here."

"What do you mean, here?"

"They were here when I bought the house. They came with the house. They are as much a part of this house as the wood and beams that hold it upright, the nails holding them together, and the foundation this whole building rests on. These paintings *are* this house."

"How on earth..." David looked around awe struck, wonder in his eyes.

The gentleman smiled. He loved to watch another art lover discover the reality of this place for the first time. So he watched David silently, waiting to see what David would be able to guess on his own.

David studied each painting carefully. He and Sarah had spent many hours in French museums enjoying famous artwork. David would never call himself an expert, but he certainly had a good eye for such things.

"It's uncanny!" David exclaimed. "It's uncanny how close these works are to something the real artist would have painted. The style, the themes, the brushstrokes, everything. The type of paint used. The apparent age of each painting, from the look of it. Who would've done this? How could they have done this? And so many, by so many different artists. I can't believe it."

"Take your time," said their host, "Enjoy each and every one of these *masterpieces*."

The way the man emphasized the word "masterpieces," triggered something in David's mind. He began to view the artwork in a different light. He looked again at a Monet. Studied it carefully, then he exclaimed: "No! Are these original works by the true artists!?"

The gentleman laughed and clapped his hands together. "Ah, yes, sir. They are!"

"Unbelievable! How! I've never even seen these in print!"

"Come, come have some wine, and I'll tell you all about this place. I'll give you a grand tour."

During the grand tour, David stopped dead in his tracks. He nearly dropped the wine glass he held. He couldn't believe it. Centuries ago, Renoir painted a picturesque scene identical to that special place in David's backyard in Malibu, which David named, "the Garden of Eden."

Here was this masterpiece, by a magnificent artist, which captured an image of that very special place, which David held so dear. The painting depicted a young couple in love, lying on a blanket, staring lovingly into each other's eyes. The woman on her back with her head turned towards the man, love reflecting in her eyes. The man lying on his side, with his head resting on his hand, propped up by his elbow, as he stared down at the woman adoringly. She had long dark hair, like Sarah. He had striking blue eyes, like David. Each of them frozen in a pose identical to the poses David and Sarah were in, when Sarah looked at David and whispered, for the first time, *"Make love to me."*

In the painting, the couple lay on the grass a few feet away from a winding stream beneath a powerful waterfall. Surrounding the couple, was an abundance of trees, lush green grass, bright flowers and fruit trees with branches filled with ripe fruit. It was the exact picture of that beautiful day that David took Sarah's virginity, in his Garden of Eden. David stared into the picture and got lost in it. David couldn't shake the feeling that, centuries ago, Renoir had predicted David and Sarah's future, and painted it.

Sarah saw what David was looking at, and it took her breath away. She knew immediately why David had stopped, entranced, lost in that picture. She walked up behind him, placed her right hand on his right shoulder, and rested her chin on his left, as she stared into the painting with him.

When David finally found his words, his voice was hardly audible.

"I have to have it," he whispered, bewildered.

The gentleman whose home they were visiting stopped to look back when he noticed they didn't seem to be behind him anymore. He saw them a short distance away, each standing mesmerized by one painting. He took his time, as he casually walked towards them.

"It is very romantic, no?"

"Oh my God," David said, "That's an understatement."

The man chuckled.

David then turned to him, "Sir, you must sell this to me. You must."

The man objected, "Oh no! No! Nothing in this house is for sale. Everything hangs where it was originally hung when the artist made his purchase with it. I cannot move a thing. I cannot sell a thing. I'm dearly sorry, sir."

"But you don't understand. I have to have this painting. I can't even explain it to you. I have to have it."

The gentleman saw the desperation in David's eyes and wondered what captured him so. Art had a way of doing that. One piece would reach into someone's soul and make them crazy about the artwork.

David persisted, "I'll give you millions, many millions. Please sir! I must have this painting!" David's eyes were nearly misty, turning ever so blue. David's eyes always became bluer with strong emotion.

The gentleman felt guilty. He knew what it was to love art so much. But he could not part with a single painting. Part of what made this place so special was the fact that these spectacular original works of art, remained in the same place they were originally hung, completely untouched, and undisturbed – a secret artists' paradise.

"You can come visit the painting any time you wish. I rather like your company. I will even set up a little table and chairs right here in front of the painting, where we can have our cappuccinos, our wine, our champagne. And you can stare at that painting as long as you wish."

"But it won't be the same," David pleaded, "Please sir, name your price. Anything, I'll pay anything."

"Sir, I understand your agony. Believe me, I understand. But you must understand how much it would agonize me to remove this beautiful piece from its original place."

David's chin dropped and his once hopeful, pleading face turned sad.

The homeowner felt even guiltier, yet. How could he deny the man his passion; but how could he part with the painting, himself? He thought of a compromise that he hoped would alleviate David's pain. "As a gift to you, I will not take any payment for it, I will personally, commission the best artist in France to create a reproduction. I have never done such a thing. But I will for you. I will even have a frame reproduced to match the original frame you see here. And you may still come visit the original any time you like."

David lifted his chin and a polite smile appeared, "Thank you, sir. You are far too kind."

David and Sarah remained at the man's home until nightfall. They made a new friend that day. The man had invited them to stay for lunch, then dinner, then a nightcap. They enjoyed his company. They had great conversation, and good laughter until it became very late, and they really needed to be on their way. As they drove away from his home, Sarah dreaded having to leave that wonderful escape, as the time neared when she would have to be calling Katelyn to coach her through White Jr.'s trial. She couldn't wait for this miserable case to be over, so that she could go back to peacefully living happily ever after with David, without interruption. Also, it was becoming more and more difficult to keep her involvement in the trial, a secret from David. She did not want to ruin his bliss, or flare his anger, with memories of White Jr.; so, she held it all inside, and didn't say a word to him.

Chapter 14

Stellar defense lawyers, such as the ones White Sr., had hired to defend his son, never roll over and play dead, after one bad ruling by a court. The team of defense lawyers representing White Jr., were now gathered around a conference room table at White Sr.'s law firm. They were strategizing over how to present the case, after the judge denied their motion to allow evidence of the alleged victim's prior conviction for prostitution.

Larry Pason led the conversation, "We can still present the victim's past to the jury. We just have to be more creative in the way we do it. I think we start in voir dire. I will ask questions of potential jurors about their prejudices, which will be designed to lead them into drawing conclusions about the victim's character. Also, just because we cannot present evidence of the criminal conviction, does not mean we cannot present evidence of our client's state of mind, and what he believed to be the case. Our client believed he had hired a prostitute to role-play. She just took it a little too far. This means, he will have to testify."

The defense team agreed with Larry. After a discussion about the types of voir dire questions they intended to ask potential jurors, the defense team turned to analyze the home surveillance video that they had not yet disclosed to the prosecution.

The video was saved to a thumb drive. Co-counsel, Michael Denez, was plugging it into a laptop and preparing to display it on the big screen TV in the conference room. Before turning it on, he explained what it was.

"This is video from surveillance cameras in White Jr.'s home in Beverly Hills. They capture the living room, where the exchange occurred. The video is both helpful and hurtful to our case. It shows an exchange between White Jr., and Kelly Luthan, which for the most part is consistent with what the alleged victim describes in the police report. It appears as if White Jr., forces her into sexual intercourse, while she struggles to get away. However, the video differs drastically from her description of events pertaining to the use of the knife. In the police report, she says that he attacked her, then, she swung her purse at him in attempt to fend him off, and that while she swung her purse, a knife that she keeps in her purse for self-defense fell out. She says that when he saw the knife, White Jr., reached for it, and said he was going to kill her after he finished raping her so that she couldn't talk. She told police that she was able to get to the knife before he did; and that she used it in self-defense before running out of his home.

"In contrast to that statement, in the video, we see that she never swung her purse at him. The knife never fell out of her purse, and our client never grabbed it, reached for it, or even saw it. He was not even aware of the knife until she suddenly slashed it across his face.

"In the video, you can see that she deliberately reached into her purse, pulled out the knife, and swiped it across our client's face before he even knew a knife was present. He quickly recoiled and put both hands over his face in pain, while she ran out of the house and drove straight to the District Attorney's Office, with the bloody knife. Our client made no attempt to chase her, but was still on the couch holding his face in shock while she exited through his front door.

"This evidence most certainly defeats the charge of attempted aggravated murder, which is based on nothing more than the victim's statement that he threatened to kill her with the knife. However, we need to review this video and analyze whether it helps prove the prosecution's case for rape. Certainly, a woman has a right to defend herself if she is getting raped. Therefore, we cannot rely solely on her use of the knife to defeat the rape charge. Let's watch. We need to decide whether we present this video in court, and if so, at what point before court, do we disclose it to the prosecution."

The men all watched the video closely, from start to finish. Kelly was in White Jr.'s home for at least an hour before any sexual activity commenced. The defense team watched every minute leading up to that point. They did not fast forward, in case something occurred to help prove she consented, despite what appeared to be a struggle and resistance.

The first clue that she went to White Jr.'s home intending to either seduce him or arouse him, intentionally, was in her clothing. Put simply, she looked like a prostitute. Her dress was very short. It was extremely tight around her body, and it was so white it was nearly see-through. Though it did not look see-through on camera, it looked like it could have been, or at least had the same effect, because of how tightly it fit against her body. She also wore very high-heeled boots, adding to her over-sexualized and seductive appearance.

When she entered the living room, it appeared as though she and White Jr., greeted each other amicably. He poured wine, and the two of them sat on the couch, drinking and conversing like old friends. There was no sound on the video; therefore, there was no evidence of what words were exchanged between them. The conversation and the wine consumption went on for an hour. At one point White Jr., laughed then put his hand on her leg. She pushed his hand away, but he persisted, and she continued to push his hand away. Then, White Jr., got on top of her as she turned and tried to reach for her purse, which was sitting on the end table. White Jr., did not punch her, slap her, or use any other aggressive or assaultive behavior towards her. The only apparent aggression was in the way he had grabbed her hips with both hands firmly, to pull her towards him and to keep her from getting away. It also appeared that he was using the force of his weight to keep her down, as she squirmed and struggled to get out of his grasp, continuously reaching for her purse. During the fumbling and grabbing and squirming, Kelly had managed to turn onto her stomach so that reaching for her purse was easier. As she attempted to inch towards it and reach for it, he held her by the hips and forced her down onto his erection. It appeared that she kept up the struggle to get away from him for as long as the intercourse was in progress. She reached, and reached for her purse throughout the entire process. When she was finally able to reach the strap of her purse, she yanked it towards her, quickly pulled out the knife and in one swift swoop, slashed it at his face. He recoiled, and she ran. It looked like a rape. It looked like date rape.

Despite what the video appeared to show, White Jr., had told his defense attorneys that he had hired her to play a role. He claimed that he just wanted her to role-play, as a girl who resisted; but he was surprised at how much she resisted, and of course, did not ever expect that she would use a weapon.

After reviewing the victim's statement in the police report, White Jr., had told his defense team that his surveillance camera would prove she was lying about the knife. He further explained that they should prepare to observe a video that looked like it might be showing a rape in progress, but that they shouldn't worry because he had hired the prostitute to play a specific role. He had asked her to play an innocent virgin, nervous about sex. He explained that he was tired of L.A. women throwing themselves at him, and putting out on the first date. He said he wanted sex to feel different for a change. He wanted it to feel more challenging. Because of his experience with the women that surrounded him and aggressively pursued him, the only way he could think of experiencing a more resistant, innocent woman, was if he hired someone to play a role. He claimed that he had never hired a prostitute before and that he was nervous. So he decided to call a woman he knew. He chose to call a woman he had previously defended in a prostitution case. He said it felt like a safe bet to call on his former client, but he was dead wrong about that.

White Jr., had explained to his attorneys that in the phone call, during which she had agreed to service him in his home, he had specifically asked her if she would resist a little during the initial advance. So, when she did, he believed it was all part of what they had agreed upon. He had no clue that she was going to come to his home armed, and ready to turn a consensual arrangement into framing him for rape.

That explanation was the backdrop against which the defense attorneys analyzed the video. After reviewing the video, White Sr., spoke first. He was disgusted. He couldn't bear to watch his son in an act, which very much resembled rape.

"This video should never see the light of day," he said.

"Let's not make such a quick decision," replied Larry Pason.

"No one can see this video," repeated White Sr., more sternly.

"Now, I think we shouldn't underestimate how valuable the video can be to show that, if the victim told such an egregious lie accusing a man of attempted murder, she must also be lying about rape. I think we should consider how this video can actually corroborate our client's version of the story, while at the same time presenting evidence that she is a prostitute, through our client's description of what he knew, in his mind, to be the transaction they agreed upon." Larry Pason, explained.

"You can do that with the right type of cross-examination," argued White Sr. "This video does not see the light of day."

Larry Pason persisted: "I think we should prepare our client for testimony that explains what is happening on the video. We need to be prepared to show the video to the jury to corroborate our client's testimony. I agree that we can wait until after we cross-examine the victim, before we decide whether or not to present the video. But we can't simply pretend that it does not exist and never prepare our client to testify about it."

All the other defense attorneys agreed with Larry, as White Sr., sat silently, crossing his arms with a scowl on his face. They knew they could not convince him of anything today because it was his own son he had just observed in a video that appeared to reflect he was committing an atrocious crime. It was too close for him to think rationally and analyze the evidence for its other values, and strategize over how to turn what appeared to be bad evidence into something that could help the defense.

But White Sr.'s mind was sharp. Despite the emotional tumult he was feeling, he could still see the case from both sides. He warned: "There is a risk that the jury will not believe him when he explains he hired a prostitute. Do not forget, the Court has not allowed us to present evidence of her conviction. If an objection is sustained in the middle of his testimony, regarding his belief that she was a prostitute, it could completely disrupt our rhythm and leave him looking like a rapist who is so foul that he calls his poor, innocent victim a prostitute, during his own trial for rape. It could blow up in our faces. I am instructing you now. You will not show this video to the prosecution. If at some point during the trial, we decide it can be a useful tool to impeach the victim's testimony, without the risk of securing a conviction for the state, then we will re-visit the issue during a recess. But for now, nobody else sees this video."

Larry responded, "We will be very careful. During his testimony, he can very easily blurt out that he knew, from prior experience, she was a prostitute. We will not ask a question that draws the objection. We will prepare him to explain the details while answering a different, innocuous question that leaves the prosecution unprepared to object. In response to the innocuous question, 'how did Ms. Luthan get inside your home,' White Jr., will explain that he represented Kelly Luthan in her prostitution case, which is why he knew to call her to engage her in this transaction. Then, when the State objects, it will be too late. The jury will have already heard it. But I agree with you. We will not disclose this video to the prosecution. If we use it, we will surprise them with it. We argue that it's impeachment evidence, and that, as such, it cannot be excluded for our failure to disclose it pre-trial."

Chapter 15

Johnny drove Kelly to the airport in her car, instead of his truck. The truck had a flat tire, a perpetual problem due to nails on the ground at construction sites.

"Why do you have to go?" he asked, during their drive.

"I told you, sweetheart, because she has nobody else to take care of her."

"Are you sure there's nobody else?"

"Yes. I'm sure."

"But I don't want you to leave again. I get so nervous at the thought of you leaving, again."

"Honey, she's on bed rest. She can't get up. Someone has to take care of her. I'm the only one who can."

"But you're not a nurse. Why can't she hire a nurse?"

"She doesn't have the money. And besides, she's scared. She wants someone by her side who cares about her, someone she feels comfortable with who will help her through this."

"How long will you be gone?"

"No more than two weeks. I promise! She is due to give birth in two weeks, but if the baby comes sooner, I can go home."

"Why can't I come with you?"

"Johnny, please. I need someone to watch the café. We're just starting to have a steady stream of customers. I don't want it to die down while I'm gone. I need you to watch our new employees and make sure they're running things properly. Please help me. Please support me. Please watch my business while I'm gone." She pleaded.

Johnny could never resist her beautiful pout and her pleading eyes. "Ok," he said, giving into her wishes one more time.

Giving Kelly everything she wanted in life was Johnny's life dream. It was the reason he borrowed money to help her open her business. It was the reason he was driving her to the airport now, even though he wanted to kick and scream, and demand that she not go. And, it was the reason he would stay to watch over her business.

When they got to the airport, Johnny parked the car and carried Kelly's bags inside. He stood in line with her while she checked in, and walked with her all the way to the security gate. That was as far as he was allowed to go. He held her tight in his arms as they said goodbye. He did not want to let her go. He gave her a long, passionate kiss that lingered with her, long after he had reluctantly walked away.

"Be good in Kentucky," he hollered back, after he had taken a few steps away from her.

"I will," she promised, and she blew him a kiss as he continued walking further away from her.

★ ★ ★

On his long drive home from the airport, a state police officer pulled Johnny over. He cursed under his breath. "What!" he said out loud in frustration, as he pulled the car over. "I'm not even speeding!" he said to himself, angrily.

As the officer approached the vehicle, Johnny rolled down the window and tried to gain his composure. Maybe he could sweet talk his way out of a ticket. His winning smile worked on women and men alike.

"Hello officer! I hope your day hasn't been too stressful."

"License and registration, sir."

"Yes, officer. Bear with me while I look for it. I'm driving my fiancé's car. I always tell her to keep that stuff in the glove compartment, but she doesn't always listen to me."

Johnny fumbled around in the glove compartment and found a folder. "Ah. This must be it!" He put the folder in his lap as he flipped through papers containing notes about menu ideas and prices for Kelly's Kafe. Finally, he found the proof of insurance that identified him and Kelly as the insureds, and which included the vehicle he was driving.

"Well, here's the proof of insurance." Johnny then reached in his back pocket for his wallet. "Here is my driver's license. I'm still looking for the registration."

The officer took the license and proof of insurance. After a quick glance, he handed the insurance card and driver's license back to Johnny, "I see that your name is also on the insurance, but I still need to see the registration."

"I'm looking, officer," Johnny said, as he continued flipping through the pile of papers in the folder. Johnny didn't notice a tiny folded paper drop into his lap, as he flipped through each paper, one by one.

"Maybe that's it," said the officer, as he pointed.

"What? Where?"

"In your lap. Something fell into your lap. Let's see what it is."

Johnny looked down and saw what the officer pointed at. Johnny began to unfold the paper, as the officer watched.

The officer recognized what it was before Johnny did.

"Whoa. That's a subpoena. You better show up for that or they can issue a warrant for your arrest."

"What? I don't know anything about a subpoena?"

"You mean, you weren't personally served?"

"No."

"Here, let me take a look." The officer read the subpoena. "Oh don't worry. It's not for you. It's for Kelly Luthan. Good thing it's not for you. L.A. is a long ways away from here, and you're headed the wrong direction. The airport is the other way. And this subpoena is for a court case that starts tomorrow."

Johnny was flabbergasted. As the officer handed him back the subpoena, Johnny took it into his hands and stared into it, unable to focus on the officer's next question.

"So, how about that registration?"

Johnny stared at the subpoena, speechless.

"Sir? The registration, please?"

Johnny ignored the officer as he read the subpoena, incredulously. Finally he spoke, but it was not responsive to the officer's question. "She said she was going to Kentucky," Johnny said with a voice filled with shock and disappointment, as he continued staring at the subpoena, blinking as if trying to clear his vision to be sure his eyes were not playing tricks on him.

Responding to Johnny's visible concern and dismay, the officer explained, "She's not the defendant in the case. She's just a witness."

"But why wouldn't she tell me?" Johnny asked, more to himself than to the officer, his eyes still bewildered, as he stared at the subpoena.

The officer could tell from the look on the man's face, that he was having a hard enough day. He decided to not ticket him for the burnt out tail light, or for failing to carry his registration.

"I'm going to let you off the hook for failing to present the registration. I'm sure you or your fiancé own the vehicle, otherwise you would not be insuring it. Also, make sure you get your taillight fixed, or they'll keep pulling you over for that. Drive safely, sir."

The officer walked away, and Johnny continued to stare in disbelief at the subpoena, which commanded Kelly Luthan's appearance at a criminal trial in Los Angeles.

Chapter 16

It was the first day of trial, and the courtroom was filled with potential jurors waiting to see if they would be selected or if they could go home. The attorneys sat at counsel table. Each of them had a list of the names, occupations, and ages of each potential juror. They also had copies of forms that Judge Johnson had each juror complete in order to make jury selection proceed more efficiently. Jurors completed forms, in which they were asked a list of generic questions about their ability to serve in a criminal case, involving these types of charges. Generic questions included questions about whether the juror had ever been a victim of these types of crimes; whether the juror knew anyone who had been the victim of these types of crimes; and whether the juror had ever been accused, arrested, or indicted for these types of crimes, and on and on. The forms also contained questions designed to ask the obvious questions, which both sets of lawyers would need answers to before deciding how to use their preemptory strikes. The questions were also designed to allow the judge to identify which select few jurors he would question individually, before turning things over to the lawyers. The jurors' answers to the form questions would help the judge identify who might be likely to show prejudice so great they could not fairly judge the case.

Judge Johnson began calling names. With each name that was randomly selected, a potential juror would take the appropriate seat in the order the judge told them to sit, starting with a chair that had white paper taped to it, with the #1 printed largely on the paper. Next to that chair, was a chair with the #2 printed on it, and so on and so forth. Upon taking the designated seat, the potential juror would be identified by that juror number from that point forward.

The judge liked to maximize efficiency in the manner in which voir dire was conducted; so instead of only selecting 12, he would select 18. As voir dire went on, and jurors among the 18 were excused for cause, another potential juror sitting in the audience would immediately replace the excused juror. That way, after the defense and the prosecution concluded their examinations, and the judge completed his decisions about who could be stricken for cause, there would still be 18 left. Then, after each side used their 3 strikes, there would remain the 12 final jurors who would judge the case. The jury box only contained 12 seats. Juror numbers 13 through 18 sat in chairs that lined the outside of the jury box. If one set of lawyers did not use all 3 strikes, the judge would excuse the extra jurors seated outside the jury box, starting with the highest juror number. However, that almost never occurred. Attorneys almost always used all three strikes.

The first potential juror whose name was called, was a little old lady. She scuffled slowly towards the jury box and took her time sitting down. When she sat, she smiled sweetly at the attorneys. She immediately noticed how young Katelyn was, and thought she looked very cute with her short black hair and her smart business suit. Katelyn's youthful face was a stark contrast to the group of five sharply dressed older men who surrounded the defendant. They all had gray hair and appeared to be very experienced attorneys. The little old lady immediately felt that this would be an unfair fight. She felt a tinge of sorrow for young Katelyn and hoped she'd be able to hold her own against the big guns who sat at the defense table. After smiling warmly at Katelyn, juror number 1 looked at the table full of defense lawyers to try to get a feel for them. She searched the faces and body language of everyone at counsel table, trying to get a sense of who she should listen to, and whose lead she should be following as the case progressed. At defense counsel's table, she noticed a very good-looking young man seated among the older attorneys. She immediately decided he must be the defendant in the case. She could see a look in his eyes that seemed to say, "help me."

Her heart went out to him. She already wanted to help him, though she still knew nothing about the case.

When juror number 1 had answered the generic question on the form, which asked: "Is there anything in your background or life experience that would prevent you from fairly judging a case involving an accusation of sexual assault," she had answered: "no." She answered in the negative, despite the fact that she was still angry about the time her son lost his job because a slutty girl he worked with accused him of sexual harassment. The accusations against her son were false, and management of the company knew the accusations were false; but, out of fear of being sued, they fired her lovely son, who would never in a million years do such a thing.

When juror number 1 completed the questionnaire, she did not believe that that experience would influence her decision in the case; because she thought accusations of using sexually explicit words and innuendo were nowhere near as awful as an accusation of rape. Sitting in the jury box, she still did not believe her son's experience would prejudice her view of the case. However, the truth was, the sight of White Jr., made her think of her own son who had been falsely accused; and she was already worried that this nice-looking young man had also been falsely accused.

The judge continued to randomly select names, and the jury box slowly began to fill up. Juror number 4 was Mr. Wilson. He owned a mechanic shop. All who knew him knew he was a very kind-hearted man. He had a nice face, warm eyes and a soothing smile. His soft heart was most vulnerable to beautiful women. Unlike most mechanics, who saw a female client as an opportunity to take advantage of someone who didn't know cars, Mr. Wilson frequently gave women discounts for his services because he felt bad for a woman who didn't have a man in her life to protect her and take care of things like taking a car to the mechanic. If a pretty girl ever cried and expressed her fear of being unable to pay the bill, Mr. Wilson would frequently give the girl free labor and charge her only for the most expensive parts.

These are the types of personality traits that usually cannot be detected in voir dire, particularly because most people are unaware of how their past experiences and natural personalities will affect their judgment in a criminal case. Thus, it doesn't matter the question that is asked, often times, attorneys will never know the deep rooted thoughts and feelings of the final twelve people who will determine a man's guilt or innocence.

The judge continued selecting names. Katelyn was nervous. Most of the names were men. She worried they would identify with the male defendant and not the female victim, despite Sarah's earlier warning that things were never that simple. Sarah had said: *"Women judge each other more harshly than men do. Find the sympathetic men on the jury and keep them. Keep the men with daughters."* There were men with daughters selected. Some of Judge Johnson's generic questions included questions about the jurors' family lives; whether they were married; how many children they had; their ages; and if they were boys or girls. Though some of the men in the jury box had daughters the victim's age, it still made Katelyn nervous that juror number 1 was the only female juror selected so far. Then finally, juror number 9 was called. A female. A young female. A college student. Perfect! Katelyn thought. Finally, a young open minded female who will believe in a woman's absolute right to control her body, and will likely be more afraid of letting a rapist go than worrying about whether he's innocent. Sarah had previously advised Katelyn: *"Young women can be good, but be careful of the old women, they always like a young good-looking defendant. It makes them think about their sons, and they instinctively protect the young men."* Katelyn remembered Sarah's advice; and she knew, from the questionnaire, that the old lady in seat number 1 had a son around White Jr.'s age; but the old lady smiled at her so warmly; and so far, there were only two women in the jury box. Despite the memory of Sarah's advice, Katelyn decided she would likely not use her strike on the old lady. For Sarah had also said: *"Get the jury to like you."* And it already felt like the old lady liked Katelyn, so Katelyn was keeping her, unless something weird or crazy came out of her mouth during the questioning.

Judge Johnson continued calling names. A police officer was juror number 10, a construction worker was juror number 11, and an accountant was juror number 12. The extra jurors numbered 13 through 18 consisted of three women who worked in the social services field; and three men, each of whom had been arrested but not convicted of domestic violence.

Katelyn hung her head. It almost didn't matter what happened during voir dire. She had to use all her strikes on the men who have histories reflecting violence against women. It did not matter how anyone else answered questions from the lawyers. She had no choice. She had to use her strikes on them. As for the women in the extra seats outside the jury box, she knew there was no hope that they would stay on the jury because they worked in social services. The defense team would certainly assume they have prejudices leaning towards protecting women, which would cause them to presume that all men accused of violent crimes against women were guilty. Katelyn knew the defense wouldn't need to use their strike on the police officer inside the jury box, because he would certainly be excused for cause.

And sure enough, as soon as the potential jurors were settled into their proper seats, the judge started with the police officer.

"Officer Mendez, do you believe that your occupation may cause you to have prejudices so great that you cannot sit in fair judgment of the accused?"

"Yes."

"You may be excused."

Judge Johnson then selected another name to replace the excused juror. It was another man. He was an ear, nose and throat doctor with no wife or children.

The judge went on to question the jurors about obvious prejudices, but nobody else expressed an opinion that would require the court to strike them for cause. Some of them sought to be excused because of demands at work, but their requests were denied after a long sermon Judge Johnson gave about everyone's civic duty to serve and the sacrifices all are expected to make in performing that duty. He ended his speech as he normally did, "Unless it is a life or death situation, I am not likely to excuse you on the basis of inconvenience, alone."

Upon concluding his general welcome, admonishments, and sermons typical in most cases, Judge Johnson turned the floor over to Katelyn Kruz. Katelyn was nervous. Very nervous. She was comfortable giving an opening statement to a jury, or a closing argument, or examining a witness in front of a jury; but the absolute worst thing, which she hated most, was addressing the jury in voir dire and asking them questions. She feared that she would insult the jurors before they judged the case. She feared she'd stumble over her words and lose credibility before the case even began. In DWI cases, she had overcome that fear after becoming comfortable with her standard questions useful in every DWI case. But this was a rape and attempted murder case. She had never handled anything so serious. Her mind was now blanking out on most of the questions that she had prepared and analyzed and reviewed during her coaching sessions with Sarah. She blamed Sam Chapman for this. He had been so cruel in the committee meeting when she raised the strategy Sarah gave her for taking the wind out of the defense's sails by getting the jury's commitment to judge the facts, despite the victim's prior conviction for prostitution.

Not even knowing that Sarah had been coaching Katelyn, Sam Chapman had barked at Katelyn during that committee meeting: *"Sorry Katelyn, but you're no Sarah Cartwright. Stay within your comfort zone, which should never be above your skill level. There's no way you can strike that balance in front of the jury. Don't even try it!"* The Committee Chair, who usually defended Katelyn against Sam's rudeness, didn't encourage Katelyn that time. Instead, he had reinforced Sam's warning. He had gently said: *"Katelyn, you'll recall when we first discussed this case when Sam was supposed to handle it, I had specifically instructed him to not allow evidence of the victim's prior conviction to be admitted at trial. You did a great job in getting that ruling. Don't lose that advantage. I'm sure you've heard great stories about how Sarah Cartwright could balance a high-wire act like the one you're suggesting, but not just any lawyer is capable of doing that. I would advise you to take the safe bet. Rely on the court's ruling, and be prepared to object vigilantly before you ever allow the defense to even hint at that evidence."*

Now, as Katelyn walked towards the jury, her mind was reeling with thoughts pondering the conflicting advice given to her by Sarah and the men on the Sexual Assaults Team. Katelyn walked towards the jury, nervous as hell. This was the time for her to decide, whether or not she would follow Sarah's advice. This was the time to decide whether she would go out on that limb. But she buckled. Her mind blanked out on that entire line of questioning. She clung instead to Sarah's first bit of advice – *"make no mistake about it, this is a popularity contest."* So Katelyn smiled. And she waited. And a fraction of a second later, every member of the jury smiled back at her.

"Ladies and gentlemen of the jury, first let me thank you for your service today. I know it's not easy leaving your families and your jobs to come to my place of business to help me administer justice. I can't express enough, how grateful I am for your service."

Katelyn went on, perfectly poised, perfectly confident, perfectly capable of the jury's trust; but she did not ask any of the questions geared towards getting their commitment to judge this case on its facts and not on the victim's past. Instead, she kept her questions safely generic:

"Can you keep your commitment to follow the law, and not allow your prejudices, whatever they may be, to interfere with your judgment of the facts?"

"Do you understand that the burden of proof is not that the State must prove its case beyond any doubt whatsoever, but that the doubt you hold must be reasonable?"

These were the types of questions Katelyn posed to the jurors.

She then made an attempt to have the men previously accused of domestic violence stricken for cause. She began with juror number 15.

"Forgive me for asking a personal question, but I must explore further whether you have personal biases that may interfere with your judgment of the case. I see that you've indicated in the questionnaire that you were arrested but not convicted of a crime involving domestic violence, is that correct?"

"Yes."

"Do you believe that you were falsely accused?"

"Yes."

"But despite the false accusation, you were in fact arrested?"

"Yes, but the charges were dropped."

"Did that experience sour your view of police officers, or any other aspect of the criminal justice system?"

"No. How could they know she lied? They have a duty to protect women, right?"

"Yes. I absolutely agree with you. But is there anything in your background, or in your life experience, that will prejudice your view so greatly that you may already be leaning towards favoring the defendant instead of the victim?"

"Actually, it's the opposite. My sister was raped when she was very young and nobody believed her. It ruined her life. She began using drugs and alcohol excessively, and now she's a mess beyond help. She was a very good girl before that. If I ever come across the guy who did it, I'll probably kill him, and I hope a jury like the people who surround me, will let me go for that."

Katelyn was astounded. She was ready to use her preemptory strike on this man, if she couldn't convince the judge to excuse him; but now, she hears he would favor the State? She paused, speechless for the briefest moment.

Larry Pason bolted out of his seat, "Your Honor! I move to

strike this juror for cause! I think it's very clear he cannot sit in fair judgment of my client."

Before making his decision, Judge Johnson asked the gentleman a few more questions, "Now, I understand that you have strong feelings about someone that has hurt your sister very badly, but will that affect your ability to presume this defendant is innocent before this case begins, and to analyze all the facts, and wait until the case concludes, before you pass judgment on the defendant?"

"Well, I mean, I think it will be a little hard for me to do that. There must be some reason why he's sitting here today."

"But you've said yourself you were once arrested on false charges."

"Yeah, but the case was dismissed right away. It never went to trial. This guy must be guilty if things have come this far."

"You may be excused."

Judge Johnson called another name. Again, it was a male juror, replacing juror number 15. Katelyn started with him when she resumed her questioning.

"I apologize, I don't have your questionnaire with me, it's still at counsel table. Forgive me for asking a personal question, but it's an important one for this process. Have you ever been accused of committing a violent crime against a woman?"

"Yeah! And she lied too! But I wasn't so lucky as the last guy. I had to pay an attorney thousands and thousands of dollars to defend me. I can't believe what that last guy just said. Of course a man can be innocent if he's sitting here for a trial! That's what trials are for! They're to give the guy a chance to prove he's innocent, when some vindictive woman is trying to gain an advantage in a divorce case or something, like my ex-wife did. She thought she'd get more money out of me in the divorce!"

Katelyn was sorry she had asked the question. *He's tainting the jury,* she worried. But she had to ask another question.

"Does that mean, your prior experience will cause you to favor the defendant and assume the victim is lying?"

"No. I didn't say that."

"Well, you may not have said it, but what I'm getting at, is your personal feelings. Might your emotions flare up during this case, due to your prior bad experience, having been falsely accused by a woman, and potentially interfere with your fair judgment of the facts?"

"No."

Katelyn was stuck. Back to square 1. All her strikes had to be used on the three men sitting outside the jury box. She didn't dare ask the other two men questions in attempt to have them stricken for cause, just in case they too gave impassioned speeches about women falsely accusing men for financial gain. She decided juror number 15 was an anomaly and would stick to the safe bet – end the conversation, and strike the three men seated in the extra row.

Katelyn concluded her voir dire. "That's all the questions I have. I thank you all again for being here today."

Larry Pason waited for Katelyn to reach counsel table and sit down before he stood. When he stood, he stood with grand authority and poise. He walked with a confident and relaxed stride towards the podium, which was placed in front of the jury. He did not stand behind it. He stood next to it. He placed his right elbow on the podium, as if using it as an armrest, and he warmly greeted the jury.

"Hello everyone."

They all smiled.

"I'm glad you're here today – because my client's fate rests in your hands. And I need good people, such as yourselves, who can be trusted with a very serious decision about a young man's life. You've already heard two men today, two of your fellow jurors, say that they too have had the awful experience of being falsely accused of a crime. You only heard from two of them, but there are more of them who sit among you. Of course, I have no intention of pointing them out by calling on them and asking them personal questions about that experience; but it's a point I make to alert you to the fact, that it is a problem more common than what you might expect."

"Your Honor, does Mr. Pason have a question? This is not the time for argument?" Katelyn interjected.

"He's allowed a short introduction, Ms. Kruz. I'll allow him to go on, but not for much longer."

Larry Pason stood straight up, turned towards the judge very respectfully and said, "Thank You Honor, I was just about to get to my questioning." He then turned back to face the jury.

"Ladies and gentlemen of the jury, what I was getting at is a very, very important question, I'm about to ask each and every one of you. My question is this: Are you the type of person – and this is not wrong or right, I just need you to be honest with me – are you the type of person, with similar views as the gentleman who just left here, who automatically assumes, that if someone has been arrested and charged, that there must be some credibility to the accusations made against him?

I will start with juror number 1 and I will go through each one of you in order. For now, all I need you to do is answer, 'yes' or 'no.'"

Larry Pason warmly smiled at each and every one of the jurors, one by one, starting with juror number 1 and gently asked, "Is that your view? Each juror smiled back at Larry and answered his question in the negative. Some elaborated: "Of course not, people are wrongfully accused all the time." Another said, "It seems like the police get it wrong, often. I would never assume someone is guilty just because they've been arrested." And another juror said, just what Larry Pason was waiting for: "Isn't everyone in America presumed innocent until they're proven guilty?"

Yes! Larry thought, *Just what I need! For that rule to come from the jury, so I don't have to preach it.* He answered the juror with smooth flattery:

"You are absolutely right. It is a guaranty provided by the United States Constitution. Now, I want to see a showing of hands. How many of you believe in following the supreme law of the land, the United States Constitution?"

100% of the hands went up.

"And how many of you understand and appreciate that the supreme law of the land requires you to presume that my client is innocent, right now, in this moment?"

100% of the hands went up, some a little more slowly and cautiously than others, but they followed the pack.

"Now, for a more difficult question. What if someone told you the State had 10 bishops from St. Peter's Square on its witness list? How many of you could still honor the United States Constitution, and still presume my client is innocent, as you sit here, right here, right now?"

All but three jurors shot up their hands without delay, knowing exactly what the defense lawyer was testing them on. Three women seated in the extra row looked at the defendant, squirmed in their chairs, then slowly raised their hands believing that was the answer the defense lawyer wanted.

"Now, just so you know, there aren't really 10 bishops coming here from the Vatican, today."

Members of the jury laughed.

"However, throughout this trial, things may come up that might trigger a personal opinion or a strong emotion you may have. What we try to do here, in voir dire, is ask you to tell us now, what emotions, thoughts or feelings you carry that could cloud your unbiased judgment of the facts. For example, what if I told you that my client has been accused by a woman of ill repute? Would that affect the way you view my client? Would you wonder why he had placed himself in a position to be in such close quarters with a woman of ill repute?

Upon hearing Larry Pason's line of questioning, Judge Johnson looked at Katelyn and waited for an objection, but she didn't move. He saw Sam Chapman sitting in the back of the courtroom shaking his head. Judge Johnson thought to himself, *"then why aren't you trying this case, big shot?"* Judge Johnson was the type of judge who did not interrupt an attorney without an objection from the other side. He believed that doing so was the same as raising objections on behalf of attorneys. It was his philosophy that, be what may, in a jury trial, justice sometimes came down to one simple rule: "May the best lawyer win." Otherwise, if a judge began to play the part of attorney on behalf of one lawyer or the other, it would drive the judge away from his proper position as unbiased adjudicator, and towards a position of advocate, which was a position a judge sitting on the bench should never take. Thus, he allowed Larry Pason to go on and on with his questions suggesting that the victim was a woman of ill repute, because Katelyn Kruz never objected, though she should have. Judge Johnson would have sustained the objection. Poor Katelyn was too young to understand the connotation carried in that old-fashioned phrase. Larry Pason had just called the victim, a prostitute.

Larry again presented this line of questioning for each juror one at a time. Starting with juror number 1.

"If those were the facts ma'am, would you hold it against my client?"

"No."

"Not at all?"

"Not at all."

Then with juror number 2, Larry asked: "If those were the facts sir, would it make you wonder if my client was less worthy of the protections of the United States Constitution?"

"No."

Larry asked juror number 3, "If my client was found with a woman of ill-repute, could you distinguish that conduct from the conduct he is accused of today?"

"Yeah."

Larry went through the jury box then onto the jurors seated in the extra row. Each of them gave the appropriate verbal answer. Larry was focused on getting the jurors to commit to honoring the United States Constitution, and presuming his client innocent; therefore, his focus was only on the words they said out loud. The four defense lawyers and the psychologist employed by the defense team, who were seated at counsel table, were in charge of watching for body language. The defense team wrote furiously, taking notes of every shift, every gesture, every facial expression that could be observed in the members of the jury as voir dire went on.

Larry Pason took his time in voir dire. Some questions required an answer from all 18 people. Some questions could be addressed to the group as a whole with a showing of hands. Larry Pason spent 3 hours examining the jurors with detailed questions, some of which were designed to identify biases, but most of which were designed to indoctrinate them into philosophies that would support the defense theory of the case. Larry Pason took his time, because he believed voir dire was the most important part of the case, as the 12 who remained would decide the fate of his client.

Finally, Larry Pason concluded his voir dire and thanked the jury with even more eloquence than Katelyn had:

"Thank you all. I trust that each and every one of you will be a fair juror. I know that you will do the right thing in this case, and never forget, that my dear client, whose fate you hold in your hands, is presumed innocent."

At the conclusion of the defense lawyer's voir dire, Judge Johnson called a recess.

"Ladies and gentlemen of the jury, please remain seated. This is a short recess to allow the attorneys a break to consider if and how they will utilize what we call a preemptory strike. Six of you will be excused after the break, and the remaining twelve will remain as the members of the jury."

Katelyn sat at counsel table. She did not leave for the recess because she knew exactly how she was going to use her strikes. She waited patiently. Sam Chapman was still at the back of the courtroom. He did not approach her to ask if she needed help deciding how to use her strikes. The D.A., had instructed him to let her make her own decisions and learn from her own mistakes, so if she had not looked around seeking him out for help, he would not move. He sat and waited. Katelyn stared straight ahead waiting for the judge to return to the bench.

The defense team hurried out into the hallway and found a private corner where they could huddle and make decisions about the jury. They would discuss and analyze each and every juror. Every person at counsel table watched every expression, every gesture, every shift in the seat of every juror who sat among the 18 selected. They all took notes profusely, while Larry Pason eloquently addressed the jury. They made notations of answers to questions, of facial expressions, of body language. Everything the human eye could observe, four lawyers notated. Four lawyers and one doctor, that is.

Dr. Jean Mastor was among the defense team today. She was a renowned psychologist with an office in Beverly Hills, California. She was hired to assist the defense team in analyzing the members of the jury, during voir dire, to help them select the best jury for their client.

Larry Pason spoke to the team first. "Now, our focus should be on the twelve sitting in the box because we know they are certain to stay if no strikes are used on them. So let's start our analysis there. Obviously, if we have to start using strikes on the people outside the box, those three women have to go. They're all in social services. We can't trust them."

"Not at all!" Dr. Mastor pitched in. "They're determined to

get on this jury so that they can fry your client. It's written all over their body language. Normally, I would ask you not to jump to conclusions based on occupation alone, but these women want blood."

"How can you tell?"

"Well, when you mentioned the phrase 'woman of ill-repute,' they each scowled. One crossed her arms tight across her chest and didn't release her arms for as long as you stood before the jury. The other crossed her right leg and turned her body slightly towards the left, as if shielding herself from you. She remained in that position with her head tilted away from you as if she no longer wanted to hear another word you said. And the third one looked right at you, narrowing her eyes with a glare that looked like it could send daggers. She then turned that same glare onto White Jr., and turned her lip up in disgust. You definitely offended them. They think you're slinging mud at the victim to gain an advantage, and they don't like it one bit.

Also, during your questioning of each of them, wherein you sought to establish cause to have them excused, each one reacted the same way. Each one snapped out short one-word answers, answering 'no' to the possibility that they may lean towards presuming guilt, while their body language said something very different. It appears to me that they want to be on this jury because they intend to convict your client."

"Wow, I hadn't noticed any of that?"

"Well, the body language was subtle and slight, but it was there."

"Did you see any other members of the jury react that strongly to that phrase."

"No. The college student did furrow her brow, but I think that's because she didn't quite understand what you meant. She's young enough that she might not understand what that phrase is in reference to."

"Do I need to worry about her? Because she's in the box. She's guaranteed to stay if I don't use a strike on her."

"I think you're ok. She seemed to smile shyly at our client. That could be indicative of a little crush."

"Yes! That's why I was leaning towards keeping her. I'm glad you saw that. My instinct was to keep the young college girl who might develop a crush on our good-looking client."

Dr. Mastor nodded thoughtfully, then raised an issue that all the men had missed. "There is someone in the box you need to worry about, a little. The mechanic, Mr. Wilson was his name. He appeared to be looking at your client rather suspiciously; and he seemed to be very fond of the prosecutor. That's a danger sign. I won't say that he looked at your client with disdain or prejudgment, but he definitely looked as if he was trying to read him, and that he carried a little suspicion in his thoughts."

The defense lawyers made note of Dr. Mastor's comments then continued with an analysis of each and every juror in the box. They started with juror number 1.

"What do we think of the old lady?"

Dr. Mastor chimed in: "She's a dream. You have to keep her and pray that the prosecution does not use their strike on her."

"Wow. That's a strong recommendation. Why so good?"

"She looked at your client adoringly. She already likes him. A lot. Also, when she first took her seat she was smiling sweetly at the prosecutor; but when you raised the issue about 'women of ill-repute,' she lifted her chin up as if she had just been given a very important bit of information. Then she seemed to give a slight nod as if she had just made a decision. After that, she gave the prosecutor a look of disapproval. It wasn't a scowl per se, and not very noticeable, because she generally has a sweet face, but she definitely looked at the prosecutor differently than when she first sat down, less favorably."

"Okay then. Juror number 1 definitely stays."

The defense team went through the list, in order. There were no other strong impressions, one way or the other. For the most part, all the remaining jurors sitting in the jury box seemed fair and unbiased.

The defense team concluded that four jurors were potential problems. So, they now had to strategize over how to use their three strikes.

Larry Pason said, "I think we all agree that the three women sitting outside the box are the worst ones. However, we need to decide if we should strike the mechanic, in hopes that juror number 15 gets into the box, or any one of those men who have previously been arrested for domestic violence."

Dr. Mastor then asked, "What's the procedure for utilizing strikes?"

We go one at a time. First the prosecution, then us, then the prosecution. We take turns.

"Ha!" Dr. Mastor gave a little laugh. "Well that makes it easy! The six extra jurors are seated boy, girl, boy, girl, boy, girl. I think you wait and see if the prosecution uses all of her strikes on the men seated in that extra row. If she does, you have to use all your strikes on the social workers in that row. If all the men in that row are gone, a strike against someone else in the jury box, will land number 18 – a social worker – in the jury box, taking the place of whoever is excused from the box."

"Excellent observation, doctor," said White, Sr. "Let's double check. Are there any men sitting in the jury box who have been arrested or convicted with any crime against women, or are they all seated in that extra row?"

In response to White Sr.'s question, every member of the defense team stopped to review the questionnaires of each juror sitting in the first twelve seats.

"No," said Michael. "None in the jury box. No arrests or convictions for any crimes among those members of the jury."

"Then we can be certain, Katelyn will use all her strikes on the three men in the extra row. We'll pay attention, however, because you never know. So, our plan now is this: Our first strike is against social worker who is juror number 14. Second strike is against social worker who is juror number 16. Third strike depends on whether Katelyn has stricken numbers 13, 15 and 17. If so, then we strike number 18. If not, if after her third strike, one of the men in 13, 15 or 17 remains, then we strike the mechanic, resulting in the man we want taking his place. But of course, if no men are left in that extra row, we have no choice but to strike social worker number 18."

The defense team walked back into the courtroom and motioned to the court's clerk. She picked up the phone and said: "They're ready." Less than a minute later, Judge Johnson returned to the bench.

"Counsel, you know the procedure. I will call the attorney's name and the attorney will simply provide the number.

"Ms. Kruz."

"Number 13, Your Honor."

"Mr. Pason"

"Number 14, You Honor."

"Ms. Kruz."

"Number 15, Your Honor."

"Mr. Pason."

"Number 16, Your Honor."

A few members of the jury snickered quietly. It sounded like the judge was testing the lawyers to see if they could count in order. The young college student had to look down and cover her mouth, she was afraid she would laugh out loud. The judge continued, as if unaware of the shifting and snickering in the jury box.

"Ms. Kruz."

"Number 17, Your Honor."

"Mr. Pason."

"Number 18, Your Honor."

The ear, nose and throat doctor who sat next to the college student decided this was a good opportunity to flirt with her. He leaned towards her and whispered, "Hey, the lawyers know how to count. Isn't that great?" She jerked her head suddenly in surprise, turning to look over her right shoulder. She was not expecting that. She gave him a polite smile but lifted her shoulder and turned back around as if to duck away from any more of his attention. He got the hint and leaned back in his chair, a little embarrassed.

Judge Johnson then announced that the following six jurors were now excused and asked that they kindly leave the courtroom. He listed them by name. Each of the jurors in the extra row stood and left the courtroom.

* * *

After the jury was selected, opening statements began. The prosecution went first. Katelyn stood before the jury with poise, eloquence and confidence. She gave a speech, which was as impassioned as the speeches she gave when convincing Judge Kline to hold the defendant without bail, then later convincing Judge Johnson to disallow any evidence of the victim's criminal conviction for prostitution. She felt a strong connection with the jury. She felt as if they trusted her. She was doing everything right, just as Sarah had instructed her.

She was so good, that the seasoned defense lawyers were getting nervous. Larry Pason began objecting profusely – meaningless, meritless objections designed to throw Katelyn off. It didn't work. She stood squarely in front of the jury, her shoulders creating a triangle of exclusion – her left shoulder to her right shoulder creating the base, and the jury box creating the point of the triangle, leaving defense counsel and even the judge, outside Katelyn's triangular bond with the jury.

Larry Pason would object, but Katelyn wouldn't budge. She would not turn her head towards him. Nor would she turn her head towards the judge. And she would absolutely not, move her shoulders so as to break the triangle. She kept her gaze on the jury and they kept their attention on her, as if the defense lawyer's objection was nothing but background noise. Katelyn would smile at the jury as she waited to hear the judge say, "overruled." And he did every time, because Katelyn stayed well within the rules of opening statement; and she knew, that just as Sarah had told her they would, the defense was objecting for the sole purpose of disrupting Katelyn's rhythm, in attempt to break the bond she was establishing with the jury. And just as Sarah had instructed her, Katelyn stood her ground, un-phased. On occasion, she would cast a slightly annoyed eye towards defense counsel as he spoke (though never moving her shoulders), then she would look back at the jury and shake her head slightly, as if to say, "Is he interrupting us again?" She could see in some of the jurors' faces they felt the same way. They seemed to be following her lead and learned to wait patiently with her until the judge said overruled, and Katelyn would pick up where she left off with the same phrase each time, "As I was saying..."

White Sr., stared at Katelyn, awed by the spectacular performance of such a young, inexperienced prosecutor. "Just like Sarah," he muttered in awe, under his breath. White Jr., turned his head abruptly, staring at his father in dismay. *"How dare, he!"* White Jr., thought. *"How dare he think of Sarah, during my trial!"* Then, White Jr., looked down, trying not to appear angry. His lawyers had warned him against losing his cool during trial and appearing aggressive in front of the jury. He was tempted to bury his face in his arms to hide his rage, but he was also afraid of looking like a guilty man trying to hide from the prosecutor's words. He picked up a legal pad, leaned back in his chair and held the legal pad in front of his face, as if reading, in attempt to hide his anger from the jury. Even now, at a time like this, his father was still putting Sarah on a pedestal.

Though the defense team never seemed to put two and two together, White Jr., knew it was Sarah Cartwright who was in that interview of the victim, with the police officer. He had heard her voice on the tape, and recognized it. Now, here he sat at his own trial, his father completely oblivious to the fact that Sarah Cartwright was the cause of his arrest, and probably was the one orchestrating the whole thing. White Jr., knew better than anyone, she sure had motive. Now, White Jr., had to listen to his father seated next to him, whispering Sarah's name, as if she herself were as great a legend as his father. The anger boiled inside him so badly, he had to hide his face, and just wait for the day to be over.

At the conclusion of the prosecutor's opening statement, Larry Pason stood and advised the court that the defense would be reserving their opening statement until after the State closed its case in chief, and before the defense began presenting its case.

"Very Well." Said Judge Johnson. "I think now would be an appropriate time to adjourn for the day. We will reconvene tomorrow at 8:30 a.m. That will be the time the first witness appears in the case. Members of the jury please report to the jury room by 8:00 a.m. sharp. The bailiff will escort you into the courtroom from there, when we're ready to resume. Thank you. You may exit the courtroom through this side door, which is to my right and to your left. It leads straight into the jury room. The bailiff will instruct you on how and when to exit the courthouse from there."

★ ★ ★

While the jurors waited for the bailiff, they sat in the jury room and made small talk. The old lady couldn't help herself. She needed to get something off her chest, "Well, I don't know why they're making us do this?"

"I think it's so we don't run into any lawyers or witnesses on our way out of the building," said Mr. Wilson.

"No. I don't mean the wait. I mean this whole trial. The lady's a prostitute, so how could she have been raped?"

"Huh!" The college student gasped with shock at the old lady's baseless accusation.

The accountant spoke up, "Now, how do you figure that?!" he asked in a tone leaving no secret as to his belief that she was a mean, crazy old lady, that might be losing her marbles.

"Well you heard him!" insisted the old woman, "The defense attorney all but told us during that jury selection. He said a woman of 'ill-repute' had accused his client of a crime."

"That just means bad reputation," said the college student, "And that's not fair to judge. This isn't the 1950s. We don't judge criminal cases based on a woman's reputation. And why should a woman have a bad reputation if she does the same things men do?"

"Sweetie," said the old lady sternly, "You may be too young to understand this. But the phrase 'woman of ill-repute' specifically means, 'prostitute.'"

"Huh!" The college student gasped again, eyes widening even larger, as she stared at the old lady in disbelief. *What a terrible, mean old lady,* she thought, *how could she say such things before the victim even took the witness stand?*

The accountant joined the conversation again. "Well, she is correct about the phrase. But she is not correct about how the defense lawyer used it. He was just asking us hypothetical questions. He did not say, 'the victim is a woman of ill-repute, now how do you feel about that?'"

"Well, darling," said the old lady, "there would be no reason for him to ask us that hypothetical question, unless the victim was a prostitute."

Just then, the bailiff opened the door and the jurors stopped talking. He instructed them on the path they were expected to take when exiting the building. Each juror stood and silently exited the door, one at a time.

* * *

The reason the defense had reserved its opening statement, was to achieve a great strategic advantage in trial. It was designed to keep the defense theory of the case a secret from the prosecution, so that it could not prepare witnesses for what was to come. So far, it was obvious that the state was relying on the favorable ruling obtained pre-trial, and had not prepared to explain the victim's history to the jury. White Jr., a defense attorney himself, had invoked his right to remain silent, upon being arrested. The State had no idea what his side of the story would be. The defense sought to preserve that advantage by reserving opening statement until the beginning of its case-in-chief.

Larry Pason had prepared great one-liners for his opening statement, such as: "If the State wants to charge my client for employing a prostitute, he will plead guilty to that charge, because that is the only crime he is guilty of, in this case." These one-liners would draw objections, and sidebars would be had. During the sidebars, Larry Pason would explain that his client was going to testify that in his mind, he believed he hired a prostitute to role-play, but that she turned against him in attempt to extort more money from him than what one job would pay. He would explain that the court cannot suppress evidence of what the defendant believed in his mind was transpiring between him and the victim, and that it could not suppress evidence of the defendant's description of the conversation between him and the prostitute, which was essentially along the lines of: "I will pay you, if you role-play," followed by her assent to the transaction.

But all this had to wait until after the state concluded its case-in-chief. Otherwise, cross-examination of the unsuspecting victim would not be as effective.

Chapter 17

The State's first witness was Detective Jones. He was the detective who had responded to the District Attorney's Office to interview the victim on the day she reported the crime. The victim had barged into the D.A.'s Office, demanding to speak to a female prosecutor. The prosecutor had taken Kelly Luthan into her office and called Detective Jones to assist with the interview.

Detective Jones was a strong, large framed man who looked authoritative and trustworthy when he wore his uniform. He always wore his uniform when testifying before a jury. Today was no different. He sat with perfect posture and spoke in a manner that commanded respect. The jury's approval of the detective was visible.

Katelyn capitalized on these strengths during her direct examination of Detective Jones. During the detective's testimony, he explained that he had observed the victim just after the rape had occurred; and that she appeared to still be under the influence of a traumatic event. This gave Katelyn the foundation to introduce hearsay statements made by the victim when she reported the crime. It was called the "excited utterances" exception to the hearsay rule. To Katelyn's surprise, the defense never objected to hearsay when the detective repeated the victim's report. Katelyn thought they could have easily argued that enough time had passed during the drive from the defendant's home in Beverly Hills to the District Attorney's Office in downtown L.A., that the "excited utterances" exception should not apply. She was relieved that the defense did not object. This allowed for a very smooth direct examination of the detective, which allowed him to explain to the jury everything the victim had said while reporting the crime. Through the detective's testimony,

Katelyn was able to achieve a goal every prosecutor aims for, during direct examination of its own witnesses. His testimony repeated and confirmed the same facts Katelyn told the jury to listen for, during her opening statement. Through the testimony of Detective Jones, Katelyn established each and every element of the crimes charged.

Katelyn also established, through the detective's testimony, that Kelly Luthan was not discovered with the knife involuntarily; rather, she offered the knife to authorities, without being asked. During that line of questioning, Katelyn asked Detective Jones:

"So, the victim told you that she was able to gain possession of the knife, and use it in self-defense?"

"Yes."

"And you say, she brought the weapon to the District Attorney's Office, willingly?"

"Yes."

"It was not discovered during a search warrant?"

"No."

"She offered it to the District Attorney's Office, on her own free will?"

"Yes."

"Immediately after the incident?"

"She was still frazzled by what had just occurred, and she told us she had driven straight to the D.A.'s Office after she was able to defend herself and get away from him."

"Did she explain why she was demanding to speak to a female prosecutor, instead of going to the police?"

"Well, I wasn't there when she said why, but apparently..."

"Objection. The witness cannot testify if he does not have first-hand knowledge."

"Sustained."

Katelyn paused, flipped through her notes, then continued her examination:

"Did you observe blood on the knife?"

"Yes."

"And was the knife sent to the crime lab to determine whose blood was on the knife?"

"Yes."

"Detective, in your experience investigating the thousands of crimes you have investigated in your career, has a perpetrator guilty of assault or robbery, ever volunteered to give you the weapon used?"

"No, ma'am."

"Criminals usually hide their weapons from police, don't they?"

"Yes."

Katelyn ended her examination of the detective there. She wanted to leave lingering in the jurors' minds, the most important point – that it was very obvious that Kelly Luthan was the victim of the crime, not the assailant.

Larry Pason could have objected to the prosecutor's last two questions on the basis of relevance; but he did not. He was saving his response for cross-examination. Larry Pason began his cross-examination where Katelyn left off:

"Detective, is it possible, that a wise criminal – one who is smarter than most criminals – could concoct a scheme to give the weapon used in her crime to authorities, in order to fool them into believing she was the victim?

"Well, uh,..."

"Just answer the simple question – is that possible?"

"Yes. Anything's possible."

"Detective, please explain to us in detail, how did the victim appear during the interview?"

"She appeared frazzled, distraught..."

"No, Detective, I don't want you to guess what her mental state was."

"I'm not guessing."

"Well, aren't you? You can't read her mind, can you? You can't know what she was really thinking, can you?"

"Well, I wasn't reading her mind, I'm describing her mannerisms, her speech, the visible affect in her demeanor..."

"Yes, yes, but could you really know whether or not she was merely acting? You're not a mind reader are you?"

"No sir. I'm not a mind reader, but I believe I've been on the police force long enough to tell the difference between someone who is faking emotional trauma and someone who was actually traumatized."

"Unless she was a really great actress, right? I mean, this is Hollywood."

"Objection. Argumentative."

"Sustained."

Larry Pason was un-phased by the objection. He proceeded with his next question as if the prosecutor and the judge had not even spoken. The smooth and seamless continuation of his examination rendered the voices of the prosecutor and the judge, mere background noise.

"Detective, what I was really getting at when I asked you to describe her appearance, was not your best guess about her emotional or mental state. What I really wanted you to tell us, is what you could see with your own eyes, regarding her physical appearance.

Did she look disheveled?"

"No sir."

"Were her clothes torn?"

"No."

"Was her hair a mess?"

"It was not."

"Did she have any physical injuries?"

"No."

"No scratches, no bruising?"

"It would be too close in time for bruising to appear."

"What about redness. Did you observe redness anywhere on her skin?"

"I did not."

"No redness? No scratching? No signs that he struck her? No signs of a struggle?"

"I would not expect to see signs that he struck her. She did not describe him striking her with his fist, or even an open hand. She described a struggle, wherein the defendant primarily used his weight to over power her and hold her in place. That type of overpowering would not leave the signs you're asking about."

"But didn't she describe him grabbing her by the hips and forcing her onto his erection? Wouldn't that leave marks, if he was holding her with so much force that she couldn't escape his grip?"

"It could."

"Did you observe any evidence on that part of her body, which would have corroborated that story?"

"She did not allow me to look. She was too embarrassed to lift up her dress."

"I thought I had heard a female voice on the interview tape. Couldn't a female officer or prosecutor make that observation instead of you?"

"We can't force a victim to comply. The victim has a right to decline if we ask her to remove her clothing for further observation."

"So, she refused to show you whether or not there were any

marks on her body that could have proven she was telling the truth."

"It is not uncommon for a victim of a sexual assault to feel that way."

"I didn't ask you what is common. I asked you if the alleged victim in this particular case refused to show you the only part on her body that you would have expected to see marks from the description of events she gave you."

"Objection. Asked and answered."

"Very well," Larry Pason quickly interjected before the court sustained the objection. "I'll withdraw. The prosecution is right. You have already testified that she refused to cooperate with the investigation, despite her initiation of the report."

"Objection," repeated Katelyn.

"I'll move on, Your Honor," Larry quickly responded.

"Now Detective, even if the victim described a struggle that would not leave visible injuries to the parts of her body that were not covered by clothing, wouldn't the struggle you described – which is based on her statement to police – have left her hair a mess and her clothing disheveled?"

"It could be a long drive between Beverly Hills and downtown L.A. sir, I assume she would have fixed her clothing and her hair during that time, or in the parking lot, from embarrassment, before entering the building after she parked."

The defense lawyer interrupted, "Ah, but you're just guessing, again. Your Honor, I move to strike the last statement the witness made, as he could not possibly know that."

"Granted. Members of the jury, you are to disregard the last remark by the detective."

"Thank you, Detective," said Larry, politely with a warm smile. "That's all the questions I have for you."

★ ★ ★

Katelyn's next witness was an expert from the crime lab. She used the expert to establish that the blood on the knife was White Jr.'s blood. She did this for two reasons.

First, it corroborated the victim's testimony, and proved that a violent exchange occurred between the victim and the defendant, negating the idea of consensual intercourse.

Second, it revealed to the jury a fact the defense would exploit in their favor if the prosecution hadn't presented it first. If the jury heard about whose blood was on the knife from the defense, it would have appeared as if the prosecution were hiding that evidence and that the defense discovered it to prove their client's innocence. Presenting it in her case in chief took the wind out of that sail.

However, even as Katelyn tried to take the wind out of the defense's sails on this one fact, Larry Pason, took it back. At the conclusion of Katelyn's examination of the expert witness, Larry Pason stood and addressed the court:

"Your Honor, we have no questions for this witness. Our whole point here is that it was my client's blood on that knife, not the victim's. Thank you."

★ ★ ★

The next witness to be called at trial was a doctor who Kelly Luthan had been advised to visit after Detective Jones had finished interviewing her. The doctor had physically examined Kelly after she reported the alleged crime. He had collected DNA evidence left by the defendant during the incident. Though Katelyn did not anticipate that the defense would dispute that a sexual exchange had occurred between White Jr., and Kelly Luthan, she nonetheless, introduced the DNA evidence with testimony by the doctor who collected it. However, the most important reason Katelyn called this doctor to the witness stand, was so that she could inquire about any injuries he may have observed, which the Detective had not observed:

"Doctor, did you observe any injuries on the victim?"

"Yes."

"Please describe what you observed."

"There were scratches and red marks on her hips. The red marks appeared to be the early stages of bruising. I'll just call them bruises. The bruises matched the look of the tip of fingers, with four round marks on one side, and one round mark on the opposite side – like four fingers and one thumb. These markings were observed on both hips, as if someone had forcibly grabbed her with both hands, by the hips, in attempt to hold her in place, as she struggled to get away. There were also scratch marks consistent with movement. If she were trying to move away from him, while he forcibly pulled her back, it would leave the same markings I observed on the victim's body."

"Are the injuries consistent with the victim's description of her attempts to get away from the defendant?"

"Yes, she did describe a moment during the struggle where she was on her stomach, attempting to gain balance on her hands and knees to try to crawl away from him, but he grabbed her by her hips, and pulled her towards him, forcibly shoving her down onto his erection."

"Thank you, Doctor. I have no further questions."

Larry Pason began his cross-examination of the doctor. It was short:

"With regard to the finger marks, is there any way to tell the difference between finger marks left as a result of the story the victim gave, or finger marks left during a passionate moment where a man grips a woman firmly, as she willingly bounces upwards and downwards, or forwards and backwards on all fours, during consensual intercourse?"

"Well, it depends on how firmly he grasped her. It would have to be hard enough to actually leave marks. He would have to be digging his hands in rather forcibly."

"So, the short answer is 'yes,' passionate sex between consenting adults could leave the same marks?"

"Yes. It is conceivable that the same marks could be left either way."

"Doctor, I know you found evidence of sexual intercourse, and you also linked that evidence to my client. We do not dispute that these two had consensual sex. My question is this, aside from being able to conclude that sexual intercourse transpired, did you form a conclusion about whether or not a rape occurred?"

"The evidence was inconclusive."

"Inconclusive. That means there is no evidence of rape?"

"No. It's inconclusive."

"Well, if it was conclusively decided that there was evidence of rape, wouldn't you say there was evidence of rape?"

"Yes."

"But there is no evidence of rape in this case, is there?"

"None that I found, no."

★ ★ ★

Kelly Luthan was the next witness called during the trial. Just as Katelyn had instructed, Kelly wore her Sunday best. Kelly was dressed in a conservative white dress, with floral print. It was long-sleeved, with a high button up neck, and had long, flowy length, which fell just below her knee. She appeared to be the picture of innocence itself. Her long blond hair was neatly pulled back in a low ponytail, and the little makeup she wore looked very natural.

She smiled shyly at the jury box as she walked passed and took the witness stand. Her presentation was demure, innocent and sweet.

During her direct-examination, the prosecutor asked Kelly Luthan easy, open-ended questions, which first asked about her current, personal background, so that the jury would get to know her as a human being and warm up to her. During a short series of introductory questions, the jury heard about Kelly's nice life in Oklahoma, before the prosecution began asking the victim about the details of the terrible crime that happened to her, here in L.A.

Katelyn's direct-examination of the victim drew from her the same statements made to Detective Jones when she reported the crime. Katelyn was satisfied with the victim's testimony. The jury had just heard the victim testify consistently with what Detective Jones had testified to. So far, the case was going well for the prosecution. Katelyn thought.

Then, the defense began its cross-examination.

Ms. Luthan, let me begin with a few more questions about your background. You say you work in a café now?

"I own the café."

"Oh you own it? That's fantastic. Congratulations. How did you get the money to open a café, you were just a paralegal before, correct?"

"Yes. My boyfriend gave me the money."

"How much was that?"

"$100,000" Kelly answered, giving the defense a lucky strike, for which they never would even dared hope. Her answer tied in nicely with their client's story. It was a relevant fact, of which the prosecution was completely unaware, because the alleged victim never told them during her interview. In an instant, Larry Pason suddenly transitioned from background questions, to discrediting the victim:

"Oh, that's interesting, that is the exact amount you asked my client for on the day you say he raped you, isn't it?"

Kelly's mouth opened wide. She blinked twice. She had forgotten about that. Caught off guard, and completely unprepared for such a question this early in the examination, Kelly stammered, "Well, uh, I,... um."

"Yes, Ms. Luthan, you asked my client for $100,000 in his living room, on the day in question, correct?" asked Larry Pason, emphasizing the word "correct" with such authority that it was difficult for the witness to respond in any other way.

"Correct," answered Kelly, still caught off guard, and unable to utter any other words.

"And now, you have been able to find a different man, with whom you are sexually involved, who has given you $100,000. Congratulations."

"Objection!" shouted Katelyn.

"I withdraw, Your Honor," said Larry Pason, never taking his eyes off the witness. He stared at her with determination, as if ready to force a confession out of her. His glaring gaze trapped her in place. Her tentative eyes transfixed on his, Kelly was immobile as a deer in the headlights. Stricken with fear and shame, she was trapped, and already judged.

Larry Pason could see that he had rattled the witness enough to go in for the kill; he continued his cross-examination without mercy:

"Ms. Luthan, you lied to police about what happened between you and my client that day, didn't you?"

"No!"

"Of course you did, you told police that he threatened you with the knife, but that's false, isn't it?"

"No, it's not!"

"Ms. Luthan, we have video."

Kelly's eyes widened and her mouth dropped again in surprise. She looked at the prosecutor, wondering why the prosecution had never told her about a video.

Katelyn jumped up, "Objection! Facts not in evidence!" Katelyn thought Larry was playing a trick that even she, as a young attorney knew how to use – pretending to have contradicting evidence to confuse the witness into telling a different story. Katelyn tried to alert the witness through her objection that there was no such evidence. It didn't work.

"Overruled," said the judge.

Larry Pason continued: "Ms. Luthan, you were not under oath when you spoke to police, but you are under oath now. If you lie today, you can be prosecuted for perjury, so I am going to ask you again, did my client threaten to kill you?"

Kelly dropped her chin, looked down at the witness stand and mumbled, "No."

"I didn't hear you, Ms. Luthan, please speak a little louder."

Kelly looked up, and a little louder said: "No."

"Then, it must be, that you also lied about the rape!"

"No! That's not true! He raped me!"

"But you said he threatened to kill you, even though he didn't, how can this jury believe he raped you?"

"I had to say he tried to kill me! They'd never believe me! I was afraid I would get arrested instead of him!" Kelly screamed.

"Why?"

"Because they wouldn't believe me!" She screamed again.

"Why wouldn't they believe you?"

"Objection! Irrelevant! Prejudicial!" Katelyn objected profusely.

"Why wouldn't they believe you, Ms. Luthan?" Larry Pason persisted over the prosecutor's objections, keeping his eyes locked on Kelly's. He knew he was on the verge of forcing the witness to say what he was not allowed to ask.

"Objection!" Katelyn repeated.

"Sustained," the Court answered.

Ignoring Katelyn and the judge, Kelly continued screaming at the defense lawyer: "Who would ever believe that a prostitute got raped?! I was convicted of prostitution, why would the police ever believe me!?"

A collective gasp from the jury filled the courtroom.

"Ms. Luthan," the judge tried to interrupt.

Kelly was too distraught to hear the judge. The defense lawyer had already accused her of being a prostitute in his questions about the money for the café. The guilt and shame she felt were overwhelming; she was now the one on trial. Her emotions were uncontrollable. She continued yelling at the defense lawyer:

"And he was a rich guy, the son of a famous lawyer! Why would they ever believe me!? The only way I could get him off me, was to use that knife! But then I was scared I'd get arrested for assaulting him! I had to say he tried to use the knife against me first! If I hadn't, they would've arrested me!"

The judge tapped his gavel on the bench, to get her attention. "Ms. Luthan, please. I had sustained the prosecutor's objection. When I sustain an objection, that means you do not answer the question. Are we clear?"

Kelly nodded.

Still poised, professional, and in complete control, Larry Pason asked the court:

"Your Honor, permission to inquire about facts to which the witness has already admitted, irrespective of this court's earlier ruling."

"Granted."

Turning to the witness, Larry Pason, asked: "Ms. Luthan, you had sex with my client in exchange for money that day, correct?"

"No!"

"Ms. Luthan, you have already admitted that you asked him for $100,000 that day, was that before he had sex with you, or after?"

"Stop that! Stop that! You creep! I'm not a prostitute anymore! And I wasn't then either! He took advantage! When I asked him to borrow that money, he put his hand up my skirt and told me to earn it! I told him, No! I told him I didn't do that anymore! But he kept going, he forced me, I couldn't get him off me, the only thing I could do, was swing that knife at him, to get away! It's not fair! I have the right to say 'no' to sex. He shouldn't be allowed to force me, no matter what I've done in my past! This is not fair!" Kelly was wailing and crying on the witness stand, as she finished her angry outburst at the defense lawyer.

Larry Pason needed to disrupt her emotional outburst quickly. The defense couldn't allow the jury to see her cry, as they would surely feel sorry for her. Larry spoke quickly and with all the smoothness of a perfect gentleman, he addressed the court:

"Perhaps we can take a recess, Your Honor."

The court granted a recess and the jury filed out of the courtroom towards the jury room.

★ ★ ★

Although they had been instructed, before the trial began, that they were not to deliberate until after the trial concluded and closing arguments had been made, the jury could not help but commence their deliberation after what had just happened in the courtroom. During the recess, they discussed what they had just observed. The old lady was the first to speak:

"See, I told you! She's a prostitute! She set up that poor boy!"

The young lady responded, "I know it makes it sound really

bad, but you saw how she cried. I don't think she wanted to have sex with him."

"She lied!" the old lady screamed at her, "She admitted that she lied! How could you be so naive! If she lied about one thing, she lied about everything!" The old lady turned to the men on the jury, "You know she's guilty! Don't you?"

The construction worker responded, "Ma'am, she's not the one on trial."

"Well she should be! Why didn't the State charge her with a crime!? They tried to hide from us the fact that she was a prostitute. You saw how that little prosecutor kept objecting. Why would they do that?"

The young lady answered, "Just because she's a prostitute, doesn't mean that anyone who wants to, can force themselves on her."

"She asked for money! He didn't force himself on her!"

The old lady looked around the room, determined to convince every one of them that they had to find the young man, innocent. She looked at the men first, "any one of you could be sitting in that young man's seat, right now. Any one of you could be bamboozled and set up by a prostitute!"

"Ma'am, I don't go to prostitutes," said the construction worker.

"Neither do I," said another man.

"Neither do I," said another juror.

"Neither do I," each one of the remaining male jurors repeated.

The old lady looked at the young lady, and pointed at her, "Your boyfriend could be sitting in that defendant's seat, right now!"

The young woman shrieked, "My boyfriend would never do that!!!!"

"Ladies, let's please calm down," said the construction worker. "It's not time yet to be judging the defendant. Also, it will never be the right time to start accusing members of this jury, or their boyfriends, of engaging in prostitution. I'll admit there is a hell of a lot of doubt in this case, after what we just saw, but we're supposed to reserve our judgment until the end of the case."

"Doubt. That's just it," the old lady said, "if any of you have any doubts that that nice looking young man raped a prostitute, then you have to find him, not guilty."

The young lady spoke up first, "I don't know, I just don't know what happened. It's too hard to tell."

The accountant responded, "Technically, if you don't know what happened, that calculates to doubt. Reasonable doubt equals acquittal. It's a simple formula. I think we all know what we have to do in this case."

"I don't," said Mr. Wilson, one of the men who had remained silent throughout the discussion. "That woman was very distraught. She sounded vulnerable, attacked and humiliated. The defense lawyer was ruthless. He should not have treated her that way. She said she was no longer a prostitute at the time she met with the guy to ask him to help her out. She was probably trying to create a better life for herself so that she didn't have to slip back into her old occupation. But he took advantage of her. I believe her. I believe that, with her criminal history, she was worried the police wouldn't believe her. She lied about the knife, to protect herself. That's different from lying to falsely accuse someone."

The old lady was baffled, "now how can you come up with all that?"

Mr. Wilson responded, "The thing that did it for me was her emotional breakdown, and the tears. Man, those tears. I really felt sorry for her. If this was just a financial transaction for her, I don't think she would've become that emotional. It looked to me like she was upset about being raped, and even more upset that people were suggesting it didn't matter."

★ ★ ★

Larry Pason looked up at the clock in the courtroom. It was 4:14 p.m., when the jury had begun filing out of the courtroom for the recess. During the recess, he had been watching the victim out of the corner of his eye to see if she had sufficiently collected herself for him to resume his examination. He could end the cross-examination of the witness, with two or three short, but very important questions. Larry Pason had observed that the victim appeared to be more collected and less vulnerable and sympathetic than she had appeared in the moment he asked for the recess. Larry decided he would finish his cross-examination today.

The judge took the bench and called the courtroom to order. Larry stood and addressed the court. "Your Honor, I know that it is nearly 5:00 p.m., but I have only a few more questions left that I do not believe will take longer than 10 minutes. I suggest that you allow me to conclude my examination of the witness today, and that we commence with the prosecution's re-direct examination tomorrow."

"That's fine. Ms. Luthan, please come back to the witness stand."

Kelly Luthan took her place on the witness stand, and the jury began to file back into the courtroom. Larry Pason wanted this next set of facts to be the last thing the jury remembered after Kelly's emotional breakdown and impassioned outburst about a woman's right to refuse sex. He had to take the sting out of that display and regain the juror's sympathies in favor of his client.

The judge reminded Kelly that she was still under oath, and told Larry Pason to proceed with his examination.

"Ms. Luthan, this jury has heard about various occupations you've had in the past, but there is one we have not yet discussed." Kelly tensed up, bracing herself for more humiliation. She relaxed when she heard him finish his question,

"Is it true that you have been an actress?"

"Yes."

"For how long?"

"Seven years."

"You were a professional actress, here in Hollywood, correct? I mean the roles might have been small, but you were an actress, correct?"

"That's correct."

"Thank you, Ms. Luthan, that's all I have. Oh, actually, there is one more question. You testified earlier that when you asked to borrow $100,0000 from my client, he told you to earn it instead, correct?"

"That's correct."

"But he did not agree to pay you $100,000 did he?"

"No."

"He offered to pay you a different sum, didn't he?"

"Yes, but I didn't..."

"How much did he offer to pay you, if you were willing to earn it?"

"I didn't – "

"How much, Ms. Luthan?"

"$1,000."

"But you wanted a lot more than that."

Kelly dropped her head into her folded arms and began to cry. She couldn't deal with this again.

The defense lawyer let her be. This time it looked like she was crying from guilt and shame. He didn't mind if the jury saw that.

"Your Honor, that concludes my examination of this witness."

★ ★ ★

The judge excused the jury. They were escorted by the bailiff back into the jury room where they were required to wait for a period of time after court adjourned to allow the lawyers and witnesses to exit the courthouse. This was ordinary procedure intended to minimize the chances of a juror accidentally running into a lawyer or a witness in the case.

While they waited, the old lady spoke.

"Do you have your answer now, Mr. Wilson? She's an actress. That's how she had you fooled with that display of emotion."

Mr. Wilson looked at the old lady and sighed.

The old lady wasn't sure she had him convinced. "Did you hear that Mr. Wilson? There was a full discussion about how much she would get paid. She wanted $100,000 but he was only willing to pay $1,000. Those negotiations don't happen before a man rapes a woman. They happen between a prostitute and her customer!"

The accountant chimed in as well, "Now we know why she had to use the knife. She had to make it look like a rape, if she was going to be able to get that much more money out of him."

Mr. Wilson finally responded, "Call me a sucker for a pretty face. I would have believed her if the defense lawyer hadn't asked her those last few questions."

By the time the bailiff returned to notify them they were permitted to exit the jury room, every other juror had expressed their agreement that the only proper verdict that could be reached in the case, was a "not guilty" verdict. They believed their work was done, irrespective of what might happen in court the next day.

★ ★ ★

Kelly had been so humiliated by the line of questioning she had just endured, that as soon as the jury was out of sight, she bolted off the witness stand and ran out of the courtroom. With all the drama and stress of what she had just endured, and with all the cameras and press and other observers in the courtroom, blocking her view, she never saw him.

Johnny was seated in the second to last row, fuming – anger and disgust coursing through his veins, turning his stomach violently, as he had witnessed the whole debacle. He glared at his fiancé, red in the face with unspeakable anger, as he watched her dart out of the courtroom, shameful, as she damn well should've been. His fists were balled up so tight with rage, that his fingernails dug into his palms, drawing blood. He ground his teeth to near dust, trying to contain himself in that courtroom full of people, lawyers, a judge and two jail deputies. He waited for the courtroom to clear before he made a move.

Chapter 18

After court, Sam Chapman approached Katelyn. He found her at her desk, settling in for a long evening at the office. He attempted to console her from the demolition that Larry Pason had just administered.

"You did your best. Don't feel bad about what happened in there. There was nothing you could've done about it. I saw how you tried to alert the witness to not give in and blurt out information the defense was suggesting. That was good. But there's nothing you can do when a witness goes south on you. You're going to lose this case. But you will still be remembered as having performed an excellent job. You had great successes pre-trial, and you performed well during trial. You did a damn good job holding your own in there, against that stellar defense team. And I think you learned a lot in this case, which you could not have learned without actually going through it, as trial counsel. You should be proud of yourself."

Sam's words were of no consolation to Katelyn. She needed to talk to Sarah. It was Sarah who had warned her about this. It was Sarah who had told her not to rely on her pre-trial victories and to be prepared for the magic of magnificent defense lawyers. Sarah was the only one who could offer her some shred of hope of convicting the defendant. She needed to talk to Sarah. After thanking Sam without much sincerity in her voice, Katelyn exited the courthouse to grab a quick bite. She planned on being back at her desk at 6:00 p.m. sharp, in hopes of catching Sarah at the time they usually held their coaching sessions.

Upon returning from a quick dinner at a nearby hotdog stand, Katelyn sat at her desk in the D.A.'s Office frantically dialing, over and over again. "Come on Sarah. Please pick up. Please pick up."

After their last coaching session, Sarah had given Katelyn her cell phone number and said:

"Trials are unpredictable. I can't coach you beyond this point. It's up to you now. And it will be up to you to think quickly on your feet during trial and roll with the punches. But, here's my number. Call me if something crazy happens during trial. I may be able to talk you through it, if there's a break in the testimony from one day to the next."

This was definitely one of those crazy unpredictable moments. So Katelyn called Sarah. Sarah didn't answer. It was 6:00 p.m., in L.A., and 3:00 a.m., in France. Sarah was asleep on her yacht next to David, which was anchored in the Mediterranean Sea, off the coast of Cannes.

★ ★ ★

After court, the defense team gathered at a bar popular with attorneys, called "Sidebar," which was inside a luxury hotel in Beverly Hills. They congratulated Larry Pason on what a fabulous job he had done cross-examining Kelly Luthan. They also strategized over how to switch gears, now that the jury was aware of the victim's past. They all believed they would be sliding in to an easy victory after the day's events; but they were careful not to underestimate the young prosecutor. They stayed at Sidebar until very late at night, strategizing over what types of questions a prosecutor might ask in attempt to rehabilitate the witness, and how the defense would respond in their own line of questioning to tear her down again. After concluding their meeting, late in the evening, White Sr., tipped the valet driver, slid into his red Ferrari, and began his short drive home.

Because he had too much to drink, he accidentally drove passed the street he would ordinarily turn down to drive to his home in Beverly Hills. This required him to make an extra right turn to loop back around. He had a lot on his mind, of course, so he drove a little too far down that road as well. Unwittingly, White Sr., drove passed the apartment of Ann Perez, where Kelly Luthan was staying for the duration of the trial. While still on that road, White Sr., noticed the time and remembered he had forgotten to call his wife to let her know he'd be home late. His knee-jerk reaction caused him to hit the gas petal hard, speeding away in a hurry to get home. The stoplight at the nearest intersection was turning red, just as he had sped passed it. The traffic camera flashed, capturing his image behind the wheel and capturing the license plate of his red Ferrari. This occurred around five minutes before midnight.

★ ★ ★

Katelyn was still at the office. She rested her elbow on her blank notepad, holding a fistful of her own hair in frustration. She stared down at that blank notepad, which mocked her, taunted her, and reminded her of how blank her mind was. She was trying desperately to come up with some type of re-direct examination that might rehabilitate the witness. Hours went by. Her mind was numb. All she could focus on now was the loud ticking sound made by the minute hand of a clock hanging in a nearby office. She never noticed it before tonight. Tick tock, tick tock – one more mocking object reminding her of the impending implosion of a case she dared believe she might win. She wanted to tear it off the wall and smash it against her desk. No, just yanking out the batteries would do. A deep breath later, Katelyn looked back at her notepad. Nothing.

Then, a sudden realization – Sarah. Katelyn tried calling her again. She wondered if Sarah could come up with a brilliant plan to rehabilitate the key witness, after the defense had just annihilated her on the witness stand. Katelyn couldn't imagine how, after the scene she had just observed in the courtroom, but she knew if anyone could help her, it was Sarah. So, she tried calling her again.

Sarah didn't hear Katelyn's frantic call in the middle of the night. She had rushed off with David the morning before, succumbing to his pestering demands that she hurry up in time to reach the yacht before their guests arrived. David always got nervous before a business meeting, no matter how experienced he was at sealing the deal and negotiating terms even more favorable than what his own lawyers could negotiate. That nervousness was the cause of his incessant nagging of Sarah to hurry up; which in turn, distracted her. Sarah rushed outside, forgetting her cell phone on the nightstand.

Katelyn called and called but Sarah didn't answer. Finally, Katelyn gave up and went home, hoping that some profound thought would come to her in the morning, before court resumed and she would have to begin her re-direct examination of Kelly Luthan.

Not hearing any of Katelyn's calls, Sarah was still in a deep sleep, after a long night of entertaining. Although entertaining on their yacht was easy, it was still exhausting. Sarah and David had a full staff on their yacht, including a butler, four chefs, several maids, four bartenders, and six servers. The yacht was the place they entertained most often. Business meetings that were sure to last for days were usually held on the yacht. It gave a more relaxed feel, allowing high-pressure situations to remain amicable so that deals could get done. Guests were invited to stay several days on the yacht so that long negotiations, which typically rolled late into the night, would not have to be disrupted. The full professional staff would keep everyone comfortable and well fed, and would ensure their drinks never ran dry. Although the staff took care of the guests, Sarah was in charge of the staff. She normally sat at David's side throughout the negotiations, but when the table went silent as lawyers re-read the language in the hundreds of pages of agreements they'd been discussing, Sarah would slip away to check that the staff had the right champagne bottles chilled to the correct temperature; the hors d'oeuvres prepared properly; and the catered dinner ready. She also made sure the staff had each guest room readied with plush robes hanging and beds turned down, with mini bars stocked and ice buckets filled. It was like serving as the manager of a mini hotel, during breaks in the negotiations.

The yacht was large and luxurious, but still modest for the south of France. It had 8 guest rooms, each of which was furnished with a king bed, two nightstands, a 40" flat screen TV, fine wood cabinets, a writing desk, and two armchairs. Each room had its own bathroom, adorned with marble tiled shower and spa, and its own theme. Some rooms were decorated with pastel colors in fine silk drapery with oak or pine cabinetry; Others were decorated with deep jewel tones in satin, set against cherry wood cabinetry and matching furniture.

The small living room was adorned with a cozy semi-circle shaped, white leather couch with a matching white ottoman in the middle, and a 60" flat screen TV.

On an upper level, was the large gathering room, which had several deep red leather sofas, love seats and armchairs that could accommodate a group of 25 people. It had a long bar, which seated 10-12 guests. Centered in the middle of the room was a 72" flat screen TV. Off to the side was a long dining table, which seated 15-20.

The yacht had three levels of deck space. The lower level was the largest. It had a large swimming pool and jacuzzi with reclining deck furniture and outdoor couches and lounging chairs surrounding the entire area. It also had an outdoor kitchen and bar. The bow of this level was designed for maximum comfort, lounging and sun bathing. The stern was where all the water sports gear was stored, from wind surfing equipment to scuba diving and snorkeling gear, to sea kayaks. Jet skis hung below.

The middle level of the yacht was meant for luxury and fine dining. An outdoor kitchen and a short bar, which served as a bartenders' supply station, were at the stern. An elegant dining table, and a long bar meant for mingling guests, were at the bow. Luxury armchairs with matching coffee tables lined the railing for a comfortable place to retire for after-dinner drinks. The luxury dining table on this middle deck is where most business meetings were held. David hated being cooped up inside for long meetings, so he held his meetings there. Attorneys and clients could retreat to the inside conference rooms on the same level if they sought privacy from the group, when a stalemate occurred. The conference rooms were beautifully appointed with the same luxury that matched the outside dining area – fine marble and granite along table legs and table tops, set against classic brown leather chairs. Crystal drinkware, fine china, linen napkins, and real silver silverware were the only utensils to be found on this level.

In stark contrast, the upper level of the yacht was designed purely for partying. It was mostly empty to allow maximum room for dancing, for those nights that David would hire a live band. Two bars and several bistro tables with matching chairs surrounded the area near the railings, while the middle remained mostly empty to accommodate dance floor space, or a large gathering of mingling people.

After a long day of negotiations, Sarah and David fell asleep quickly. There was still more to discuss in the morning, and their guests/business associates were spending the night.

The next morning, Sarah got up to do it all over again. She woke before David, and hurried over to the kitchen on the middle level to ensure the staff had properly set the table and prepared the champagne brunch. Negotiations would begin again at brunch.

Brunch was cheerful, as the businessmen had already agreed on the most sensitive terms the night before. They were relaxed and telling jokes, while the lawyers bickered about language the businessmen thought was meaningless to anyone else in the world but lawyers. When Sarah's champagne glass was empty, she snuck to the stern and walked behind the bar to reach for the strawberry flavored soda, which she poured into her champagne glass. It was the same color as pink champagne, and served to cover up the fact that she was not drinking alcohol. When she returned to the bow, she heard David jovially arguing:

"I know, I know, we're going to make tons of money on this movie. You've already convinced me of that, or I wouldn't have agreed to invest as much money as you suckered me into last night. But, when my lawyer says the semicolon needs to be replaced with a comma,... " David threw up his arms and laughed, as he finished, "I have to listen to her!"

"But my lawyer disagrees," said the other gentleman.

"Yeah, but since I'm the sucker whose putting the most money into this deal, I think my lawyer gets to punctuate the sentences in this encyclopedia, I mean, contract." David then raised his glass, nudging the gentleman who sat across the table from him to toast, which would be understood to be his assent.

The man looked sideways at David, raising an eyebrow as if pondering his decision, then he raised his glass and clinked David's glass. The two men drank, and David's lawyer nodded with victory at the other man's lawyer.

Sarah sat next to David and held his hand. He smiled down at her. As she looked into his happy blue eyes, she knew. The time was now right to tell him about her pregnancy. She had made it through the first trimester, and now felt safe sharing the happy news with David. But she wouldn't do it on the boat. She wanted to share an intimate moment with him at home. They would have a candle lit dinner at their chateau, on the small table for two, set on the romantic balcony off their master bedroom; and she would tell him then. She looked forward to it.

As she visualized the moment she would share the happy news with David, Sarah looked blissfully into David's beautiful blue eyes, not knowing how disappointed she was going to be in days to come.

Chapter 19

It was 8:30 a.m., and the jury was entering the courtroom in a single file line. The judge was on the bench. The five defense attorneys were settled in at counsel table. Katelyn Kruz sat alone at the State's side of counsel table. And the witness stand was empty. The defense attorneys whispered excitedly amongst themselves. A few of them looked around the room and shook their heads as if answering, "no," to a pending question.

When the jury was settled in, the judge commanded, "Ms. Kruz, call your next witness."

Larry Pason bolted out of his chair: "Actually, Your Honor, although I had said yesterday afternoon, that I expected to complete my cross-examination then; it turns out that the defense has a few more questions for the alleged victim. In order to completely exercise the defendant's right to confront his accuser, it is necessary that I continue my cross-examination of the alleged victim."

Larry Pason didn't really have additional questions for the victim. However, when he saw that the victim was missing from the courtroom, he decided to make the record appear as if the defense had not completed its cross-examination, so that it could cause a mistrial, if the prosecution failed to produce the witness.

"Very well," said the judge, "Ms. Kruz, please call Kelly Luthan back to the witness stand."

"Your Honor, I request a recess."

"Why?"

"Well, it appears the victim may have been delayed. She is not here yet."

"Did you excuse her from her subpoena, yesterday?"

"No, Your Honor."

"Then she is required to be here. I don't grant recesses for people who are late to their required court appearances. Do you know why the victim is not here? Is there a good excuse for it?"

"I assume she encountered bad traffic, Your Honor."

"Everyone who is in this courtroom today, encountered bad traffic getting here. This is L.A."

This, thought Larry Pason, *was the perfect opportunity*. He stood to address the court:

"Your Honor, I move for a mistrial. My client has a constitutional right to confront his accuser. He is being denied that right with the State's failure to present the witness for further cross-examination. The State has failed to proceed with its case. The jury has been empaneled and sworn, and therefore jeopardy has attached. The State cannot deny my client his right to a speedy public jury trial; then seek to try the case again. The defense has the utmost interest in seeing this case move forward immediately, without delay. The first part of our cross-examination is fresh in the jury's mind. Delay will only serve as a detriment to my client, and will benefit the State. Delay will deny my client his right to a speedy trial and effective confrontation of his accuser. I request a mistrial, with a specific finding that there is no manifest necessity that would permit a new trial. I ask the court to find that the mistrial is the result of the prosecution's failure to move forward with its evidence."

Katelyn Objected: "Your Honor, please. The witness is only a few minutes late. The defendant is not being denied any rights here. And counsel overstates the reach of double jeopardy. There are many alternatives the court can consider, including granting a recess or finding manifest necessity for a new trial, depending on the circumstances. Not having heard from the victim, I am at a severe handicap in responding to defense counsel's sudden motion."

"I will grant a two-hour recess," said Judge Johnson. "If Ms. Luthan is not here by then, I will declare a mistrial. The issue of manifest necessity can be determined at a later date, if and when the State seeks a new trial." Judge Johnson then tapped his gavel to indicate that he would take no further argument on the matter. He then instructed the bailiff to escort the jury to the jury room and bring them back in exactly two hours.

Katelyn rushed to her office and called Kelly's cell phone number. She did not know where Kelly was staying, and she had no other contact information for her. She called the cell phone number every five minutes, continuing her futile effort to reach Kelly.

Meanwhile, the defense team gathered in a conference room at White, White & Smith, a few blocks away from the courthouse. They were practically celebrating already. Despite the jubilation, one attorney questioned the wisdom of the motion they had just made.

"Was it a good idea to seek a mistrial? If the State is granted a new trial, there is no way we will be able to re-create what happened in court yesterday. The witness will be more prepared. The prosecution has seen our strategy and will prepare the witness to keep her composure. They'll coach her to stay calm and avoid the outburst she made. But if we proceed and complete this trial, with this jury, we are almost guaranteed victory, after what happened yesterday. We may never get another shot at making the witness breakdown like she did."

White Sr., responded sharply, "Of course it was a good idea! You always request a mistrial if the victim fails to appear. If you're lucky, the victim will turn up dead before the State can commence a new trial."

Larry Pason chimed in, "Also, I do not believe there is any way the court can find manifest necessity for a new trial, under these circumstances. Double jeopardy will prevent the State from trying this case again, without exception. If the alleged victim does not show up in two hours, this case is won, for good."

White Sr., added: "And my son will get out of jail, today."

★ ★ ★

Two hours later, a mistrial was declared. Nobody in the courtroom knew yet, that the night before, Kelly Luthan had been brutally attacked in Ann's apartment. A neighbor had called to report what sounded like domestic violence. During the 911 call, she had frantically pleaded for emergency response: "You better hurry! It sounds awful! It sounds like someone is being murdered! That woman is screaming for her life! Please hurry!"

When the police arrived on the scene, they discovered a horrific, bloody crime scene. Blood was smudged in various spots on the walls, evidencing a terrible struggle. A pool of blood lay beneath the victim.

They found Johnny on the floor, holding Kelly's limp, non-responsive body in his arms. He was covered in her blood. He was shaking and crying, "Kelly, why? why?" He sobbed, as he rocked her limp, bloody body. "Why, Kelly, why?" he wailed on between sobs. It was difficult for the officers to get him to say anything else. One officer turned on his audio recording device as the others secured the crime scene. Another officer called for an ambulance, though the amount of blood that had been spilt made him believe it was far too late for that.

Two officers took Johnny into custody, while the others began interviewing the neighbors. As the two officers escorted Johnny, drenched in Kelly's blood, out of the building, Ann walked in. Her face turned ashen when she saw him. She could see the crime-scene tape blocking the entrance to her apartment, and she ran towards it. Two officers stopped her, and she began screaming at them, demanding to know what happened.

"Did he kill her! Did he kill her! I knew it!" she screamed frantically, "I knew it! I knew he was abusing her!"

"Ma'am, please calm down. Calm down for just a minute."

"What happened! Tell me what happened!" she demanded.

"Calm down ma'am. I'll be asking the questions. Do you know one, Miss, Kelly Luthan?"

"Yes," Ann cried, "she was staying with me."

"What can you tell us, ma'am."

"She called me one day, asking me to make up a story for why she had to leave in a hurry to come help me. She told me not to say I was in L.A. She needed an excuse to leave him, and she didn't want him to know where she went. Oh God, he killed her, didn't he?" Ann began sobbing uncontrollably. The officer decided to conclude the interview later. He took her phone number and moved on to interview the next witness. The officers continued knocking on doors and questioning all the neighbors.

★ ★ ★

At the police station, Johnny sat with an unseeing stare, motionless and speechless. They had not yet arrested him, but had placed him in an interview room with a one-way glass wall, which allowed the officers to watch him, though he could not see out.

"He hasn't invoked his rights yet, so we can still talk to him," said the officer to his sergeant.

"So, why haven't you yet?"

"I think he's in shock or something. He won't speak. He's not being responsive to our questions. He just stares straight ahead without a word."

"Well, just go sit in there across the table from him. Give him something to drink. Wait for him to speak to you. Try tea, not coffee. Some people find tea more soothing."

The officer went back into the interview room, placed a cup of tea in front of Johnny, and sat down across from him. The officer relaxed in his chair, holding his own cup of coffee in his hand, and waited.

Ten minutes passed before Johnny moved. Then finally, he reached for the cup of tea, lifted it to his mouth, but did not sip. He let the aroma and steam fill his nostrils and soothe him. He closed his eyes at the memory of smells he had enjoyed at Kelly's Kafe. After a few moments, Johnny spoke:

"Kelly likes tea."

"Likes, or liked?" asked the officer.

Johnny grimaced at the officer's words. It felt like he'd been punched in the gut by a heavy weight boxer. Tears flooded out of his eyes, and a desperate sob burst out of him as he cried. His chin hung low, and his shoulders shook with the force of his sobbing.

"Shit," thought the officer, *"Too soon."* He waited while Johnny wailed on. Finally, when it seemed like Johnny's crying began to simmer down, the officer said:

"Tell me what happened today."

Johnny began taking quick short breaths in attempt to stop crying. He tried to catch his breath from all the sobbing. When he caught his breath, he took a sip of tea. Then he took another sip of tea. He stared over the cup. The officer was directly in his line of vision but Johnny's eyes were not focused on the officer. It seemed as if Johnny didn't even see him sitting directly in front of him. As Johnny's eyes glazed over, his mind replayed scenes from the courtroom earlier that day. Almost as if to himself, Johnny whispered, "She's a prostitute."

"Who?"

Johnny narrowed his eyes with gut-wrenching pain, and he answered, "My fiancé. I found out today that my fiancé is a prostitute."

"You never knew before?"

"No," Johnny whispered:

"Is that what sent you over the edge? Is that why you attacked her?"

The officer's words ripped Johnny's mind from memories of the courtroom and forced it back to that terrible scene at Ann's apartment. He threw his hands over his face and began to scream: "No! Kelly! No! Oh God! Kelly!" He crumpled to the floor in a ball and began crying uncontrollably.

"Goddammit! Not again!" thought the officer. He tried waiting this out too, but the man just wailed on. He wasn't going to stop. The officer tore out of the room in frustration.

"Goddammit! I lost him again! I need a shrink for this one!"

"What's wrong, Mr. Sensitive?" the sergeant asked, sarcastically, "Forget how to interview a suspect?"

"No. That's not what I mean!"

"Going soft, are you?"

"No Goddammit. I'm just not going to get any answers out of him today. Look! He's catatonic again. Look at him. Now he's just staring straight ahead, again. I don't think he's blinked in five minutes. Try getting information out of him, now! You do it. You go try."

The sergeant went into the interview room, but he was even less successful than the officer. Johnny wouldn't move off the floor. He had curled up into a ball. His head buried between his arms, which were wrapped around his knees. Not a single movement, not a single sound could be drawn out of him.

The sergeant came out of the room and gave instructions to the officer. "Let's put him in the holding cell. Let's keep him there until morning. He's not asking for a lawyer, and not asking to leave. We don't have to make any official decisions about arrest yet. Just keep him in the holding cell and we'll try again tomorrow. The victim's friend had said that she believed he'd been abusing her. These guys always feel remorse after they've gone too far. He'll be ready to talk to us tomorrow."

★ ★ ★

The morning after Johnny had been taken into custody, and around the same time the judge had declared a mistrial in White Jr.'s Trial, the investigating officers gathered to share and review information they had obtained during their investigation of the attack on Kelly Luthan.

Officer Smith shared the results of the witness interviews:

"The old lady that lives across the hallway from the crime scene kept insisting that the young man could not have done it. She claims that the violence was ongoing when the young man entered the building. She said she heard the screaming and the ruckus inside the apartment, and came out of her own apartment so that she could locate the sound. She wanted to be able to tell police which unit it came from. While she was in the hallway, she saw the young man enter the building. She says he heard the noise as soon as he entered the building and began running as fast as he could towards the sound. The old lady pointed at the door and said to him, 'there, I think it's coming from there.' And that's when the guy we took into custody last night began slamming his shoulder against the door and kicking it in, frantic to get inside. She then went back into her apartment and closed her door because she didn't want to get caught in any crossfire.

She also insists that we should be looking for an older man. She says that less than 30 minutes before hearing the struggle from the apartment across the hall, she had opened her door at the sound of a knock. She saw a white-haired man, with blue eyes. She guessed he was in his 60s or 70s. She could not tell because he seemed to be very physically fit. She also estimated that he was about 6 feet tall. She said he was stocky with broad shoulders.

During my interview, she kept saying to me, 'No, no, no. The man you took away tried to save her. He was trying to save her.' "

Officer Ricardo then interrupted Officer Smith's summary: "My tape recorder capturing sound from the crime scene, at the time we arrived, corroborates that description of events, as it relates to the man we have in custody. I didn't notice this at the time, because it was too hard to understand him from all his wailing and crying. But listen to this.

Officer Ricardo played his tape recorder. The officers listened. On the tape, they all heard Johnny cry as he repeated himself. It was difficult to make out the words, through his gasps and sobs, but through careful listening, they heard him say: "Kelly, why,... [sobbing]... why didn't you... [sobbing]... tell me? Why Kelly? I could've... [a sob, and a gasp]... been here. Why Kelly? I could've ... huh, ... huh... protected you. Why Kelly, Why? I could've... [a sob]... protected you. I would've,... ah , aaah, Why?... [gasps and sobs] would've protected... youuuu, aahhh, why?... [sobbing]... Why didn't you tell me, Kellyyyyy, aaahhh, whyyyyy?"

The officer stopped the tape recorder. "All I kept hearing him say at the scene, was 'why.' But in listening to the tape, it's clear. He was grieving. He was regretting not having been there to protect her."

The lead investigator responded, "So the forced entry we saw, was him trying to get inside to save her. It was not the assailant, breaking in. The assailant was let in by the victim. She must have known him, been comfortable with him. Did the old lady say whether she saw the white-haired man enter the apartment?"

"Yes. She said that when she opened her door, she realized the man was not knocking on her door but the one across the hall. He turned and smiled at her while he waited for that door to open. The old lady described a young, beautiful woman matching Kelly Luthan's description, as the one who opened the door and let him in."

"And you say, she estimated that it was only about 30 minutes later that she heard the commotion and saw the young man running down the hall trying to save her?"

"Yes."

"Do we know if the man in custody observed a second man while the assault was in progress?"

"Not likely, the old lady said she heard a window break while the man in custody was still attempting to gain entry. We observed broken glass on the first floor window, with most of the glass fallen on the outside. This shows a blow from the inside by someone seeking to create enough space to allow him to exit. Most likely, the perpetrator heard the sound of someone attempting to enter the apartment, then fled out the window.

We have a statement from another witness that says she also heard commotion and glass breaking. She lives in an apartment further away. She said that she looked out her window trying to figure out where the noise was coming from. She estimates that within about five minutes or less, of hearing the glass break, she saw a man speed down the street in a red Ferrari. It was very late at night and there were no other cars on the road. The description she gave of the driver matched the description given by the old lady of the man who Kelly Luthan let into the apartment, before the attack. She could see the driver as he passed under a bright street lamp."

"Alright then," said the sergeant, "we release the fiancé and we're now on the lookout for an old man with white hair, a red Ferrari, and possible wounds from broken glass. Check all traffic cameras in the area for a red Ferrari on that road, around the time of the attack. Get the license plate number, and interview the driver."

After the meeting, the sergeant released Johnny from his holding cell. He no longer treated him as a suspect, but now treated him with the carefulness he treated family members of crime victims.

"Here are your things, and here is a number you need to call. Our victims' advocates will fill you in on all the details regarding your loved one. I'm so sorry you're going through this. Please make use of our victims' advocate program. They will help you through this difficult time."

Johnny didn't say a word. He gathered his things, held on tight to the business card of the victims' advocate, and walked out of the building.

During their investigation, the police sifted through all traffic camera footage of all traffic lights in the vicinity of Ann Perez' apartment, from the evening Kelly was attacked. It was not long before they discovered a photograph of a red Ferrari speeding passed a red light, around the time the witness heard glass break in Ann's apartment.

Officer Smith began hollering, "Serg! Serg! Come look at this! You won't believe it!"

The sergeant came rushing over to Officer Smith, knowing what case he was working on.

"What is it?"

Officer Smith handed him the photograph, "Do you recognize this man?"

The sergeant squinted. Photographs from traffic cameras were never very good. "Well, I can't tell you exactly who it is. But it's definitely a man in his sixties or seventies, with white hair, driving a red Ferrari. It sure looks like our prime suspect."

"Yep. Recognize anything else about him?"

"No."

"This should help. Here's the information on the vehicle owner."

The sergeant stared at the papers and his eyes grew wide. "No way! No. You don't think?"

"What else? Motive. Opportunity. We can place him at the scene, at the time of the attack. What else could this mean?"

"Make the arrest. I'm sure he'll invoke his rights, so we won't get any information out of him. The crime lab won't process the evidence gathered at the scene for a few more weeks, but we have to get him off the street before he flees."

The license and registration, which the sergeant held in his hands, as he gave these orders to the officer, identified White Sr., as the owner of the vehicle. Upon discovering the photograph of White Sr., in his red Ferrari, time-stamped around the time of the attack, the police wasted no time in making an arrest. By then, the police had already discovered through a search of the victim's name, that she was the alleged victim in White Jr.'s trial, and that a mistrial had been declared as a result of her absence in court. They immediately jumped to conclusions, not realizing what great success the defense had achieved in court, the day of the attack.

★ ★ ★

Sarah's beautifully planned day was interrupted by a call from Detective Jones. After several days of entertaining David's business associates on the yacht, she had returned home and listened to all of Katelyn's voicemail messages about the case going down in flames, which were later updated with a text message explaining that there was no need to call back because a mistrial had been declared. Thus, when Sarah saw Detective Jones' phone number appear on her cell phone screen, she had no idea what a tremendous disruption it was about to cause in her day.

"Hello?"

"Hi. How are you?"

"Wonderful. And yourself?"

"Well,... things just keep getting more interesting around here."

"What happened?"

"White Sr., has been arrested."

"For what!?"

"Attacking Kelly Luthan."

"What do you mean? That's impossible! He would never do such a thing! He's the most gentle, kind-hearted man I've ever met. How could this be?"

"The arresting officers think he wanted to kill her to save his son. That's pretty strong motive. They can't be argued with. They say no one, other than White Jr., would have stronger motive to attack her; but he was still in jail at the time, so it must have been his father, White Sr."

"But there was a mistrial."

"The attack occurred the night before the mistrial, after the first day of testimony."

"The officers are wrong! I heard Katelyn's frantic messages. The defense was winning the case. They had that case won. I could tell from the messages, Katelyn was in over her head. There's no way he would have gone to those lengths at that point in the trial."

"Well, the guys wanted to get him off the street fast. They've made an arrest before the crime lab has processed the evidence collected from the scene. They got really eager after an anonymous call came in from a delivery guy who had been following trial coverage in the local media. He said that while walking by their conference room after making a delivery, he overheard White Sr., telling his defense team that the motion for a mistrial was their best option, and that if they were lucky the victim would turn up dead."

"Defense lawyers always say stuff like that! That doesn't mean anything!"

"You have to admit it sounds really bad, Sarah."

"I'm not convinced by a delivery man who is unfamiliar with the common parlance of criminal defense attorneys."

"White Sr.'s son walked out of jail, a free man, after that woman was attacked and failed to appear in court. You can't argue about motive."

"Have they looked at any of the men in her past? Her former

customers, anyone else?"

"Not that I'm aware of."

"How could they miss that!?"

"They can place White Sr., at the crime scene around the time of the attack."

"How?"

"Traffic camera caught him speeding passed a red light, making him look like an assailant fleeing in a hurry."

"Oh my God. This is terrible. This is just terrible. I'm coming home."

Sarah hung up the phone remembering the charming, gentle old man who had made so many attempts to recruit her to join his law firm. She knew him professionally and personally. She had attended many of his parties. He was too jolly. He was too sweet. He was too proper, and appropriate. She remembered his interactions with his wife. She remembered what an old-fashioned gentleman he was in his interactions with all women. The only time he was ever known to deviate from showing a woman the utmost respect, was in the courtroom, during cross-examination, when his duty to his client required it; and even then, he was known to gently impeach a female witness, which usually won over the jury and was even more effective than other lawyers using aggressive tactics. It was not possible that he could brutally attack a woman, for any reason.

Sarah sat at the edge of her bed, sick to her stomach. This couldn't be happening. It was bad enough that White Jr., had been freed, and his victim brutally attacked. But now, White Sr., was in jail? Deep down Sarah knew that it was impossible that he was guilty. The police rushed to judgment without carefully analyzing the evidence. How could they arrest the first man they suspected? The victim was a prostitute. There could have been lots of different men who might have attacked her.

Sarah Cartwright was such a strong believer in truth and justice, that she believed the only thing worse than watching a guilty man walk free, was watching an innocent man pay for a crime he never committed. Her stomach tumbled with nausea. Overwhelming guilt washed over her. Could this be her fault? Did her selfish decision, made in a moment of weakness, set about this chain of events? Sarah pondered events transpiring from a moment, in which she made a decision she'll always regret. She thought of events leading up to White Jr.'s trial for the rape of Kelly Luthan; and she thought of the way she, herself, left L.A., and never looked back. Had she made different choices, would the victim have remained safe in Oklahoma? Would White Sr., have been spared the trial of his son, and an arrest for a crime, which Sarah was certain he was incapable of committing?

Sarah sat on her bed, staring out her window where the beautifully set table was waiting for her and David. The candles were already lit, and David was downstairs. Just before receiving the call from Detective Jones, she was about to call David up to join her for an elegant, romantic dinner on the balcony off their master bedroom, where she would be sharing with him the happy news of her pregnancy – a special evening, ruined, with one phone call from Detective Jones. Sarah was too sick to her stomach to celebrate now. This day was too awful. Her special moment with David couldn't happen now.

Also, she now firmly believed that she had a duty to correct her mistakes, which she believed led to this chain of events. She now believed she had to travel back to L.A., to prevent any further injustice from occurring. She needed to make sure White Sr., was released from jail. Deep down, in her heart of hearts, Sarah knew, that warm, tenderhearted, man could not be guilty.

Sarah did not know how much the stress of going back to L.A., might affect her pregnancy, especially now that White Jr., was free. But she had to do it. She could no longer make another selfish choice that might cause others to suffer. She had to return to L.A., which meant, she couldn't tell David about her pregnancy. Not now. Sarah slowly stood, walked over to her balcony, and blew out the candles. She then sat in the chair where she was supposed to enjoy a lovely private dinner with David, and she cried. She placed one hand on her belly, afraid of what might happen next, worried, that she might never get the chance to tell David about this pregnancy, scared that she might lose another baby.

Chapter 21

Sarah and David flew back to L.A., in their private jet. During the long flight, Sarah pondered, many times, whether she should tell David about her pregnancy. She never did. *Not like this*, she thought, *I don't want to have to tell him like this.* She silently gave herself a deadline. *Whatever happens in the investigation, I have to tell David, no later than two weeks after today*, she thought to herself. *No, three weeks*, she amended. She looked down at her growing belly and wondered if David had noticed. *Of course he noticed*, she thought to herself, *He probably just thinks I'm getting fat.* Her stomach had not expanded very much, but it had definitely grown fuller than her tiny waist typically was. David knew Sarah's body like the back of his hand. She was certain he noticed. Before her last miscarriage, he had noticed the changes in her body, before she had. *Of course, that was because they had taken the pregnancy test together, so he was looking for it*, she rationalized. Sarah sat silently on the long plane ride back to L.A., and wondered whether her husband noticed the change; and if so, why he hadn't asked her if she was pregnant. *Was he also afraid to find out?* she wondered, *Was he also afraid of being disappointed again?*

Uncertain about the degree of stress that awaited her, Sarah decided it was best to not discuss her pregnancy with David, until she was certain it would not be compromised. Thus, her final decision was to wait.

* * *

To avoid the longer drives into downtown to meet with Detectives and analyze the case, Sarah asked David if it would be ok to stay in their home in Beverly Hills, instead of their home in Malibu. Ever the loving and supporting husband, David said, "yes." He was not the least bit fond of Sarah's decision to help White Jr.'s father; but David was not the type of man who tried to control his wife. He kept his anger to himself, not knowing how to express his feelings to her. He tried to bury the anger with overcompensating gestures of support. However, he worried every day about a possible encounter between Sarah and White Jr. So, he hired private investigators with concealed weapons permits to follow his every move. This was the secret compromise he had reached with himself, in his own mind.

The morning after they landed, Sarah was on the phone with Detective Jones, ready to begin the investigation that would prove White Sr.'s innocence. David never spent so much time away from his wife. He had to keep himself busy enough to avoid overhearing her on the phone, working on that case. He got home late enough at night that there would be no time to discuss each other's days. Nobody hated White Jr., more passionately than David. He couldn't imagine that any kin of his could be a decent person. But David loved and respected his wife. He had seen the pleading in her eyes, when they were still in France, which told him, this case was too important to deny her. He had survived life with her as a Deputy District Attorney before. What was one more case? He kept telling himself. He also rationalized that it would also be good for him to be back in L.A., reconnecting with old business contacts. While Sarah went about her business, David went about his.

* * *

At the police station, Sarah and Detective Jones analyzed the evidence that had been gathered in the case, to date. They reviewed the witness statements and discussed the physical evidence located at the crime scene. The only DNA sample that had been retrieved was a single hair found on the floor near the victim's body. It was a white hair. Therefore, it obviously did not belong to the victim, her fiancé who'd been found hovering over her, or the friend whose apartment she was staying at. The sample was retrieved with the belief that it belonged to the perpetrator. It was sent to the crime lab, but the crime lab was backed up. It would take weeks before they had an answer as to whether the hair belonged to White Sr. Sarah knew in her gut that it did not. She hoped to solve this case and give White Sr., his freedom as soon as possible, and long before they had to wait for the crime lab to run its tests.

"Hey, Detective, don't you have a contact with the FBI?"

"Yeah. Why?"

"Don't they owe you a favor?"

"Sure, they do favors for me all the time, but this is a local crime. Why would we need their help?"

"Could you call in that favor, and maybe see if they could test the DNA faster than our crime lab can?"

"Sure."

Detective Jones made a quick phone call. After his call, he walked over to Sarah.

"Done. He'll process our evidence with the highest priority."

"That's excellent. Thank you."

"Now let's head downstairs," said the Detective, "The neighbor who described an old man entering the apartment before the attack is about to view the lineup. We're going to see if she identifies White Sr., in the lineup. The Deputy D.A., on the case says he wants more than just a traffic camera picture placing him at the scene of the crime. He wants the eye-witness who saw him enter the apartment."

Sarah quickly stood and followed Detective Jones.

When they entered the room, they saw an old lady, who appeared to be in her 80s, standing nervously in front of the glass. Behind the glass, a line of men began walking into the room, in single file. They each stopped in the place they were ordered to stop.

Seeing the men walk into the room behind the glass, the old

lady stepped backwards and turned her head.

"It's ok, ma'am," said the officer who accompanied her, "They can't see you. Only you can see them."

"Oh," sighed the old lady, "It's so clear through that glass. It feels like they can see me."

"I assure you. They cannot. Please come back and stand where you can get a good look at each of these men. Take your time. All you have to do is tell us if you see the gentleman that you say entered the apartment across the hall from you, before the attack that day."

"Ok," the old lady said cautiously. She slowly stepped towards the glass. To test the accuracy of the officer's assurances, she waved. The officer looked at her, perplexed, wondering if the investigation should rely on this witness. Then, she explained herself, "I just wanted to make sure you were right, that they really can't see me. I guess someone would have waved back if they could."

The officer tried not to laugh. "That's a good observation," he said, respectfully. Whatever the witness needed to do to make herself comfortable, he would accept. Then he gently asked, with a sweet smile, "Do you believe me now?"

"Oh, yes. Oh. It's not that I didn't believe you. I just wanted to make sure you were right."

The officer smiled warmly at the old lady, "Do you now feel sure I'm right?"

"Yes," she smiled shyly.

"Are you comfortable taking a look and letting us know if you see the man in this lineup?"

"Yes. I can do that."

"Ok. Just take your time"

"I will."

The old lady stared. She looked at each one of the men in the lineup. She wanted to be very careful not to identify the wrong man. She took her time looking at the grey-haired men and the white-haired men. She was sure the man had white hair, but she wanted to be thorough.

As she continued her observation, she began explaining her thoughts out loud, "Well, I know the man had white hair, not grey hair. But I'm looking at the two grey-haired men anyway, just to be sure. And I'm certain it is neither one of them. Now, the rest of the men have white hair and are about the same height as the man I saw, but those two look a little too thin. The man I saw, though, older, was strong and healthy looking. There, I think that's him." The old lady concluded, while pointing at White Sr.

"Number 3?" asked the officer.

"Yes," answered the witness.

The officer pushed a button and ordered: "Number 3. Please step forward."

White Sr., stepped forward. Sarah's heart sank. She couldn't stand to see him that way. He looked pitiful, his chin turned down, his eyes sad, his brows furrowed, and his shoulders slouched, almost as if he'd given up on life entirely. He was just the shell of the man she once knew. She stood in the back of the room, waiting to hear what the witness would say next.

The witness squinted her eyes and leaned towards the glass. "I think that's him," she said.

The officer pushed the button again. "Number 3, step back." White Sr., stepped back and Sarah and Detective Jones went back upstairs.

When they reached his desk, Sarah sat in Detective Jones' chair, and he sat in the visitor's chair across the desk. He had a long professional relationship with Sarah, and he was used to following her lead, as the Deputy D.A., serving on various crime teams, leading investigations. Sarah was always more hands-on in the investigative stages than other Deputy D.A.'s. She always wanted to ensure an airtight case could be developed before presenting a case to grand jury. This made the officers respect her. Detective Jones had an enormous amount of respect for Sarah; so, he let her sit in his chair and he was happy to sit back in the visitor's seat, allowing Sarah to take the lead.

They sat across from each other in silence for a few moments before Detective Jones spoke:

"Well, we have a positive I.D."

"No we don't."

"What do you mean, Sarah? You heard the lady."

"Yeah. I did hear the lady. She said she *'thinks'* that's him."

"Yeah, she said she thinks that's him. That's a positive I.D. She pointed at him and everything. She confirmed it when he stepped forward."

"No she didn't."

"Were you and I in the same room!?"

"Yes. But you weren't listening carefully. The witness emphasized the word 'think.' Didn't you notice that?"

"I heard her say, 'I think that's him.' Just like I might say, 'I think you're being irrational, Sarah.' You're getting too caught up with this hope that White Sr., is innocent."

"Detective, that was NOT a positive I.D. That was an uncertain identification. The emphasis she put on the word 'think' was the type of emphasis, which connotes uncertainty. It was not a casual use of the word think to convey an opinion. It was an expression of uncertainty. The uncertainty was so clear in her voice. I can't believe you didn't pick up on that."

The detective sighed and leaned back in his chair. He folded his hands behind his head in resignation. There was no arguing with Sarah when she got this way. "So, now what?" He asked.

"I'm going to review the police reports again. Tomorrow, we'll go out and interview each witness, after I've read what they told police in their first interviews."

"Fine. I'll leave you to that. Meet back here tomorrow morning?"

"Yes."

"Ok. See you then." Detective Jones stood and walked away, leaving Sarah to her work.

Sarah reviewed every police report written in the case, again. She had read them all before, to get a general gist of the evidence so far. But this time, she was reading the reports with a focus on witness interviews. What did they say? What didn't they say? What did the police ask? What didn't they ask? Sarah was going to identify the possible wholes in the investigation to develop further questions, which could shed new light on the case.

With a legal pad and pen in hand, she flipped through each police report, and began taking notes. She spent hours analyzing each witness interview and making notes of questions that popped into her mind, which were unanswered in the reports. She worked on this until it was dark outside. Then she remembered she hadn't eaten in hours. *The baby*, she thought, *How could I? How could I get so immersed in this work, that I forgot to feed my unborn child?* She scolded herself. *This isn't just about me any more.*

Sarah put her pen down, looked at her watch and stood up. She looked down at her notes and decided she had done enough for the evening. It was time to go home and get something to eat.

Sarah reached into her purse for her cell phone. She looked at the screen and was disappointed to see that David had not called or sent a text message. She quickly sent him a text:

"Where are you, love?"

"Busy," his text replied.

That was unusual, Sarah thought. David was never that short with her.

"I'm coming home, sweetie. Are you home yet?"

"No." Another cold, short reply. Sarah was disappointed but

tried not to get angry. She gathered her things and went home.

Their home in Beverly Hills still had the same staff operating it from before they left for France. Sarah was grateful. The chef had a warm meal waiting, and Sarah was famished. She ate alone, checking her phone constantly to see if David would call or text. He didn't.

After dinner, she moved to the extra comfy sofa in the living room, in front of the TV. She turned it on and flipped through the channels mindlessly. This was the first time during her marriage that she was left alone at home for so long in the evening. This was their quality time together. She was always with him during their evenings, whether entertaining business associates, or at home cozying up with him. She didn't like this separation, which began after they had come back to L.A. She dialed his number. He didn't answer. Instead, a text message popped up on her screen:

"In a meeting." Nothing more was said. Sarah dropped her phone on the couch in disappointment and grabbed the remote control. She flipped through the channels, annoyed and irritated, more at David's absence than at the lack of anything good to watch on TV. Nothing but reality show this, and reality show that. Finally, she stopped on a channel showing a reality TV show about women who, judging from the title, must have lived very close to her home, because it was based in Beverly Hills. "I guess I'll eavesdrop on my neighbors," she said out loud as she dropped the remote control on the coffee table and curled up on the couch.

Sarah watched several hours of the same reality TV show, of which the network was running a marathon for the evening. She was in the middle of the final episode of the third season, when she fell asleep on the couch. She was woken up by the women on TV, shrieking at each other again in another angry argument at another social event. Sarah turned off the TV and checked her phone; still, no word from David.

She sent him another text: "Are you coming home, soon?"

"Don't wait up," his text replied.

Sarah went to bed and fell asleep alone for the first time in their marriage. She didn't even realize that it was her fixation on the White Sr., case, which drove her husband away. She had set her alarm to wake her early the next morning. She planned on leaving so early, that she knew David would still be asleep when she left. This made her sad, but she was determined. She had to finish investigating this case.

★ ★ ★

The next day, Sarah and Detective Jones left the police station together to conduct more thorough interviews of the witnesses. After reviewing police reports of witness accounts, Sarah had more questions. They drove to the apartment complex, in which Ann Perez lived, and began interviewing all the neighbors who lived on her floor.

They started with the old lady who had identified White Sr., in the line up. She lived directly across the hallway from the apartment in which the crime occurred.

When the old lady opened her door, a white cat with long hair darted out of her apartment and ran down the hall. "Snowflake! Snowflake, get back here!" she hollered after the cat. Sarah watched the cat run down the hallway; then noticed how much of its fur was embedded in the carpet. As the old lady continued calling after her cat, Sarah turned to Detective Jones and mumbled under hear breath, "I hope it was human hair we sent to the FBI for testing."

Detective Jones muffled a laugh with his hand. He couldn't imagine the cops who processed the crime scene could've made that mistake, but it was a hilarious thought. Sarah's keen mind, full of alternative theories, always served her well when she led teams of investigators in solving complicated cases. He appreciated and respected that about Sarah. And he also appreciated the amusing thoughts her open mind could conjure up, as well. But Sarah was not amused. She looked at the Detective with serious concern in her eyes, as she explained, "That cat hair gets on a shoe walking down this hallway, then into that apartment, and falls off the shoe inside..." The Detective just smiled broadly at Sarah and shook his head.

"Is something amusing, sir?" the old lady asked Detective Jones, frustrated with the fact that her cat was lingering by the front door of the complex, ready to bolt outside at the first opportunity.

"Oh, I'm just tickled by your cat ma'am. It's such a beautiful cat, and what great spirit it has. I love the independence and curiosity that a cat can exhibit like that." He schmoozed her, knowing a cat lover would eat that up.

"Yes. I love it too. But it can be a chore to deal with."

"I'll help you ma'am. Do you mind if I go pick up Snowflake?"

"Yes. Thank you. I would appreciate that. I can't chase after him anymore and when he gets like this, it's so much trouble."

"I'll get him." Detective Jones hurried down the hall, as the old lady warned, "Watch his claws though. He's not fond of strangers!" Detective Jones lifted a hand in acknowledgement of her warning and gently picked up Snowflake.

He walked back towards the two women, with Snowflake cradled in his arms. The cat made itself comfortable and began to purr.

"Oh, he likes you!" the old lady said with surprise. "Would you like to come in?"

"Yes, ma'am, thank you."

Sarah and Detective Jones walked in and sat on the couch. The old lady offered them tea, but they politely declined. She sat across from them, in an armchair. When Detective Jones released his hold of Snowflake, the cat jumped onto the coffee table and pranced across the table as if all had gathered to watch it parade around.

Detective Jones began the conversation, "Ma'am as we stated

earlier, we're from the LA City police department, and we just have a few questions to follow up on your earlier interview."

"Well, I've already told the police everything they asked me."

"I understand, but often times, at the scene of the crime, only a preliminary interview is taken, then later we realize there are a few more questions that could have been asked. Or sometimes, due to the excitement of what's happening, a witness forgets to mention a small detail. We're here to interview you in a more calm environment, without so much commotion going on, to see if there is anything else you can tell us."

"Ok."

"Why don't we just start with you telling us what you remember from that evening?"

"Yes. The police hauled away the wrong man. I was trying to tell them it wasn't him. He was trying to save her. The young man, I mean. But then that Ann Perez, came home and saw the crime scene tape and the blood on the young man and she just went crazy. Yelling at the police officers, interfering with their investigation. She was hysterical. She made it difficult for them to do their work. So while she was screaming at one officer, two other officers dragged that poor young man away. I had to wait for the other officers to finish interviewing other witnesses before I could explain that they had the wrong guy. They knocked on every door in this long hallway. So it took them a long time. It must have been 2:00 in the morning by the time I got anyone to listen to me. I kept coming in and out of my apartment to see if an officer was ready to speak to me. I had to stay up really late, waiting for them."

Sarah interrupted, "Tell us about the man who you think did it. What did he look like?"

The old lady answered her question with the same description she gave during her first interview.

Sarah continued, seeking more detail, "Was there anything unique about him? Anything that stood out, which might distinguish him from other men in their 60s or 70s with the same color hair, same height and same build? What other distinguishing factor did you notice?"

"Uh, well, let me think... Ah, yes, this could be a distinguishing factor, he was Russian."

"How do you know he was Russian?"

"From his accent."

"He had an accent?"

"Yes. I heard it when he spoke to her. She was surprised to see him, but she interrupted him and quickly asked him to come inside. It was obvious that she didn't want me to hear their conversation."

"Why didn't you mention his accent to police, before?"

"They didn't ask me what he sounded like. They only asked me what he looked like."

"I see. Had you seen him visit this apartment before?"

"It's hard to tell. So many men come in and out of that apartment. And they are usually, older, well dressed men, wearing expensive clothing. I assume they're all wealthy. They look wealthy. They're usually driving expensive cars. I've complained to management about how many different men Ann entertains in that small studio apartment of hers. But they won't do anything about it. They tell me she has a right to host visitors. Well, I think her 'visitors' pay her to host them, if you ask me. It's not right. It's not normal, such a young woman, and so many different, older, wealthy men. She's definitely up to no-good. Something like this was bound to happen. I hope they'll finally evict her after this."

Detective Jones and Sarah continued the interview for an hour. The witness did not provide any additional helpful information, besides the fact that the perpetrator had a Russian accent. But that was significant. White Sr., was not Russian, and did not have an accent.

As they exited the old lady's apartment and walked down the

hall, Sarah gloated.

"Your positive I.D., just made an about-face."

"Yeah. I know."

"White Sr., does not have a Russian accent."

"I know. How could they have missed that in the initial interview?"

"You heard the lady. They didn't ask her what he sounded like."

Sarah and the detective then burst into laughter, remembering the old lady's excuse. This was why follow up interviews were so important. Witnesses don't lead. They follow. If the right questions are not asked, significant information can be left out. Sarah was proud of her interview skills, and needed to gloat a little more.

"How much do you want to bet, that if we put a Russian man in one of those suits White Sr., typically wears to court, that witness would tell us, she *'thinks'* the Russian man is White Sr.?"

"Enough, Sarah, enough. You've made your point."

Sarah laughed.

"Ok, who do we interview next?" Detective Jones asked, changing the subject back to business.

"Let's talk to the jogger who let the perpetrator inside the building."

Sarah and the detective stopped at the end of the hallway, and knocked on the resident's door located nearest the building entrance, which remained locked until a security code was entered.

The resident did not answer.

As they waited, the detective pondered with Sarah the results of the prior interview.

"You know, that DNA sample is no longer important."

"Why, because your friends at the FBI don't have Snowflake's DNA in their database?"

Detective Jones laughed, "No."

Their conversation was interrupted when the resident answered the door.

"Hello, we're here from LAPD, and we'd like to ask you a few more questions about what happened in this building, last Wednesday evening. Can we come in?" asked Detective Jones.

"Well, I was just on my way out. Can this wait?"

"How about we walk you to your car?"

"Ok."

"Tell us about the man you let into the building."

"Which one? I let two guys in. The one the police hauled away and an older man before that."

Sarah answered him: "Let's talk about the older man before that. Did you speak to him?"

"Not really. I was on my way inside the building and he was walking up to the entrance as I punched the security code in. When I opened the door to let myself in, he just walked right in and walked straight to the apartment down the hall."

"Did you try to stop him, I mean this is supposed to be a secure building?"

"No. That apartment gets frequent visitors by men dressed like him, who fit his age range."

"What does 'dressed like him,' mean?"

"You know. Business-y, professional. He was dressed in an expensive business suit. He looked like an elderly, wealthy businessman. Not someone who makes you fear for your security. I guess I just assumed he was one of Ann's regular guests. He didn't look menacing or anything."

"Did you say anything to him?"

"No."

"Did he say anything to you?"

"Yeah. He said, 'thank you.' When I opened the door.

"Did he have an accent?"

"No."

"No? Or you're not certain?"

"None that I heard. I wasn't really paying attention. It was the young guy the police hauled off that I was worried about. He was sitting in his car for hours just watching the building. He looked real angry. He sat in his car with a bottle of liquor, drinking right out of the bottle, staring at the building, as if trying to decide what he was going to do to someone inside. I was worried one of the women in the building had a stalker. I called management, but they told me they couldn't do anything if the guy wasn't on the premises. He was in his car, across the street, on public property. When I went back out for my jog, he was standing on the sidewalk. As I jogged away, I saw him catch the door before it shut behind me and let himself in."

Sarah interrupted him, "We're not that interested in the younger man. But please think real hard about the older man you let in, are you sure he didn't have an accent?"

"I didn't hear one."

"How certain are you?"

"I don't know. I guess I can't be 100% certain. He only said two words as he passed by. I was still behind him, and he was facing straight ahead. So I can't tell you with any certainty what his voice really sounded like. Sometimes you don't hear a person's accent unless they say more than a few words to you."

Sarah was satisfied with that answer. He didn't completely contradict the old lady's description. "Thank you for your time." She said, concluding the interview.

Detective Jones and Sarah left the witness at his car and walked back towards the building.

"So," said Detective Jones, "Our perp may or may not have a

Russian accent."

"He does."

"Why so certain?"

"I trust the old lady who was standing face to face with him, more than someone he passed by who wasn't paying attention."

"The same old lady who I.D.'ed White Sr.?"

"That was not a positive I.D."

"Ok."

"Whose next on our list?"

Sarah and Detective Jones continued their interviews. They spoke to every neighbor who lived on the same floor as Ann. They also interviewed the neighbors who lived on the floor above that to see if they had heard or seen anything. The remainder of their interviews did not turn up anything new or different from what appeared in police reports.

★ ★ ★

The next morning, the FBI agent called Detective Jones on his cell phone. Detective Jones felt his phone buzz in his pocket as he stood in a long line at the coffee shop, waiting his turn to order a much-needed double espresso.

"Detective Jones speaking," he answered.

"I have a match for that sample you sent me," said the FBI agent.

"Who does it trace back to?"

"I can't tell you."

Gritting his teeth, Detective Jones paused. He wanted to rip that FBI agent up and down with a string of cuss words, but he was stuck in a crowded coffee shop and didn't want to make a scene. Instead, he clenched his teeth to hold back the tirade, and asked simply, "Why not?"

"I'm just calling so you know I didn't forget about you. I ran the sample and I have a match, but I can't tell you anything more than that. It will compromise an investigation we're involved in."

"Is there anything else you can tell me?"

"No."

"Am I supposed to say, 'thank you,' or should I say something else?"

The FBI agent chuckled, "You can say whatever you want."

"No, I can't. I'm in a crowded coffee shop. I'll say what I want next time I see you."

"I'll be looking forward to it," the FBI agent joked, "Talk to you later."

"Bye."

Detective Jones walked back to the police station, and slowly climbed the stairs to his office, still gritting his teeth in anger over the call he just received.

Sarah was seated at his desk, a blank notepad in front of her. She stared out into space while she tapped her pen on the notepad. He knew that look well. That was the look of Sarah searching for thought, trying to decide on her next move. He placed a paper cup in front of her.

"Here, this might help," he said as he placed the cup down, "a double tall mocha."

Sarah looked up at him. He held his own drink in his hand. She hadn't asked him to bring her anything but she appreciated it. She smiled at him and thanked him. He noticed however, that she did not pick up the cup and drink from it. Instead, she moved it to the side as if to put it away, out of her reach.

"What's wrong? Did your time in Europe make you too good for American-made espresso drinks?"

"No," Sarah smiled, "I'm on decaf now. But thanks anyway."

"Decaf, huh?" Detective Jones glanced at Sarah, scanning her from head to toe, as the word registered in his mind.

Detective Jones pulled out the visitor's chair opposite Sarah and placed his cup on his desk.

"I got a call from the FBI."

"And?"

"They have a match but they can't help us."

"Shit!"

"It's not that big of a loss though, is it Sarah?"

"Of course it is!"

"Nah. Think about it. Two neighbors say that elderly men in business suits frequented the place. Multiple white-haired men entered that apartment. Matching the DNA to another elderly man, can't prove White Sr. ,was not there. It can only prove that others were also there at some point in time or another, which is what neighbors are saying anyway. Even if the one hair that was found is the DNA of another man, it can't exonerate White Sr."

"It can if he has a Russian accent."

"Well, there's nothing we can do about it now. We just have to wait for our crime lab to tell us who it belongs to, then follow that lead."

"What about blood from the broken glass? That proves more than just presence inside the apartment, that identifies the perpetrator who fled at the time in question."

"None of the glass was retrieved when they processed the crime scene."

"Why not?"

"Presumably, there was no blood. Presumably, he used something other than his arms or legs to break the glass. White Sr., did not have any injuries to his arms or legs."

"So, why aren't we looking for someone who does? That's the biggest mistake cops can make, sometimes. They look only for the evidence that proves the man they have in custody is guilty. They don't look for all evidence, whatever it speaks to. We need to head back there."

"But they've returned possession back to the resident. The crime scene is no longer preserved. I'm sure she cleaned up the glass."

"We can look outside. There might be specs of glass left. Remember, he broke the window to exit, leaving most the glass on the outside."

Chapter 22

FBI Agent, Andrew Scott, had a lot of respect for Detective Jones. A few years back, Detective Jones was instrumental in discovering evidence, in an unrelated criminal investigation, which allowed the FBI to foil a horrific terrorist attack that was being plotted by a terrorist cell within the United States. Agent Scott would never forget Detective Jones for that. Most officers would have missed that little shred of evidence, while executing a search warrant in a white collar crime case, involving illegal banking transactions. But on the suspect's computer, which was seized under the search warrant, Detective Jones saw hints of evidence of what he thought could be something much more serious. He immediately shared it with the FBI. "I don't know what any of this means, but I have a strong feeling your resources will unveil its meaning," he had said, when he contacted Agent Scott and showed him the evidence. The evidence had given Homeland Security the link in the chain that was needed to identify and take down all members of the plot. This was the type of local law enforcement, federal agents would never forget.

So when Detective Jones had contacted Agent Scott for assistance in solving a local crime, Agent Scott wanted to help in whatever way he could. He had already told Detective Jones that the official position of the FBI was that they could not assist because doing so would compromise their under cover agent's identity; however, Agent Scott wondered if an off-the-record conversation with Detective Jones might help lead him in the right direction, without having to compromise the secret agent's identity.

So, at midnight on a Thursday evening, Agent Scott called Detective Jones' home phone number.

"Hello," Detective Jones answered, gruffly. He had just barely fallen asleep.

"If I told you I had Cuban cigars, would you let me come over?"

"I don't know. Why should I host a federal agent who thinks his cases are more important than mine?"

"Because. The cigars are Cuban."

Detective Jones smiled, "Well, I guess if the cigars are Cuban..."

"Alright! I'll be right over!"

"Make sure you bring a bottle of whisky too!" shouted Detective Jones before Agent Scott hung up.

"Done," promised Agent Scott.

Forty-five minutes later, Detective Jones and Agent Scott were sitting in Detective Jones' smoking room. It was the man cave of all man caves. Several big screen televisions were situated on the walls, in such a way that, any one of them could be comfortably viewed from the lush leather armchairs, which served as the room's primary seating. The armchairs were slightly angled towards each other, allowing for a relaxed conversation between old friends, while also providing comfortable lounging while watching several different games on the various televisions. To the left and to the right of each armchair, were cup holders and ashtrays placed within a comfortable reach, without taking up space on the armrests. This was designed to accommodate both right-handed people and left-handed people.

Detective Jones explained the amenities of his man cave to Agent Scott:

"The double sided cup holders and ashtrays are for my red-headed, left-handed friend who thinks he's a disadvantaged minority for being both left-handed and red-headed."

Agent Scott roared with laughter at the image, and Detective Jones went on:

"I told him – 'you don't have to be a minority in here!' I also said, 'and look! We can smoke in here too!' This is one of the only places remaining in California where you can smoke inside, have a drink, and watch a game. That's why I made sure both sides of all the chairs have ashtrays too.

And I placed the TVs in the perfect spots on the wall so I don't have to decide which football game to watch during football season. I get to see it all! One day, I might invite you over during football season. But probably only if you bring more Cuban cigars."

"I'll bring 'em!" said Agent Scott, enthusiastically.

The men relaxed in their chairs, feet propped up on matching ottomans, each of them holding a cigar in one hand, and a glass of whisky in the other.

"I hate Jack Daniels," said the federal agent.

"That's cause you're a pretty boy," said Detective Jones.

"Hey, just because I like top-shelf scotch, doesn't make me a pretty boy."

"Real men drink Jack Daniels," retorted Detective Jones, "I'm glad you brought the Jack, or I wouldn't have let you in."

"I know. That's why I brought Jack, instead of Chivas Regal."

"Ha!" snorted Detective Jones, "Chivas Regal, huh? Is that what your regal ass drinks?"

Agent Scott responded with a friendly punch to Detective Jones' arm and the men laughed.

The men continued with small talk, and catching up with each other, until Agent Scott finally opened the subject of his visit:

"So, what's so special about the murder case involving the dead prostitute? I thought you were due for retirement a few months ago, but you're still working on this case."

"Well, it's not a murder case yet, but it can become one any minute now. The victim is in a coma. Doctors don't think she'll survive. And yeah, I am past due for retirement; but I have to help a former Deputy D.A., solve this case, before I retire. It's very important to her, and for the right reasons too. She strongly believes, the man who has been arrested, is innocent. She feels a responsibility to help free him. It's a noble cause, and I'd like to help someone I have a lot of respect for, achieve this goal – which is very important to her, personally. Also, I know the guy. Although he's a criminal defense attorney, I really like the guy, and don't believe he did it. Don't even believe he's capable of it. And you know, after being on the job for so many years, we start to think anyone is capable of anything. But on this one, I just don't believe old White Sr., is capable of committing murder, or attempting to commit murder."

"So, for now it's nothing more than an attempted murder case?"

"That's right."

"You know we can't compromise an agent's position, unless we're looking at charges that will put our target away for life. Attempted murder won't do that."

"I know."

"So, what if I gave you information off the record, but told you, you couldn't use it in the prosecution of the suspect? Do you think that could help your cause in any way?"

"Well sure, I could find the same evidence through a different path. If I know it exists, I'll know what I'm looking for. I'll find it and prove it some other way, not through your source."

"Well, I couldn't let you interview any other witnesses, because if certain people find out the mere fact that you know the information, it could compromise our agent's safety."

"Ok. So, I might not be able to make an arrest, but I might have what Sarah needs to convince the D.A., to dismiss the case against White Sr., and have him released from jail. I think that's her primary concern. If she can accomplish that one bit of justice, I think she'll be satisfied, even if we can't reach the real culprit. So long as you promise us, you'll get him one way or another, I think we can wait for him to get what he deserves from the feds, when you determine the time is right."

"Will the D.A., dismiss such a high profile case, based on evidence that can't be disclosed?"

"Yeah. White Sr., is his old friend. I think at this point, he wants to do what is morally and consciously right, and not what is politically right. I think he'd hang his hat up and retire if he had to, if it meant saving his old friend. He just won't do it without knowing for himself the facts that justify his release. Of course, he won't jeopardize his career to save an old friend, if his friend is actually guilty."

"Of course not. But my evidence proves without a doubt that the guy you have in custody is innocent."

Detective Jones sat straight up in his chair with a bolt, which startled Agent Scott. He grasped each armrest firmly with both hands and postured towards the agent aggressively, "What evidence do you have!" demanded Detective Jones.

"Now, settle down. I can't get into too much detail," replied Agent Scott.

"Come on, Scott! You have to tell me! A woman might be dead! An innocent man accused! You have to tell me!" Detective Jones was furious at Agent Scott's intention to withhold information. Until then, he had no idea that the evidence the FBI held, could provide such certainty with respect to what happened.

"Calm down. I'll tell you, but without specific details. I'll just tell you the conclusions that can be drawn from the evidence. I can't tell you names. I can't tell you dates. I can't quote what the assailant said, and you cannot repeat to anyone my summary of what he said, because only three people were in the room when he said it, and our under-cover agent is one of them. The perpetrator is the other. So if the perpetrator ever finds out that his words were repeated, he only has to kill two other people to eliminate witnesses, and our agent is one of them."

"Fine, use vague terms. Just tell me enough that Sarah and I can convince the D.A., to release an innocent man."

"As you know already, the DNA evidence your guys collected from the scene matches one of the targets we're investigating, who is involved in organized crime. He's actually the main target of our investigation. We've never had an agent penetrate his inner circle so closely, and we've never been so close to building a case we can pursue against him. That's why we cannot give you the evidence to solve an attempted murder case, especially where local police have already created reasonable doubt by arresting an innocent man, first. Multiple arrests confuse juries. We don't have enough confidence that a guilty verdict will be rendered if that case is charged; so, we cannot divulge the evidence..."

"Oh, get on with it! I don't need to hear any more bullshit about why you can't give us what we need to arrest this scumbag! Just tell me what evidence you've been keeping from me!" demanded Detective Jones.

"Fine. Our target matches the description of the man you've arrested. From a distance, you could easily mistake one for the other. And, though I will not divulge his ethnicity, he speaks with an accent that a witness could describe as Russian."

"Ok, That creates doubt that White Sr., is the real criminal. What's the evidence that proves without a doubt that White Sr., is innocent?"

"Our target made a drunken, oral confession, witnessed by our under-cover agent, close in time to the date the crime was committed. He referred to the victim by her first name, described the location of the crime, and angrily stated that a prostitute made him kill her. He complained that if the 'dumb bitch' hadn't resisted, he would not have had to do it. Apparently, he was angry that she would have the nerve to deny him, after he had bought her diamond earrings a long while ago that were so expensive, they were supposed to serve as a retainer of sorts, to keep her available at all times, any time. He said he'd forgotten all about her, until he had seen her walking in Beverly Hills. Thinking he'd call on her for a quick and easy lay, he followed her, saw what apartment she had walked into, and knocked on the door."

"Disgusting!" Detective Jones interjected.

Agent Scott went on: "He always wears a suit, and tries to present himself as a sophisticated businessman. More than likely, the victim had no idea who she was dealing with when she had made that arrangement with him, a few years back. She likely mistook him for an ordinary businessman.

He made this confession only to two other people, with whom he believes all his criminal secrets are safe. He spoke to them as if he were merely venting to them about a bad day, the way someone angrily tells a story to their friends about bad traffic and being cut-off on the freeway. The brutal assault was that insignificant to him.

He thinks he killed her. So why charge the attempted murder case, only to give him a reason to seek her out and finish the job? Let him think she's dead, and let us take him down for something else.

Our secret agent has been able to establish a relationship with him, which is so close, that he speaks that comfortably in front of him about such an atrocious crime. That is why the confession cannot be used without compromising our agent's position."

"What if she dies? We just let this scumbag walk around free?"

"There's no statute of limitations on murder. As long as my under-cover agent stays safe, you will still have your evidence of the murder case. It can be pursued at a later date — after we conclude our case."

"Are you sure you're close to nailing this guy to the wall?"

"Very close."

Chapter 23

"Are you two, fucking crazy!" the District Attorney hollered at Sarah and Detective Jones, as he jumped out of his chair, throwing his hands up in the air. Detective Jones and Sarah stood in his office with the door closed, bracing themselves for this outburst, but determined to convince him, despite how little they were able to tell him.

"You want me to dismiss this case, but you won't tell me why!?"

"We have told you why, sir," answered Detective Jones. "The FBI has solid evidence that another man committed the crime."

"Who!"

"They wont tell us."

"What's the evidence!"

"I can't tell you."

"Do you know how preposterous you sound?"

"Yes."

The District Attorney threw his hands up, in exasperation.

Then, Sarah interjected, "But you know it's the right thing to do."

The District Attorney shook his head and slowly began to sit back in his chair, "But I can't. I – " He kept shaking his head. He placed one hand over his forehead and covered his eyes, as he sank in his chair, "I – I just can't."

"You can," Sarah encouraged him.

The District Attorney shook his head and mumbled, almost as if to himself, "This case is in the media. They're reporting on our long-term friendship. They keep saying, 'long-time friend of the District Attorney: arrested for attempted murder.'"

The District Attorney kept shaking his head. He rested his elbows on his desk and placed both hands over his face. He rubbed his temples as if he had a bad headache.

Sarah repeated herself, "You can."

"How!" Slamming both fists against his desk, the D.A. looked up and demanded: "You just tell me, how the fuck I'm supposed to dismiss this case, without being able to say one word as to why!"

"You dismiss it in the best interests of justice."

"Oh is that right?" he mocked, with stinging sarcasm in his voice, "It's that easy, is it Sarah?"

Sarah stared at him, stern determination reflected in her face. With a forceful and unwavering voice, she looked him straight in the eye and said, "Yes. It's that easy."

The District Attorney looked at her and smirked. He shook his head again.

Sarah persisted, "I'll sign the dismissal. Your name doesn't have to be anywhere near it."

"You resigned. Remember?" the D.A. stated, resentment and annoyance clear in his voice.

"So deputize me again," Sarah said, raising her right hand.

The District Attorney looked at Sarah. His face began to relax, the contemptuous look gone now, admiration slowly appearing in his face. He stood and administered the oath, which every Deputy District Attorney was required to take before serving in his office. He ended with that familiar question: "Do you so solemnly swear or affirm?"

"I swear," stated Sarah.

"Godspeed," said the District Attorney. And Sarah was off.

Sarah and Detective Jones rushed out of the office. Sarah

instinctively headed towards her old office. Of course, someone else was sitting in her old chair. She stopped, speechless for a moment. Though illogical, for a split second, Sarah was surprised to see that the office was now occupied by someone else.

Detective Jones politely asked the new occupant to move.

"What's this about?"

"We just need your desk for a few minutes. District Attorney's orders. We won't be long. You know Sarah Cartwright, don't you?"

"Oh, Sarah. Yes, yes of course. I've heard of you. Of course, I'll just go get a coffee. Take your time."

Sarah sat at her old familiar desk, and began typing frantically. As she typed the motion to dismiss, Sarah asked Detective Jones to head down to the jail and wait for her text message giving the word that they were to release White Sr.

★ ★ ★

As Detective Jones stood at the counter near the intake center at the jail, he shot the breeze with the officers manning the desk, and waited for Sarah's text. He had no idea what was happening inside the jail.

★ ★ ★

Inside the jail, White Sr., was finding it more and more difficult to concentrate on his young cellmate's question. The cellmate was so excited to share a cell with the iconic defense lawyer. He had been star struck since the day White Sr., was placed in his cell. He never stopped chattering – always asking White Sr., about one legal theory or another, asking him about constitutional law, or simply chattering about life on the outside.

As the cellmate continued to chatter, White Sr., noticed the room seemed to be going dark, from the edges of his peripheral vision and closing in. The chest pain he had experienced during his son's trial, now returned. But this time it was sharp and sudden, and extremely painful. He closed his eyes and grabbed his chest. Then the pain spread to his left arm, he was losing consciousness...

"Hey man! Are you ok? Hey, White! Are you alright man!" the cellmate asked him frantically, as he watched the old man's face turn ashen.

As White Sr., fell to the floor, gripping his chest, another cellmate exclaimed, "Dude! I think he's having a heart attack!"

The two cellmates began yelling for help:

"Guard! Guard!" they yelled frantically.

Nobody came.

"Guards! Guards!" they continued to yell.

No one responded.

"Guards! I said God-dammed Guaaards!" one of them screamed at the top of his lungs.

Still nobody came.

Inmates in nearby cells heard the commotion. "What?" one of them hollered.

"It's White Sr. He's dying! Help!"

Inmates in neighboring cells all began clamoring, making as much noise as possible. White Sr., was an icon and a hero among the local criminal population. Inmates in every cell of that cellblock joined in.

"Help! Help! Emergency!" they yelled.

"It's an emergency! Emergency! He's dying! Help! Guards!" they continued screaming.

The inmates began shoving beds against walls, kicking and slamming whatever they could, to make as much noise as possible, as they continued hollering, "Help! Guards! Help!"

Finally, a jailor slowly walked through the cellblock, following the pointing fingers of inmates in other cells, leading him over to the cell, which held White Sr.

"What's your problem?" he asked, when he reached White Sr.'s cell.

The cellmates pointed at White Sr., whose body lie motionless on the floor. The guard immediately radioed for medical assistance.

But it was too late.

Chapter 24

White Jr., was devastated to hear about his father's death. He immediately rushed over to his parents' house to console his mother.

He walked in through the front door. He could hear crying coming from the kitchen. As he walked down the hallway and towards the kitchen, he could see his mother seated at the oak table, where he had shared so many meals with his father and mother. She sat hunched over with her hands covering her face, as his sister cradled her and tried to comfort her.

"Mom," said White Jr.

She looked up, a little startled at the sound of his voice. As her eyes focused through the tears and rested on her son's face, she felt nothing but rage.

"You!" she screamed, "You killed him! You killed your father! This is all your fault! You worthless, no-good, rotten..." She couldn't finish her words. Sobs took over. She cried so hard she was shaking, she couldn't get any more words out.

"Mom, please," White Jr., stepped towards his mother.

She stood up, shoving her daughter's arms off of her, clenching her fists, she screamed, "Get out! Get out! Get out of here, and don't you ever come back!"

"But mom..." White Jr., tried to plead with her.

"No!!!!" she screamed. This time she picked up the crystal sugar bowl, that always rested on the center of the table, and flung it at him. Sugar flew across the room and fell all around as the crystal bowl continued its trajectory towards White Jr. He jumped to the side and out of the way, as his mother continued screaming, "Get out of here! You're not my son! You are no longer my son! You killed him! You killed your father. It was you. You filthy swine, keeping with no good whores, getting arrested. Your trial is what got him arrested! Your trial is what killed him!"

"But mom,... it was a heart attack, mom."

"Yes! A heart attack, because of you!!!" she pointed with wrath. "My husband died, in jail! Instead of in my arms! Because of you!!!!"

His sister made no attempt to calm her, or stop her. She just glared at White Jr., with equal hatred in her eyes.

White Jr., stared at his mother in disbelief. His lower lip quivered as he tried to hold back tears. He inched backwards, cowering away from his angry mother. He couldn't believe it. He needed his mother's love more than anything now, after losing his father. But she showed him no love. Instead, she blamed him. She even hated him. The pain was unbearable. In that moment, White Jr., knew, he had nowhere to go where he could be loved.

His family had rejected him. No one would console him about his father's death. There was nothing left to do but leave. White Jr., watched his mother as he continued inching backwards and out of the kitchen. Once out of her sight, he turned and ran. Where he was going, he didn't know. He ran out of the house and just kept running and running, for miles. He had to get as far away as possible.

Finally, he found an empty park and leaned against a tree. Then he slid down it and buried his face in his hands, as he sobbed, mourning not only the loss of his father, but the loss of his mother too, and the whole life he'd lost, as a result of his arrest.

★ ★ ★

Three days later was his father's funeral. White Jr., decided to numb the pain with excessive amounts of drugs and alcohol. He was not welcome at the family home, and he was not welcome at the funeral. He had heard about the funeral from the priest of his church. Knowing he would not receive word from his mother or his sister, White Jr., had stopped by the church each day after his father's death, in attempt to find out about his father's funeral arrangements. It was the church he was baptized in, and the church his father had taken him every Sunday, as a child. The day before the funeral, White Jr., had found the priest and asked for the details of his father's funeral. Then he sat in the pews, looking up at the alter, wondering whether his father was angry with him, too.

On the day of his father's funeral, White Jr., waited outside his mother's house. He watched them leave, then went inside. He found the keys to his father's Ferrari and went into the garage to sit in the driver's seat. Although he had his own Ferrari, he needed to sit in his father's car today. As he sat there, he drank more booze and began talking out loud.

"I'm sorry, dad," he blubbered, "I'm so sorry I couldn't make you prouder of me. I'm sorry about the mess I got into. There was just so much pressure. I couldn't live up to your standards. I couldn't be like you. I'm sorry, dad. This is all my fault, isn't it? Mom says it's my fault you're dead. I'm just so sorry. I don't know what to do anymore."

White Jr., turned the car on but left the garage door down. He wondered if it would hurt less if he inhaled enough gas fumes to suffocate to death, than it would if he placed the gun to his head and pulled the trigger.

He pulled the gun out of his jacket pocket and turned it around in his hand. He stared at it. He wondered who the gun was registered to. He still had it in his possession from a time when one of his clients asked him to store it for safekeeping, without providing any further detail. As long as he was not told the gun was used in a crime, he believed he could not be liable as an accessory, or for tampering with or concealing evidence. He would argue that he was merely storing it for safekeeping. Also, attorney-client privilege prevented him from ever revealing the fact that his client had asked him to "store" the gun. That was the key word, "store." The client did not say, "hide this for me." He merely said, "store it," which served as another justification for White Jr.'s storage of the suspicious weapon.

White Jr., looked at the handgun and wondered if it was stolen, or if it belonged to his client. He wondered if people would know he committed suicide, or if this would trigger another murder investigation. Trying to be the heroic defense lawyer that his dad had been, he wiped the gun down, to remove anybody else's fingerprints. He was compulsive about it. He wiped it so compulsively, it served to polish the gun, leaving it almost shiny. Finally, he put the gun on the dashboard and put both hands on the wheel, and his mind wandered.

He wished he could be at his father's funeral. He wanted a better goodbye than this. He narrowed his eyes in deep thought. Then he opened the garage door, and put the car in gear. He tore out of the garage and sped down the road. *The hell with anyone who tried to deny him his attendance at his father's funeral,* he thought.

By the time White Jr., got to the church, people were leaving the services and getting into their cars. The procession to the cemetery was beginning. He waited until the church parking lot was empty. Then, he followed the funeral procession. As they reached the cemetery, White Jr., lagged behind everyone. He was afraid of how his mother might react if she saw him, so he kept his distance. He walked slowly up the hill to where the crowd gathered around his father's grave. He found a tree within earshot, and hid behind it.

As the priest continued his sermon at the grave, White Jr., heard wrestling in the grass. He looked to the right and saw her. It was a woman dressed in black, from head to toe. Her face was covered with a black veil, but he knew exactly who it was. She also stood next to a nearby tree, within earshot of the sermon. White Jr.'s gaze fixated on her. Forgetting why he came, he stared at the woman in black.

She is the one who needs to die, today, he thought to himself. *Not me. Her! That's the bitch who's responsible for my father's death!* His mind was reeling with rage. He stepped slowly towards her, like a panther stalking its prey. When he reached her, he wrapped his left arm around her face, quickly placing his hand over her mouth, forcing her against him to restrain her movement. With his right hand he placed the gun against her side. "Sarah!" he hissed between gritted teeth, "You're coming with me, you whore."

Sarah could feel the metal object against her side. She knew it must be a gun. Fearful of how close it was pointed at the baby she carried inside her, she complied with his demands.

Before he released his hand from her mouth, he whispered in her ear, "You're going to do everything I say, or I'll kill us both, right here and right now. I don't care who sees me, because we'll both be dead before anyone can reach us."

Fear coursed through Sarah's veins. He was suicidal. This was the most dangerous situation of all. *Think, think. Stay calm.* She thought to herself. *Comply with his demands until you can gain the upper-hand.* Afraid to make any move that might set him off, Sarah nodded her assent, in hopes of calming him down.

He slowly moved his hand from her mouth, caressing her face and her neck. "Sweet, Sarah," he whispered, with his mouth pressed against her ear, "You're mine, now."

Sarah didn't move. Frozen with fear, she waited to see what he would do next. She focused her attention on his left hand. If he squeezed her neck, she'd have to struggle, but how would she get out of the way of the gun in time? His hand rested on her neck, but he did not squeeze. He slid his hand down her chest and towards her left breast. He cupped her breast and whispered again, "Ah. Yes. Mine." He whispered lustfully, pausing with emphasis between each word, as he squeezed her breast possessively. Sarah almost vomited. She steeled herself, forcing composure. She was forced to allow his hand to roam freely over her body, with his sick and twisted whispering, because of the gun at her side. She could not move.

She could not react. She could not vomit. She used every bit of her will power to stand still. With his hand still firmly possessing her breast, he whispered again in her ear, "You accused me of raping that prostitute. I know it was you. I recognized your voice on that tape. You ruined my life. You killed my father. Shouldn't I make all that trouble worth something?" He squeezed and rubbed her breast as he spoke into her ear, his thumb swirling around her nipple and digging into it. She was afraid she couldn't keep from vomiting, which might cause him to panic and pull the trigger. She began taking short deep breaths to keep the vomit from rising.

"You wanted to accuse me of rape? Maybe I should rape you." His hand slid downward. "Oh, you've gained a little weight." His face was still pressed against her ear, whispering as she stood motionless. "That's ok, Sarah. I don't mind the weight gain." He moved his hand to her side, sliding his fingers across her back, and looping his left arm into her right arm, never removing the gun pointed at her side, which was now completely hidden under their linked arms. He pressed the gun deeper against her side.

"Come with me," he demanded. "Walk next to me as if we're a couple. Keep that veil over your face."

She complied with his demands.

David's private investigators, who also served as security detail, had kept a far enough distance from White Jr., that he didn't notice them. They couldn't see Sarah's face, and never saw the gun that White Jr., carried. He had used the sleeve of his jacket to cover his hand and the gun it held. Now, it was even further concealed by their linked arms. David's security personnel watched. They had no idea that it was Sarah under that black veil. From their distant view, it appeared that White Jr., and the unidentified woman, were merely a couple behaving inappropriately at a funeral.

They walked towards their own vehicle, which was parked several cars away from the red Ferrari that White Jr., drove. They kept their eyes on White Jr., as they watched him enter his vehicle in the most peculiar way. He did not walk the woman to the passenger side of the vehicle. Instead, he had her enter the driver's side then scoot over to the passenger side. He kept his arms wrapped around her as she entered, and he climbed in closely behind her.

"What a sicko," Joe said to the other security man hired by David.

"Yeah. Not the way you'd expect a man to act at his father's funeral, is it?" said Jason.

"Let's follow more closely. This looks too strange."

"Yeah. I agree. At first it looked like he was trying to hump her in the driver's side, then I think he just kind of shoved her over. I'm not sure this is what it appears to be."

The security detail quickly entered their vehicle and pulled up close behind White Jr. White Jr., did not notice them behind him.

"Keep your veil on Sarah," White Jr., said as he rested his right hand on the center console, with his gun pointed at her. He kept his left hand on the wheel, with his face turned slightly toward Sarah, allowing him to keep a view of both her and the road.

"Where are you taking me?" Sarah asked, as the red Ferrari peeled out and sped down the street.

"Shut up!"

Sarah closed her mouth and looked out the front window.

"Do you think you have a right to speak, bitch!? Do you think you're entitled to know anything!" he screamed at her.

"No," Sarah whispered, "I'll let you decide." She tried to calm him, "I'm sorry. I just thought we could have a friendly conversation. I was curious that's all."

"Curious, huh? You're too smart to be curious. I know you Sarah. Do you think I don't know you? Every question you ask has a purpose," he sneered. "Where are we going," he mocked. "Where are we going? That's for me to know and you to find out. Now why would you ask such a question? Are you trying to alert someone?"

"No. Of course not. How could I?" Sarah said calmly.

White Jr., then forcefully yanked her purse off her shoulder, with the same hand that held the gun. "Oh, how could you?" he mocked, "Because I'm nowhere near as smart as you, the apple of my father's eye, I could never figure out how you could send a message about where we were going."

That was too close for comfort. Sarah decided to adjust her strategy. She had to be more docile. She couldn't try to talk to him. Any little thing was going to set him off.

White Jr., knocked the purse into her lap, with the gun. Sarah tensed up. Another move, too close for comfort.

"Dump your purse out!" he screamed, "Show me what's inside!"

Sarah quickly opened her purse and flipped it upside down to allow all the contents to fall into her lap.

"Oh gee," White Jr., said sarcastically, "What a surprise. There's a cell phone in there. I'll tell you where we're going Sarah. We're going somewhere that cell phone can't track us. Now be a good little girl and throw it out the window." As he gave this order, he shoved the gun into her side. Sarah quickly grabbed the cell phone and threw it out the window. The wind from the open window was forceful. It whipped the veil up, exposing her face.

"Keep that veil down!" White Jr. screamed at her. She grabbed the veil with one hand and closed the window with the other. But it was too late. David's security personnel had seen her face.

"That's David's wife!" exclaimed Joe.

"Where?"

"In the car! With the subject. That's David's wife!"

"How can you tell, she's covered in black?"

"When she opened the window, it lifted up her veil and exposed her face. Didn't you see that?"

"No, I was watching what flew out the window. It looked like a cell phone."

"This is a kidnapping, Jason. David's wife would never go with him, willingly. We need to call for back up."

"It didn't look like a kidnapping. Are you sure she's not dressed that way to intentionally hide her identity so that she could rendezvous with this guy?"

"Trust me. Call for back up. I'm going to get a little closer."

"Should I call our guys, or the police?"

"The sirens might spook him and make things more dangerous. Call some of our guys. Tell them to catch up to us and to get in front of him."

They followed White Jr., as he drove through the city, getting on and off the freeway. He didn't seem to be going anywhere. He just kept driving around the city, looping back and forth from one direction to the other. He didn't seem to have a plan. It was easy for back up to catch up to them. Jason gave their location. Their back up personnel sped up to the area and quickly located the vehicle. Two cars got in front of White Jr., discretely creating traffic congestion in order to slow him down. Jason and Joe remained behind.

"We need to box him in, if we can," said Joe.

"No," argued Jason, "Let's just keep following two in front, one behind. If we box him in, it will make it obvious."

"We need to have a plan. We can't just keep driving around in circles without a plan." Joe then picked up his cell phone and gave the command. "One of you get to the side of him, and one of you get in front of him. I'll be behind. He's in the left lane, so this will work. I don't want any cars between us. He needs to be boxed in so he can't move around us."

The other two cars followed orders and soon White Jr., was boxed in. The car in front of him drove too slowly. The car to the right of him drove even with his speed, and the car behind him was tailgating. Because Sarah had stopped speaking, so as not to trigger another angry outburst, White Jr., was now more aware of his surroundings. He realized that all three cars were black BMWs.

"There's too much black around me. Why do these cars all look the same?" White Jr., said out loud.

Sarah didn't respond.

"Come on, brilliant Sarah. Help me solve this riddle. Why are all three cars that surround me, the same color?"

"Lots of black cars in L.A.," Sarah mumbled.

"Oh, it's just a coincidence? Well let's test your theory."

White Jr., honked and flashed his lights at the car in front of him. "Get out of the way!" he hollered. The car wouldn't budge. He revved his engine and tailgated so badly, he nearly bumped into it. Still, the car wouldn't move, and wouldn't pick up speed. White Jr., laid on the horn, and hollered again, "Get out of the way! Get out of the way!" Still, the car was un-phased. Then, he swerved at the car to the right of him. But it too was un-phased. It kept its pace even with his, and would not leave the lane next to him.

"These cars aren't afraid of an erratic driver, Sarah. Most cars would get the hell out of the way. I think they're following us. What should I do about that?" He tapped his gun against the dashboard, as he asked the question. The driver of the car to the right saw the gun and notified the others. "He's armed. Act accordingly."

White Jr., taunted Sarah. "Huh, Sarah? What should I do about that?"

Worried that White Jr., was about to start shooting people, Sarah gave him an alternative. "Just wait for an opportunity to turn left. Don't use your blinker, jerk the wheel suddenly and try to get away."

"Wow, spoken like an experienced criminal. Have you ever evaded police before?"

Sarah didn't respond.

"Of course not," White Jr., answered for her. "Your a perfect little princess. Perfect princesses don't run from the police," he mocked her. "But I like your idea. However, there aren't many opportunities to turn left on the freeway, though, are there Sarah?"

"There will be a split in the freeway further north. Signal as if you're switching to the right lanes. The other cars will move in that direction. At the last minute, cut to the left."

"That will fool car numbers one and two," White Jr. said, as he pointed his gun, first at the car in front, then at the car to the right. "But how about car number three, behind us?" he pointed his gun at the rear view mirror, to indicate car number 3.

Sarah was quick with her reply, "That will leave only one. It's easier to loose one car."

"Wow, if I didn't know any better, I'd think you were hoping to get away with me." White Jr., said as he caressed her thigh with his gun. Sarah took a deep breath and held it. Scared to death the gun might go off, she watched it closely. As White Jr., rubbed the gun up and down her thigh, Sarah debated. Despite her fear, she debated whether it was possible to grab the gun without getting shot. As she watched, debated and calculated, she held her breath, waiting for the moment the barrel of the gun was pointed downward. She wondered whether a shot to the knee could still endanger her pregnancy due to loss of blood. Suddenly, he lifted the gun off her leg and switched hands. The gun was now in his left hand and the steering wheel in his right.

"I'm going to have to put the gun away for this. I trust you won't jump out the car door, because you'll get run over by one of these fine men who are trying to save you."

White Jr., placed the gun in the pocket of the driver's side door and placed both hands on the wheel.

With his eyes on the road and his attention on the cars that surrounded him, Sarah took the opportunity to reach her right hand into her pants pocket where she left the cell phone with the European phone number. She slowly pulled the cell phone out of her pocket, and swiftly slid her finger across the screen to unlock it.

An empty text message addressed to Detective Jones was still open. He was still in the habit of communicating with her on this number; and their last text communication was still pulled up. Sarah quickly typed one word and pushed send. Her message said nothing more than: "help." She flipped the switch to silent and slipped the phone back into her pocket, just as White Jr., turned to look at her.

"What are you fiddling with over there!"

"Nothing, I'm just nervous. I sit on my hands when I'm nervous."

"Keep your hands where I can see them!"

Sarah quickly placed both hands on her thighs to appease him.

The freeway split was approaching, and White Jr., turned on his right signal. He looked to the right and steered the wheel to the right, getting close to the dividing line, inching towards the vehicle to his right. The first and second cars followed his cue. They both gradually moved towards the right and allowed room for White Jr., to move one lane to the right. The four cars moved in unison like military aircraft flying in formation. Then, as they moved closer to the freeway split, White Jr., slammed his foot down on the gas petal, increasing his speed to an alarming rate, as he swerved left, aiming straight at the concrete divider. As the divider got closer and closer at a heart-stopping rate of speed, Sarah screamed and closed her eyes. Impact was imminent. Sarah's life and the life of her unborn child were over.

Just before impact, White Jr., jerked the wheel left, and barely missed the center divider. Joe yanked his wheel to the left and followed in hot pursuit. The other two cars were already passed the divider and onto the other freeway.

"Ha! He's still on my tail!" White Jr., was in a Ferrari. It could outrun the BMW that followed him. He hit the gas even harder and traveled at top speed, weaving in and out of traffic, losing Joe and Jason.

Jason called the police, and frantically reported the kidnapping, describing the vehicle, the freeway they were on and the direction they were traveling. A radio alert was then announced to all patrol cars in the vicinity. It coincided with Detective Jones' receipt of Sarah's text. He was riding passenger in a patrol car, on his way to interview a suspect in another case.

"That's Sarah!" exclaimed Detective Jones, "We have to respond to that."

"Sarah who?" asked the patrol cop.

"Sarah Cartwright, former Deputy D.A. She just sent me a text that said "help" and that's White Sr.'s car they described. White Jr.'s probably driving it. They're close by. Let's follow!"

Detective Jones contacted the station and demanded they track Sarah's cell phone. An officer at the station tracked the movement of her cell phone and remained on the line to direct them to her. With lights and sirens, Detective Jones and the patrol cop raced towards the location.

"They're heading east now. They're traveling very quickly," said the officer on the phone. Detective Jones and the patrol cop followed. They called for back up, requesting that all officers near the location join in and follow the cell phone's path.

White Jr., continued his erratic, full speed race to nowhere. He laughed like a maniac. "What do you say, Sarah! Should we go out with a bang? How would you rather die, traveling full speed in a Ferrari then slamming right into a concrete divider? Or by gunshot? They'd both make a bang, wouldn't they?"

He was crazy. She had to calm him down before he killed her and her unborn child. Her heart raced, her mind raced, what could she say? Then, she remembered his sick words at the cemetery.

"No," Sarah responded, in a controlled voice, forcing calmness into the tone. "Not like this. Not in the car. Take me somewhere quiet, where we can be alone."

White Jr., slammed on the brakes, slowing the car down to about 80 miles per hour. The needle dropped, 70 mph, 60 mph. *Thank*

God, thought Sarah. *Safer speeds.* She continued, as he looked at her, searching her face. She looked right at him. The freeway was empty ahead. It was safe for her to hold his gaze for a few more seconds.

"You said you wanted me. Take me. Take me first. But you have to pull over."

White Jr., said nothing. He turned his gaze to the exits he was passing on the freeway. She knew she'd reached him. He was still traveling at the lower speeds. She could see the wheels turning in his mind, as his eyes searched the exit signs and the freeway overpasses. Sarah assumed he was looking for a place to pull over.

The further east they traveled, the more sparse and desolate the freeway exits appeared. Where would he stop?

"I know," he said, almost under his breath. He continued staring out the windshield at the open road, with both hands firmly gripping the wheel. A few miles later, he pulled off the freeway and traveled down a windy road.

"I know a place that's real quiet, Sarah," he said in a low voice, his eyes still on the road. "No one will find us," he said in a sinister tone, "My former client doesn't even use this place anymore. He abandoned it. Said it was too far out of the way. He'd rather risk being caught than have to come out here all the time. Then, finally he was."

White Jr., took his eyes off the road to look at Sarah, "caught, that is. He was finally caught. That's why he was my client. I found out about this place when he cursed himself for not having stayed there. The perfect hideaway to store masses of drugs and stolen goods. Why not use it for our purpose? It'll be overgrown with trees and shrubbery now. It was then. That's why he used it. Nobody could find it, unless they knew what they were looking for. It's practically buried under the trees. It's an old warehouse from the 1800s. He didn't need locks and bolts to protect his goods. He used the secrecy of the trees, and the power of armed guards. It's an old building that's falling apart. But we don't need anything that fancy, do we Sarah?" He placed one hand on her thigh and squeezed. Sarah struggled not to grab his hand and throw it off her. She had to hold it together long enough to get out of the car.

"We're almost there," whispered White Jr., as he slowed down and turned down a dirt road. He was right. Enormous overgrown trees lined both sides of the dirt road. The branches hung low and intertwined to cover the path. It looked like nothing but impassable forest. Taking a risk, Sarah opened her window. White Jr., jerked his head to the right. Before he could bark an order at her, she smiled. "We're alone now. I don't need this anymore, right?" His face softened and his eyes widened in anticipation. Sarah took off the veil and threw it out the window just as they reached the branches, towards which White Jr., drove. She needed to notify anyone who might be following them, that they should continue passed the trees that created a false dead-end.

White Jr., was focused on nothing more than the image of Sarah unveiling herself. He didn't notice that she'd tossed the veil out the window. His eyes fell from her face and rested on her chest.

"More?" he asked.

"Not yet," she smiled.

White Jr., hit the gas a little harder and plowed through the branches, bending them and breaking them with the speed of his car, leaving a whole where he had traveled. After they had passed through a thick barrier, they reached a clearing. About three trees deep, the prior occupants had cleared a path. Tree branches stopped short at the road, and the dirt road led directly to a dilapidated building.

"Our final destination," said White Jr.

The morbid sound in White Jr.'s voice made the bile in Sarah's stomach reach her throat. She swallowed and tried to gain her composure.

He parked in front of the building and grabbed the gun. He pointed the gun at Sarah as he exited the vehicle. Now, you come out this way. There are too many places for you to run and hide around here, I can't have the car separating us."

Sarah slid across the center console and into the driver's seat, while White Jr., stood just outside the door holding the gun with both hands, pointing it straight at her. As she slid into the driver's seat, she tried to calculate how quickly she could put the car in reverse and speed away. The keys were still in the ignition. She sat squarely in the driver's seat, but realized he had turned off the car. There wouldn't be enough time. She couldn't outrun a bullet if she had to start the car first.

Sarah put one foot out of the vehicle and slowly stepped out of the car. White Jr., took two steps back, never taking the weapon off her.

"Stay in front of me," he demanded.

She obeyed.

"Now walk in through the front door."

She did as she was told.

"Let's go up the steps," he said.

She walked towards the steps. She let one shoe fall off her foot at the bottom of the stairs, to alert followers which direction they'd taken when they went inside. She clunked up the stairs with only one shoe on.

When they reached the top, he instructed her to turn left. She took a few steps to the left, then let the second shoe fall to indicate which direction they had turned. At the end of the hall on the left, was a closed door. They went through it and White Jr., closed the door behind them.

"There," he said, "Now, we have some privacy."

Sarah walked towards the window and sat on a barrel that looked like it was still there from the 1800s. Oddly, she wondered what the barrel had contained, during its hey day.

White Jr., stood in front of the door and watched her. He lowered the weapon now. Sarah sat with her hands in her lap, trying to look demure. If she could get him to relax, he might drop the weapon. With her legs dangling off the barrel upon which she sat, she crossed her ankles, and swung her feet like a child. She looked up at White Jr., trying to force innocent curiosity into her eyes. It worked.

"You look so pretty like that," White Jr. said, as he lowered the gun all the way down. It was still in his hands, but now it was pointed at the ground.

Sarah didn't say anything. She kept her hands in her lap and continued to swing her feet.

"So innocent," he whispered, "Just like, when,..." White Jr., cut himself off. "Never mind that!" he suddenly snapped, "That was then, and this is now. Let's enjoy now."

He slowly walked towards her. The gun still in his hand, pointed at the ground. Sarah looked into his face, but kept her peripheral vision on the gun. She couldn't look directly at the gun, or it would alert him to her plan.

He stopped in front of Sarah, but still out of her reach. He looked her up and down, taking in every inch of her with his eyes. After a long period of silence, he said:

"What now, Sarah?"

She held his gaze with her eyes, then slowly allowed her eyes to travel down his body, stopping at his groin. She stared for a few seconds, glanced up into his eyes, then dropped her gaze back to his groin.

"Oh I see, what you're saying," he said.

Sarah didn't speak. She kept her gaze on his groin, teasing him, with quick lifts of her eyebrow to peak up at his eyes, then back down to his groin. Sarah was gambling. She was betting that he would use two hands to unzip his pants, instead of one. She had to keep his focus on unbuttoning and unzipping his pants.

White Jr., set the gun down on a metal table to the right of him.

It was out of Sarah's reach. He then moved both of his hands to his pants. Sarah leaped off the barrel and lunged for the gun. "Oh no you don't!" White Jr., yelled as he shoved her back with both hands. She landed on the barrel with her hands behind her, leveraging the barrel as her base, she picked up both her feet and forcefully kicked White Jr., as hard as she could. He fell backwards, reaching for the table upon which the gun rested, he tried to grab the table to stop his fall, but his hand slipped off the slick metal and he landed hard on the ground. Sarah grabbed the gun and White Jr., slid backwards. "No, Sarah. No." He wasn't so sure he wanted to die now. Staring into the barrel of that gun, in someone else's hands, scared him. He didn't want to die. He wanted to live.

He scooted backwards as fast as he could, as Sarah stood menacingly with the gun in her hand. "Please don't, Sarah. Please don't," he begged.

Sarah stared at the pitiful excuse for a human being lying on the ground before her, and her hands shook with anger. Memories of every attempt he had made to destroy her and the man she loved, came flooding into her mind. She was angry. She pointed that gun at him, shaking with rage. The sick and twisted experience he had just exposed her to, was the last straw.

"I'm sorry. I wasn't in my right mind. It was my father's funeral. My mother blamed me. I wasn't welcome there. She says I killed my father. I was using drugs and alcohol all day before his funeral. My father's funeral, Sarah! Please. Please Sarah, don't shoot. Forgive me," he begged.

As White Jr., crawled backwards Sarah walked towards him menacingly, gun pointed directly at him. He had crawled to the other side of the room. When he felt a solid surface behind him, he reached up searching for the door handle. But he had crawled in the wrong direction. His back was to the wall. The door was on the other side of the room.

"Please,..." he continued begging.

Sarah was unaffected by his pleading. All she could think about was how he had threatened the life of her unborn child. All she could think about was the risk of him doing it again. She couldn't let this happen again. He was a menace, and the world would be a better place without him.

Then she heard sirens, tires squealing, and the sound of police exiting their vehicles and storming the building.

"See, Sarah? Do you hear that? You don't have to worry about me anymore. I'm going to jail."

"No, you're not," Sarah said.

"Why not?" he asked, trembling with fear.

"Because, they won't hold you long enough. Your stellar defense team will convince the jury you temporarily lost it, the same way you're trying to convince me now."

"No! Sarah! Please!" he begged.

Sarah heard footsteps clamoring up the stairs. She heard Detective Jones' voice holler, "There!" He had spotted her clue.

Just as Detective Jones barged through the door, Sarah pulled the trigger.

He saw everything. White Jr., sitting on the ground, leaning against the wall, one hand raised defensively; Sarah standing over him, a few feet away, out of his reach, safe from danger, pointing the gun directly at him. He saw the flash of gunfire and watched White Jr.'s head jerk backwards upon the impact of the bullet. He witnessed an execution.

Detective Jones had gotten through the door first. The other officers were a few steps behind him. Immediately after the gun shot, the other officers filled the room, with guns drawn. They'd heard the shot and were prepared for an exchange of fire. It took them a few seconds to assess the situation. The kidnapper was dead, and the victim stood with the gun in her hand, pointed at the ground.

They lowered their guns and watched as Detective Jones slowly took the gun from Sarah's hand. He turned to the other officers in the room, and explained, "She shot him in self-defense. I saw the whole thing."

Not a single officer in the room thought to question the detective's conclusion.

He continued, "I'll get her to a hospital. She may be in shock. The rest of you take care of this."

Detective Jones walked out of that room with Sarah. He held her by the arm and walked her down the stairs. They didn't say a word to each other until they reached the patrol car they'd be traveling in.

"I'm not in shock, detective."

"I know, Sarah. But there was no need for you to stay for possible questioning."

"Will I not be questioned, later?"

"No. I saw the whole thing. It was self-defense. He lunged at you, reaching for the gun, and that's when you fired. It's that simple."

"That's not what happened."

"Yes it is. I saw it. You were in shock right after. So maybe you'll have difficulty recounting events. But I saw it. Got it?"

"Got it."

"Besides, nobody questioned you at the scene. I was the only officer who witnessed anything. I'll write my report. Case closed."

"Case closed," Sarah repeated. Then she asked, "Can you drive me to see David, now?"

"Yes. But shouldn't we get you to a hospital to check on the baby, first?"

Sarah snapped her head to the left, staring at the detective in surprise: "How did you know?"

"What else could get you onto decaf?"

Chapter 25

David raced to the hospital where Detective Jones said he would be taking Sarah. Before David had received Detective Jones' call, David's security detail had already informed him of the kidnapping, and explained that the police were tracking and following her cell phone movements. But that had not made David feel better. His wife was in danger. And he was angry; angry and scared to death. It felt like an eternity had passed before he had heard from the detective.

Now, he was relieved that she was out of harm's way; but he was still afraid about how badly she may have been hurt. The detective told him she was physically fine, but David had to see it to believe it. When he reached the hospital, he parked his car illegally and ran inside.

"Sarah Cartwright!" he demanded, as he ran to the front desk. "I'm her husband! Where is Sarah Cartwright?"

"Calm down sir, a nurse will escort you to her, in a minute."

"Please. I need to see her now! Just tell me what room?"

"She's not in a room, sir. She's only here for a quick check up. She's in a quad. You will be escorted to her, shortly."

Just then, a warm-natured nurse approached, "Are you Mr. Nolan?"

"Yes."

"I'll walk you over to your wife, sir. She keeps asking for you."

"Is she ok?"

"Yes. And the baby is just fine, too."

David stopped.

The nurse looked back at him, "Are you coming sir?"

"Baby? Did you say, 'baby?'" David stopped. And he thought his heart stopped too. He put one hand on his chest, and opened his eyes wide, unable to take his next breathe. All at once he learned that his wife was pregnant, just after enduring the news of her kidnapping, which placed both his wife and *his child* in grave danger. It took him a few minutes to catch his breath.

"Oh. I'm sorry. I didn't know you weren't aware. She's nearly four months along. I thought you would know."

Now David's cheeks reddened with anger. Four months? His wife had kept this secret from him for four months? She came to L.A., and endangered his child, all the while keeping it a secret from him that she was even pregnant at all? David was livid.

"Sir? Are you coming along?" the nurse repeated her earlier question.

"Uh, Yes. I'm sorry." David picked up his pace and followed the nurse.

His anger kept raging through him, as he followed the nurse down the long hallway. *How could she?* He thought to himself. *How dare she!* He amended. He felt his blood boil as worry and anger mixed together. Then, finally he rounded another corner, and there she was, seated at the edge of an examination table, her ankles crossed, her hands folded and pressed between her knees, her soft brown eyes still wide from the ordeal she had just experienced. When he saw Sarah, all anger, all frustration, all confusion disappeared. There sat the woman he loved, safe and sound. He felt nothing but relief. David rushed towards her, wrapped his arms around her, and held her tight for a long moment. He held her face in his hands and looked into her eyes. He kissed her lips, several times.

"Sarah, I love you, Sarah. Oh Thank God, you're ok." He held her again in his arms, holding on as if afraid she might be taken away at any moment.

Sarah squeezed him tight in return. "I love you too, David."

David pulled back to get another look at her. He placed his hand on her belly and looked into her eyes with the proud smile she'd seen before, the first time they were pregnant. David stared into Sarah's eyes with his sweet closed lip smile, and his beautiful blue eyes became misty.

"Our baby," he said, with his hand still on her belly. "When were you going to tell me?"

"I, uh, I..."

"Shhh. It's ok, Sarah. All that matters is that you two are all right. That's all I care about, right now."

"Oh David!" Sarah cried, as she burst into tears. The stress of the days' events caught up to her now. She fell into her husband's strong arms and cried harder than she'd ever cried before; sobbing with such force, it shook her whole body.

"Sshh Sarah, shhh. I'm here. You're ok. We're ok. Our baby is ok. I'm here, Sarah. Don't cry."

Sarah continued to cry until her sobs became more controlled, then quieter, then gone. Her cry died down to gasps, as she tried to catch her breath. David held her, as he waited for her to regain her composure. When she was calm, he held her face gently, looked into her eyes and said, "Now let's get out of here."

Sarah nodded.

"Let's go to our sanctuary, Sarah. I miss our Garden of Eden."

"Yes!" Sarah whispered excitedly through a wide smile and watery eyes, "The Garden of Eden!"

"We can both use that right now, can't we?" David said.

"Yes," Sarah nodded. She took her husband's hand as he walked her outside the hospital and drove her to the beautiful grounds that surrounded their home in Malibu.

Chapter 26

After several weeks of bliss in their Garden of Eden, Sarah and David woke up late, on a Wednesday morning, in the luxurious comfort of their Malibu mansion. Sarah wanted an omelet, and David wanted French toast. Both were too lazy to cook; and they were stuck. They had not yet staffed the Malibu mansion, out of a desire to enjoy their sanctuary alone; but today, Sarah was missing the staff.

As Sarah lay in bed feeling exhausted from the eventful evening, in which David had indulged her, the night before, she wished for a fully staffed kitchen downstairs.

"I'm hungry," said David.

"Me too," said Sarah.

"I'm huuuungrryyyy," whined David.

"Me too," repeated Sarah.

David gave her a look that said, "Well what are you going to do about it," and Sarah thought to herself, *I have spoiled him way too much.* When she didn't respond to the question in his face, he whined again: "I want some of that stuffed French toast you make." Sarah picked up a pillow and swung it at him. "Take me out for breakfast!" she demanded. He wrestled the pillow out of her hand, pinned her to the bed and pressed his face against hers like an affectionate tiger. "Feed my other appetite, first," he hummed in her ear. Then they tussled, for one long, beautiful hour.

Taking advantage of David's bliss, after their romantic tussle, Sarah put one hand on his chest and whispered in his ear, "Take me out to breakfast." David smiled contently and said, "Anything you want."

They went to Sarah's favorite breakfast place in Malibu, where they blissfully ate their breakfast on a balcony above the sand, close to the crashing waves of the ocean. Sarah sipped on her decaffeinated tea, and David gulped his black coffee, after they finished eating. Sarah stared out at the water, and her mind began to wander to things she hadn't thought about in weeks. It dawned on her that she was never updated on the status of Kelly Luthan. She knew she'd been in a coma, but she wasn't sure if she made it. For some inexplicable reason, Sarah had a nagging feeling to follow up on that.

"I think I'll go into town, today," she said to David.

"I can't join you. I have a golf game with important business associates. It's just a guy thing today though, so it's probably better if you're not there."

"Why not?" Although relieved at the excuse this gave her to go into town alone, Sarah was annoyed at his statement that it would be better if she didn't accompany him to golf.

"Come on, Sarah. You know I sometimes get made fun of for having my wife with me all the time."

David's boyish eyes made her laugh. "Why are men so childish?" she asked.

"It's not childish. Just sometimes, guys have to be guys and we can't do that with women around."

"Why not?"

"We have to be on our best behavior in front of women, especially you. Some of my friends are afraid of your prim and proper Miss Deputy D.A. thing you have going on." David motioned with his finger, drawing an imaginary circle around Sarah.

"But I don't practice anymore."

"I know. It's just, knowing you did. It makes some of them nervous. They can't tell the same jokes in front of you. And today is going to be a guys' day. Don't be offended. I don't take any just-the-guys' days that often."

"Is Todd going to be there?"

"How'd you know?"

"It's always Todd who whines about wives and girlfriends being present. He's even done it in front of me. Tell him to grow up and get a steady girlfriend."

"Ha! I'll tell him you said that. But you understand, don't you? This is actually his business deal, I'm just there for the support; so, I kind of have to do things his way."

"Fine." Sarah gave in. "I'll see you at dinner time then."

They left the restaurant and David dropped Sarah off at home. She got into her car and made a phone call to the victims' advocates office. They informed her that Kelly Luthan was still in a coma and told her what hospital she was in. Sarah hung up the phone and drove to the hospital.

* * *

Sarah slowly walked towards Kelly Luthan's hospital room. She didn't really know why she was there, but something inside her compelled her to visit the other victim of White Jr.'s crimes. She didn't know what she would get out of the visit, but she felt that she had to do it.

Sarah walked into Kelly's room and saw her lying on the bed, eyes closed, a feeding tube connected to her, and a monitor beeping a steady rhythm, proving she was still alive. Sarah stopped just inside the door and stared. She didn't see the man sitting in the chair alongside the wall, to the left of the door. His voice startled her:

"Are you also a prostitute?"

Sarah jumped and stared at the man incredulously. She inched backwards towards the door.

"I mean, she and all her other friends in this godforsaken city were all prostitutes, weren't they?"

"I'm not a friend of hers."

"Who are you? And why are you here?"

"I'm the Deputy District Attorney to whom she first reported the rape."

"Oh, so you're even stupider than I am!" Johnny laughed a wicked, angry laugh.

From her vast experience interacting with crime victims, Sarah immediately recognized that the man was not abusive, mean or even angry. He was hurt. *He must be the fiancé,* she thought. She spoke carefully.

"Sir, may I ask about your relationship to the victim?"

"She's not a victim! She's a conniving, lying, plotting prostitute! And that's what got her here! I don't know who did this to her. First, they arrested me, then, an old man. Then, the case against the old man was dismissed. Who knows who could've done this to her. I'm sure it was her filthy past that brought this on!"

"Would you feel more comfortable if I called her the patient? She is lying in a coma."

Johnny looked at Kelly and his face dropped. He mumbled, "Or we can call her Kelly."

"How do you know Kelly, sir?"

"She was my fiancé."

Sarah looked at Kelly's left hand. The diamond ring was still there.

"She still wears your ring?"

Johnny looked at Kelly's left hand and nodded.

"I know you're very angry, right now – angry with her, with her past, with her circumstances; but, can I assume you still love her?"

Johnny's eyes welled up with tears, but he said nothing. He kept his strong arms crossed, protecting his emotions with an exterior form that exhibited pure masculine strength. The water in his eyes did not fall.

"I assume that you wouldn't be here, sir, if you didn't still love her."

One teardrop fell from Johnny's right eye. It slid down his cheek. He remained still, tensely seated upright in his chair, arms crossed over his chest, motionless, staring at Kelly, not answering Sarah's question.

Sarah saw an open bible sitting on an end table next to the chair the man sat in. She then realized that the differences between the man sitting in that chair and the woman lying in that bed were as wide as the differences, which had existed between her and David when they first met – differences of which Sarah was completely unaware; ignorance of which she was most grateful. She shared her story with the man who sat silently in his chair. Though he never responded audibly, as she spoke, his tears betrayed him, indicating he was in fact listening and that her words reached him. Sarah began:

"You and I have a lot in common. I'm a religious girl who fell in love with a man whose lifestyle fell far below my moral standards. I would have never accepted him. But I thank God, every day, for the ignorance he blessed me with, when I first met my husband, and had no idea about his crazy, partying Hollywood lifestyle. I would have judged him immediately and cast him away. I would have missed out on the greatest love of my life. I would have lost my soul mate.

You're right about this city. It is a godforsaken place. It makes good people do bad things – well, bad in our eyes, that is. Sexual freedom and multiple partners is nothing I would ever approve of. Before he met me, my husband was a notorious womanizer, indulging in a different woman every night, and sometimes even two or three, together in the same night. He was lustful; but not out of need, only out of pleasure. So, I really don't know whose past is worse – my dear husband's or your dear fiancé's. Your fiancé may have engaged in similar behavior, in her past; but for different reasons, financial reasons. Whose moral character was worse? We can debate. Whose soul was more corrupted? We can wonder. But there is one thing I can tell you, for sure. My husband is a changed man, who loves me, respects me, and makes me happier than I have ever been in my life. He does that with no effort at all. His mere physical presence by my side makes me that happy. He is committed, faithful and trustworthy to me, because I am just as special to him. I am his soul mate, too.

So, I thank God that I never knew about his past before I fell in love with him and began to trust him; because it is not his past that affects me. It is our present, and our future."

Johnny heard every word, felt every word, and identified with every word Sarah said. He remained motionless, arms crossed, staring at Kelly during the entire speech. Evidence of Sarah's words sinking in, was apparent in his face. His expression changed as the details changed; and with Sarah's final words, softness appeared in his face, softness and understanding.

Sarah walked out of the room without saying goodbye.

★ ★ ★

While leaving the hospital, Sarah realized she hadn't been to church in a very long time. She needed to stop in, on her way home. When Sarah entered the church, she lit three candles. With the first candle she lit, she said a prayer for the health of her unborn child. With the second candle she lit, she said a prayer for David's health and her own health, and for a long life together filled with bliss and lots of healthy children. Sarah also prayed for forgiveness for the bad choices she had made, in moments of selfishness and weakness.

With the third and final candle she lit, she said a prayer for Kelly Luthan and her fiancé. She prayed that God would ease the man's pain and bring him comfort and understanding. She prayed that the couple would not be denied true love or the opportunity to live happily ever after. Sarah cried while praying for this other couple. She prayed with all her heart. Thoughts of what could have happened to end her and David's beautiful love story filled her mind; and she hoped that God would not allow such tragedy to happen to someone else.

She ended her prayer with a request that God give that poor man she saw in the hospital, his love back.

As Sarah prayed in the church, Kelly opened her eyes, at the hospital. Johnny was seated in the chair next to her.

"Johnny," she whispered.

Johnny bolted upright in his chair. When he saw her open her eyes and heard her voice, his heart filled with hope and love and forgiveness. Right then and there, Johnny knew, he still loved Kelly. He didn't hate her. He hated what was happening to her. What he was really angry about, was the thought of possibly losing her again. Now that her eyes were open and she was speaking, there was hope again! There was hope that he could have his one true love again. He knew in that moment, no matter what Kelly had done, he would forgive her. All he wanted to do was love her.

"Forgive me, Johnny," she whispered. "Please forgive me, I've done terrible things," she said, weakly.

Johnny held her hand with both of his, "I forgive you. Don't worry, Kelly. I know everything, and I don't care. I forgive you."

Kelly shut her eyes.

"No!!!!!! Please don't!!!!!! Nurse! Nurse! Doctor! Please somebody get in here!"

Two nurses and one doctor came rushing in.

Johnny hollered at them in a panic, "She opened her eyes and spoke, and now her eyes are shut again! Why!? Please bring her back!" Johnny cried.

The medical staff began their hurried work to check her vital signs and began chattering medical terminology back and forth to each other. Johnny couldn't understand the technical language.

"Please," he begged, "Please bring her back."

Johnny heard the heart monitor flat line. A loud, flat beeeeeep rang in his ears. "No." He was so weak with despair, the word barely came out of his mouth. Then he hit his knees and he prayed. With his hands folded, he looked up, and he begged, "God, please. Don't take her from me. I'll do anything. God, please," Johnny begged.

Then he promised, "God, if you leave her with me, I'll take her as she is, I'll take care of her. I'll never take her for granted or resent her, I'll just love her as much as you would. Please, God, don't take Kelly from me."

The high-pitched sound of the flat line continued on; and Johnny bargained, "God! take my business, take all my money, take my legs, paralyze me, take everything you can take from me, but God, please don't take Kelly."

As Johnny begged, and bargained, and pleaded with God, the medical staff used the defibrillator to shock Kelly's heart back into beating. Then he heard it. The monitor returned to its steady beeping sound. Johnny rose with tears in his eyes, and looked at the medical staff, waiting for confirmation that they had saved her.

"She's been stabilized. All we can do now is wait," the doctor said.

Johnny collapsed into the same chair he'd sat in for weeks. He slumped in the chair with exhaustion, induced by the roller coaster of emotion that had just coursed through him.

The doctor continued, "Sometimes this happens. We don't know why. Sometimes a patient comes out of a coma, then slips deeper into it, or,... or, uh,... um, passes on, after coming out of the coma. But Kelly made it through this. We're hopeful she'll remain stable."

"Remain stable," Johnny repeated, blankly. "That means stay the same?"

"Yes."

"Will she speak to me, again?"

"We don't know."

Johnny sighed then remembered his prayer. "I said I'd take her as she was. She's still alive, and I am grateful."

Chapter 27

Three months had passed since Kelly flat-lined in that L.A., hospital. Johnny was back home in Oklahoma. He had arranged to have Kelly moved to his home, with long-term outpatient medical care tending to her needs. She could breathe on her own; therefore, she did not need to be hooked to a machine. It was merely as if she were in a permanent state of sleep. She could breathe, but of course, could not eat. Johnny arranged for medical staff to visit their home, several times a day, in order to administer nutrition and tend to Kelly's hygienic needs. He believed that being home in Oklahoma, where her family and friends could come visit her, was the best way to ensure Kelly would come out of the coma. The private medical personnel that he hired would come check on her regularly and kept her as healthy as possible, as she slept. Every night, before going to bed, Johnny would kiss Kelly and whisper the same request, in her ear, "Wake up, only when you're ready to, my sleeping beauty."

On this one Sunday morning, Johnny was in the kitchen frying eggs.

"Ouch! Damn!" he cursed when he burnt his hand on the pan, trying to crack an egg against it.

"Here, let me."

The sound of her voice made him jumped out of his skin. He turned around, stunned.

"Why do you look like you've seen a ghost?" she asked.

"K-K-K-Kelly?" he said, in complete shock and disbelief.

"Yes. What's wrong?"

"Oh my God, Kelly! You're awake!?" Johnny ran to her and

grabbed her. He couldn't believe it. It was a miracle.

"Ow. Why are you squeezing me so hard? Why are you so surprised I'm awake?"

"Don't move. Just stand still. Uh, I mean, come here. Come sit down on the couch. I want you to be careful. Let me call the doctor."

"Doctor? Why? Johnny, why are you acting so funny?"

Johnny realized that Kelly had no memory of what had occurred. It was as if she had just woken up and nothing had ever happened. He felt unequipped to tell her about the ordeal.

"Let's just relax a minute. I'll have the doctor explain everything." Johnny was so afraid that this time would be like the last time, and that she might suddenly, without warning, slip back into a coma. It left him frantic with fear. All he could think to do was to have her sit on the couch and not move until the doctor came.

Johnny tried to make small talk while they waited for the doctor, but he just stared at Kelly, in stupid wonder.

Kelly giggled, "Stop staring at me."

Johnny smiled at her with tender eyes, still in awe of what he was seeing. "I can't," he said.

"You're looking at me the way you used to, when we were in school, when you were still nervous to talk to me."

Johnny laughed out loud, "That's exactly how I feel!" Johnny was as nervous as a schoolboy speaking to his crush for the first time; but the feeling was even more intense than that, because today, he wasn't afraid that she wouldn't like him. Today, he was afraid she might disappear. Johnny gazed at her, delicately caressed her beautiful face, and kissed her lips gently. Kelly indulged in the attention and savored his kisses, as she patiently waited to see what the fuss was all about.

END

Suggested Book Club Questions for White Jr.'s Trial:

1. Do White Jr.'s post-trial actions shed light on his guilt or innocence, or was he merely suffering from a mental breakdown?

2. If you believe the jury reached the correct result, was it for the right reasons or the wrong reasons?

3. Did the prosecutor's office as a whole behave in a fair and just manner?

4. During those courtroom moments where it seemed that Katelyn was winning, was she winning on her own merit, or did she catch a lucky break?

5. What do you think of Sam Chapman?

6. Was Sarah justified in her actions, or did she cross the line?

7. Ultimately, was justice served in this case, or has there been a miscarriage of justice that remains unaddressed?

OTHER BOOKS BY THIS AUTHOR

Join the author's fan club for pre-orders and other offers at:
SummerAugustine.club

Available Now:

A BRUSH WITH LOVE, A BRUSH WITH THE LAW

In a companion novel, *A Brush with Love, A Brush with the Law,* Summer Augustine reveals the events that led to White Jr.'s arrest. Readers who wish to test whether they were right or wrong about him; and to learn whether Sarah's motives were pure in ordering his arrest and dismissing the case against David Nolan (as discussed between Detective Jones and Jack Wayne) should also read: *A Brush with Love, A Brush with the Law.*

Coming Soon:

THE SUSPECT

Jack Wayne is next in line to become District Attorney of Los Angeles County. A career prosecutor whose sole ambition has been to faithfully serve the public, Jack Wayne is about to face an immense threat to his hard-earned career. He agrees to investigate an invisible criminal—the mysterious female voice who is suspected of leading a white-collar crime ring targeting wealthy young inhabitants of Los Angeles. Stepping out of his role as prosecuting attorney, Jack does something very different. He goes undercover to draw the suspect towards him, not realizing that her crime ring transcends borders and affects not only the wealthiest inhabitants of Los Angeles, but of Europe and the Middle East. Chasing down leads across the globe, Jack suddenly finds himself answering for the suspect's crimes in a jurisdiction far away from Los Angeles. A seductive vixen, whose greatest talent is con-artistry, the suspect has captured him first.

Their favorite painting is gone! David Nolan stands accused. Who else could have done it? It was Renoir's painting of the future—David's future with Sarah, predicted and painted in 1890. According to David, it depicts the future and the past. Having seen it for the first time in 2015, he swore it captured the most precious moment in David's love story with Sarah when they first met. Livid and out of his mind with rage, the painting's owner demands: "No one else had stronger motive to steal it than David!" There's just one problem – the painting's owner is also David's alibi. So, who really done it?

To check out the books coming soon, please visit the link below: SummerAugustine.club

About the Author

Summer Augustine is a trial lawyer of 20 years, who began her legal career as a Deputy District Attorney; then later became a civil litigator, handling complex business law cases. She is no stranger to the courtroom or the drama that brings people there. She hopes to share her passion for the law, life and love with her readers through a series of novels, *Prosecutors – LA,* which is also being developed for a television series. (the novels can be enjoyed independently and out of order). Summer Augustine has lived on the west coast of the United States her whole life, including Los Angeles. She loves world travel, art, and history. She spends her free time sipping champagne by the pool, unless her nieces and nephews are visiting, then it's tea parties and remote control airplanes.

To follow the author on her various social media accounts, please visit her website:
SummerAugustine.com

Stay up to date on new releases and special offers by joining her fan club:
SummerAugustine.club